Better Left Unsaid

Princess Berry

This is for those who value the happiness of others
above their own.
Your joy is just as important.
Don't light their fire only to let yours dim.

Contents

Spotify Playlist

1. *In the Stars* - Benson Boone

2. *Visiting Hours* - Ed Sheeran

3. *Like That* - Bea Miller

4. *this is what losing someone feels like* - JVKE

5. *Scared to Live* - The Weeknd

6. *Close* - Nick Jonas

7. *Nobody Gets Me* - SZA

8. *Dangerously in Love* - Beyonce

9. *Glimpse of Us* - Joji

10. *I Can't Help It* - JVKE

11. *Running* - NF

12. *Hrs and Hrs* - Muni Long

13. *Don't Blame Me* - Taylor Swift

14. *For Tonight* - Giveon

15. *I Found* - Amber Run

16. Ferris Wheel - Imagine Dragons

Hello reader! Thank you so much for giving this book a chance. It means the world to me! Although I believe you should go into any book blind, I feel it is only fair that I warn you of some of the contents within this book.

Although this is a hockey romance, it does deal with a couple of tough topics. Such as anxiety, panic attacks, and familial death. Therefore, I ask that you think of yourself.

As much as I want you to enjoy this book, I think you should take care of your mental health first.

With that being said, please enjoy the book and Happy Reading!

Prologue

Six years ago

I sit on the steps of our house. The sun had set an hour ago. It's almost pitch-black outside. Cassandra is on her way to pick me up for our dance rehearsals. She's running late, which is weird. Cassie knows how important it is to get to rehearsals early, considering she's the one who instilled it into my brain. She always says *early is on time, and on time is late*. Something I live by now.

She's now two hours late. I'm starting to get worried because Cassie is never late. Then a car finally turns onto our street, blinding me with its bright lights. I place my hands over my eyes, shielding them from the light. "You're so freaking late, Cassie. I hope you brought two Straw-frazz for each hour you're late, or there *will* be hell to pay," I threaten. Standing from the steps, I lean down to grab my duffle bag from the ground.

As I approach the car and the lights are no longer burning into my retinas, I notice it isn't Cassandra's. It's a police vehicle. They park on the side of the curb.

Is Cassandra in trouble? Is that why she's late? I can't wait to hold this over her head. Cassie never gets in trouble. She always follows the rules.

The police officers exit the car and walk toward me. "Hey sweetheart, are your parents home?"

"Sir, you do realize I'm fifteen. Not six, right? You don't have to talk to me like I'm a child." A tight smile appears on his face, as if he's holding something back. "Is Cassandra in trouble? I want to be the one who tells my mom. She would have a cow!"

"We would like to speak to your parents, now. We're sorry, but it's important." He has a serious look on his face, with his brows furrowed and his lips thinned. She must have done something pretty terrible.

"Yeah, they're home. I'll go get them. One second." I run into the house with the cop trailing behind me. I call for my parents. "There are police officers outside. I think Cassandra got into trouble with the law," I say while smirking, but my parents don't think it's funny. I open the door to let my parents out.

"Luna, knock it off," my dad commands. I immediately wipe the smile off my face. I start to follow them outside, but my dad holds his hand up, warning me to stay in the house.

"Actually, do you mind if we talk inside?" One of the officers ask.

"Sure." My dad opens the door and lets them in. "Luna, upstairs. Now." My dad commands.

I exhale with defeat and follow my dad's orders. I make it halfway up the stairs when I hear Cassie's name, halting me in my steps. I knew she had done something stupid. I hide behind the banister to listen to the conversation. I just needed to know what I could hold over her head.

She always talks about how I get in trouble or how Dean gets in trouble. But neither of us have ever been in trouble with the police.

"She was leaving a café when a car ran a red light, speeding. Unfortunately, she was halfway through the crosswalk. The hospital... They d-did everything they could. There was too much blood lost, and she died on the table. Truly, we're deeply sorry for your loss. When you're up to it, we need you to come down to the hospital to verify her identity." Then my mother's wails sound as she slumps into my father's arms.

"Oh God!" my mother screams, the kind of scream coming from the pits of her soul. My dad clutches her in his arms as the tears start to fall down his face.

My bag drops onto the staircase, sounding off a loud thud. Both of my parents turn to me, their mouths gaping. The shock paralyzes me, and the world blurs as reality shatters. This has to be a dream. This can't be real. She's just in trouble for doing something stupid and reckless. That's what I told my parents. She's not dead. She can't be dead.

I feel my body move down the staircase slowly, gripping the beam for balance. "Mom, she was supposed to take me to rehearsal. We were practicing for Swan Lake. She was the swan. Mom, she was the *swan*." I can hear myself speaking and feel my lips move, but it's like I'm not moving at all. Is this what it means to have an out-of-body experience? To see your life happen in real time, but not to live it at all.

I watch as my mom rushes to the staircase as she tries to hug me, but I push her away. I didn't want to be touched. I didn't want to believe I just lost my best friend.

"No, it's a prank." I murmur, shaking my head. "These aren't even real cops. You know Cassie likes to pull pranks. Officer, please tell Mom it's just a prank. Please tell her Cassie is in the back of your car. Please. Ple-" The tears choke the words in my throat, halting me from saying anything else. The pain hits like a relentless storm, and I struggle to comprehend a life without Cassie by my side.

The door slams open and Dean, my brother, enters. "What happened?" Dean looks around the room as the officers clasps their hands behind their back staring at the ground in silence.

My dad walks around the officers, gripping Dean by his shoulders. He explains what happened to Cassie, and I watch as Dean's back crashes into the door. I look at my mom and then at the officers in front of us. This was actually happening, not some twisted dream that I'm having.

I can't breathe. My legs give out, and my mom does her best to catch me before we both tumble onto the last step. Her hand tightens around my shoulders as my chest rumbles with tears.

"I'm going to leave my card with you as well." The officer says, laying his card onto the table in the middle of the living room. "Please, call me with any questions you might have. We can wait outside to take you to the hospital."

My dad nods his head as the police officers walk outside to wait.

My mom helps me back up the stairs and into my bed. I twist onto my side and let myself succumb to the buildup of tears and cry myself to sleep. I pray when I wake up, it'll just be another bad dream.

I wake up the next morning, shuffling from under the covers, and grab my phone. I'm expecting a text or a call from Cassie. She had an apartment near her campus, so she would normally text me good morning. There's nothing. Then I'm back under my covers, looking at the picture on my nightstand of Dean, Cassie, and me. Tears start to well in my eyes.

Cassie wasn't just my sister; she was my best friend. Even though there was a five-year age gap between us, no one could tell. She involved me in everything she would do, from dancing to eating or even hanging out with her *much* older friends. She was so cool to me. She stayed in the city to go to school near us just so she could take me to dance practice every day. Her apartment was probably twenty minutes from our house.

Cassie was also the most popular person in school, she won homecoming queen two years in a row and then turned around and won prom queen her senior year. That popularity carried on everywhere she went. There wasn't a single person Cassie met who didn't love her. She had an inviting personality that no matter who you were, you just loved her.

I have no idea how I'm supposed to keep going without her. I scroll through our messages, re-reading our last conversation.

Cassie <3

Hey cutie, I'm picking up some bagels, and then I'll head over. I'm gonna be a couple of mins so forgive me, ok?

I love you, and I will undoubtedly bring you a straw-frazz lemonade. only if you forgive me.

How can I not forgive you if you bribe me with a straw-frazz? You're not fighting fair, Cass :(

> *that's the point, cutie!! I'll see you in 10 min, be on the steps*

> *love you Cassie <3*

> *I love you, too, Teddy Bear <3*

> *See you soon babes! ON THE STEPS*

> *Or no straw-frazz for you!*

> *Gee okay, mom*

> *Ha ha bye teddy bear*

That's the last message I will ever receive from Cassie. Which breaks my heart even more. I wish she would've just came home. I wish she hadn't stop for those stupid bagels. Maybe she wouldn't have crossed the street. Maybe she would still be alive. I just want to hug her again.

There's a knock on my door and my brother walks in. He climbs into bed with me, not saying a word. Lying on his back, staring at the ceiling. We lay in silence for a while, neither of us wanting to speak.

Dean and Cassandra weren't as close as we were. They had their own little relationship. I was closer to

Dean than he was to her. I didn't mind it though because I loved them more than I loved anyone else. So, if I got to enjoy them separately or even together, I didn't mind it.

It's clear that he's hurting, but he doesn't express his emotions well. We're twins, but we're so different. Where Dean hides his emotions, I wear mine on my sleeves. Seeing him cry yesterday was a new one for him. He doesn't do it often.

"I'm here for you, Jay. It's you and me," he whispers, it's so quiet that I think he didn't say anything at all.

"I can't believe she's gone. She was just getting bagels. She was getting—" I can't finish my sentence as tears take over.

"I know." His voice cracks. He slides down and wraps his arms around my shoulders, bringing me closer to his chest. He squeezes me tighter, and I just lay there crying.

I think about how I will never be able to go to rehearsals with her again. There won't be any more late nights at Tom's Pizzeria. I just want one more phone call with her. One more laugh out of her. One more day of her calling me Teddy Bear. I want another hug from her. I just want my sister.

It's been three months since Cassandra died. We buried her. We mourned her. Yet, it still feels like I just found out about her death. No matter how much time passes, I can't seem to move past her not being here every day. Time stalled after her death, and so did I. Today is my first day back in ballet classes since everything happened. I couldn't bring myself to do any of the things that we used to do together. It didn't feel right.

I put on my pointe shoes, lacing the ribbons around my ankle and calf. Then I move the barre into the middle of the room, just as Cassie always sets the room up before we warm up together. I stare at the barre as I try to remember her. Her smile would take up her whole face. Her long, curly hair that touched the middle of her back. She had just dyed it black because she wanted to stand out when she performed Swan Lake. A part of me wanted to dye my hair black too, just so I could look like her. But she voted against because she loved my brown curls so much.

I gaze into the mirror, wiping the tears that fell. This is harder than I expected it to be.

As I finish my warm-up, I start to cry again. It's been like this for months. Anything that reminds me of

Cassie makes me cry. Her room, which I pass by every day in the house. Her car sits on our street, not to be touched, per my father's orders.

Mom wants to sell it, but Dad and I fought tooth and nail to keep it. We agreed when I was of age, I could have it. Until then, it sits on the street. Anytime I walk past it, though, I think of her. I long for the smell of her. Her warm embrace. Even to hear her laugh just one more time. I just want her back.

Since I haven't been to rehearsals in months, I lost my position in the winter showcase. Cassie won't be performing as the swan, so it doesn't matter anymore to me. I wanted to perform alongside her as one of the company dancers. I wanted to take part in one of the biggest moments of her life.

I collapse to the ground, allowing my emotions to consume me. I hastily wipe my tears when I hear the bell above the door ring. Paris enters. She swiftly places her duffle bag on the bench and joins me on the floor.

Paris was Cassie's best friend. They met in the studio when they were both twelve. It broke her almost as much as me to learn about Cassie. From the instant they met, they were inseparable. Despite how cliché it was, they really were like two peas in a pod. They did everything together. When Cassie dyed her hair black,

Paris followed. Paris eventually became like a second sister to me. It's something I'm really grateful for at this moment.

"Hey, teddy bear," she says softly. It was nice to be called that again, but it wasn't the same feeling I got when Cassie said it.

"I'm sorry. I didn't mean to start crying." I wipe the remaining tears off my face.

"It's okay. Don't apologize." There's a beat of silence before she speaks again. "I figured I would find you here. I come in here early every day, hoping to see you." She gazes into the mirror.

"Why?" I ask.

"I wanted to check in on you. Plus, you're like a little sister to me." She smiles. "We lost a sister, and I haven't been able to see how you've been doing. You haven't been to the studio in a while. I thought about stopping by your house, but I didn't want to intrude."

"I can't. I'm sorry. I just couldn't bring myself to this studio, knowing she wouldn't be here. I miss her every single day." I sob.

She doesn't say anything; she just stares at me. "I get it. But you're not alone, teddy bear. You never will. I'm here for you, as are Dean and your parents. You don't have to go through this alone, ever. Okay?"

"I know. I just... I don't know." I haven't been able to handle my emotions recently. I've started to have panic attacks anytime I think about Cassie. I become so overwhelmed and I just cave in on myself. Which is why my parents made me start seeing a therapist. It's helped a little, but not a lot. Will this ever pass or am I going to feel like this forever because it feels like it.

Paris stands up and stares into the mirror. "All Cassie ever talked about was becoming a principal dancer. She would always talk about how she sees you and her performing on stage together on some big stage in front of a crowd of thousands." She looks down at me, smiling.

"She told me that once. But there's no way I could become a principal dancer. I'm not Cassie. She was way better than me." I sniffle.

"You're just as great. Honestly, you were better than her when she was your age. She even said so." She squats to my eye level, "Look, teddy bear, I really do think you have the potential to become an amazing dancer. Your sister would want you to."

I look into the mirror, trying to see what my sister saw, but I don't really see it. But if Cassie saw it, that's all that matters. I stand up and grab Paris's hand, resolved. "Can you help me become just as great as Cassie?" I beg.

Paris was just as good as Cassie at dancing. If anyone could help me improve my dancing, it would be her.

"Of course, love." If Cassandra's dream was to become a principal dancer, then it's my dream too. I want to live the dreams she couldn't. I want to make sure her name is carried on. I always said I wanted to be Cassie when I grew up, and now I will be.

I'll become a principal ballerina for Cassie. It's the least I could do.

Chapter 1

Luna

"**P**lease... God, end me now. Put me out of my misery," Gia cries out, as she tosses her long, burgundy waves on the table.

"Stop being so dramatic." I grab the paper out of her hand. She's been taking these practice exams I created to prepare for her midterm. I make them occasionally for myself, too, to help me study. Today, we're studying college algebra.

"No, Luna. I'm serious. This is hell. Like actual hell. I hate college. Why am I here? Like seriously." She rolls her eyes and stands up. "It's because of this stupid-ass society that tells us we *have* to go to college for us to be *somebody*. I mean, look at my dad. He didn't go to college, yet he's one of the richest men in the Boston tri-state area. So, please tell me why the *hell* I'm in college."

"Because you won't be able to access your trust fund." Her eyebrows furrow. "It was your father's stipulation. You won't be able to access any of the money they have for you unless you get a college degree." How did she forget that? I don't know. It's quite literally the only thing she ever talks about.

"Right. All the *hypocrisy* is coming back to me now. His father never gave him stipulations for his trust fund. Why do I have to have stipulations for mine?" I'm not touching that with a ten-inch pole. She knows that her father and her grandfather are two totally different people. I won't lie, her dad's an ass. He likes to control everything she does, and she tries to rebel against every single thing he has set for her life.

She sits back down on the couch in my living room. I hand her the practice test after grading it. "Hell yeah! An 87!"

"Shouldn't you aim higher?" I question.

"Nah, I know what I'm capable of. Anything above an 87 is asking for the impossible." Gia isn't dumb. She is probably one of the smartest people I know. This is one of her ways to rebel against her father. He knows she's smart as hell, so he expects greatness from her, so she dumbs herself down.

"Okay, well, I have to head to the studio." We've been studying since 8:00 a.m. I know she hates getting up early, but it was the only time I could squeeze her in with my busy schedule. According to my planner, I was supposed to be in the studio thirty minutes ago.

"Oh, okay. I'm going to go home and take a fat nap. I feel like I deserve it." I laugh as she starts to pack her backpack.

Gia and I have been friends since we were five. We've been going to the same school since the fifth grade. We've been through everything together. She's my better half, literally. She's the fun and loose one, whereas I'm the uptight schedule follower. I'm meticulous with scheduling. Gia hates how much I work. My schedule consists of school and dance, with barely anything in between. So, I occasionally allow her to disrupt my schedule with an impromptu party or hockey game.

Let's be honest, though, the only reason she even likes going to hockey games is because of my brother. Gia has had feelings for Dean for years now. Ever since he hit puberty in high school, she's been in love with him. She says she would never do anything about it because he's my twin, and that's crossing a line she could never cross back over. Which is fine with me because everything about that stresses me out.

"You could always just sleep here until I get back," I tell Gia as she continues to pack her books away.

"No, that's okay. I have a Tempur-Pedic bed, and it's calling my name." She stops to look at me. "No offense."

"None taken." Gia's family is richer than mine. My family is what one would call comfortable. They make enough money to save and still pay for us to go to school and our apartments. Dean lives in a house with other hockey players, so his rent is pretty cheap. I live in the off-campus apartments called Treasures Grove. It's not really expensive. Considering the other prices we looked at, I'd say we got a good deal.

Gia also lives in Treasures Grove, but her apartment is on the other side of the world. She stays in the new building. Since it's new, it's more expensive. I think she pays about $3,000 a month. I've gone over a couple of times, and I'd say she's getting her money's worth. She has a one-bedroom, one-bathroom apartment. It features granite countertops and a tile floor throughout. With floor-to-ceiling windows overlooking the Boston State University campus. It's an astounding view, but it's even more stunning at night when the hockey stadium lights are on.

"Okay, I'm going to go. Love you. Text me when you want to get dinner tonight," Gia says as she heads for the door.

"I don't think I can tonight. I have dance, and then I need to write a ten-page paper that's due in two weeks." I grab my keys off the coffee table and my duffle bag from the floor.

"No. Unacceptable. You have to eat." She frowns.

"I'm sorry, but school comes first." I know it's an unhealthy habit. Something she tells me all the time, but I can't help it. It's easy to get so wrapped up in my work, I just go to bed without eating. It's not that it really bothers me, but it does for her.

"Screw it. I'll bring dinner by later tonight." With that, she leaves, leaving me no room to object to her future intrusion.

"Dammit." I don't really want her to come over tonight. I love spending time with Gia, but she can be a bit of a distraction. Especially when I have a lot of work to do, like tonight. I put on my shoes and headed out.

I walk into the studio and walk straight upstairs. Million-to-One Dance Studio has been my life since

Cassie's death. I made a vow to her that I would do everything in my power to become a principal ballerina. This semester is my chance.

Our studio hosts a winter showcase every year. The studio invites various dance company directors to come see the production and browse for potential dancers they would invite to their studio. This semester, I could actually get signed by a company. I just need to be perfect.

Technically, I could wait another year since I'm only a junior, but I don't want to. By the end of this year, I could really make Cassie proud. It's not really a burden. It's just this crushing weight of needing to succeed. Okay, I heard it. I know that's what a burden is, but I need to succeed and make Cassie's dream a reality. I need to make her proud.

I just need to.

All she ever wanted was for us to become ballerinas together on some big stage. Since she can't be here to hold up her side, I'll do it for the both of us. There's no room for failure or mistakes.

Is it stressful? Yes.

Will it be worth it in the end? Also, yes.

I quickly pulled my sweats off and slipped on my pointe shoes. When I look up at the clock on the wall,

I realize I'm almost an hour behind schedule. I try to let the smell of old wood from the floors calm my nerves. As I tie my ribbons around my ankles, I take three deep breaths to slow my heart rate.

It's not working.

All I keep hearing is this little voice in my head saying, *"On time is late, and early is on time"*. It plays on repeat in my head over and over again. I hate being late for anything. It's been instilled in me that I have to be early for everything. Helping Gia was important, but I shouldn't have let it run over my schedule. I'm normally meticulous when it comes to scheduling, but when it comes to Gia, all of that goes out the window. She's my best friend, and I would do anything for her. *Almost* anything.

Standing up from the floor, I brush the loose curls from my face with my palms, and I walk toward the barres stacked perfectly against the mirror on the left side of the room. I carry the barre into the middle of the room and stare at myself in the mirror. Letting my eyelids fall to a close and taking another deep breath as I remind myself why I'm doing this. What I'm trying to achieve.

When my eyes open, I fall into the first position and start working through our warm-up exercises.

My body goes through each step as if it's second na-ture. Despite the level of responsibility I've imposed on myself, I actually like dancing. Cassie introduced me to it when I was younger. Nothing else has ever appealed to me. Purely dance. It's easy to become engrossed in the moment and forget about everything else.

As I move, each step becomes a brushstroke, painting emotions on the canvas of my soul. Music is like the partner in this silent conversation, and with every twirl and leap, I feel a liberation, a language spoken without words. In the dance, I find an expression of joy, passion, and beautiful poetry of movement that transcends the boundaries of spoken language.

There's a ring from the bell that hangs over the door downstairs. When I look at the clock, it says it's only 10:40, so no one should be here yet. Class doesn't start until noon. So, I should have almost an hour to myself. I turn toward the door to see who's coming.

"Dean?" It is my brother. Why the hell is he here?

"Hey, Jay!" he responds.

I roll my eyes, turning back to the mirror. "Stop call-ing me that." I hate that name. I always have. I always will. He just doesn't give a damn.

"Sorry to bother you, but I have a favor to ask." He steps fully into the room.

"What?" Rising into a relevé.

"Can I borrow your apartment? Just for, like, an hour or two?" He stops two feet away from me, looking in the mirror, waiting for my answer.

"For what reason?" I ask as I step into a grand plié.

"Just some stuff." He's looking down at the ground, like he's up to something suspicious. I scrunch my eyebrows. "Look, it's not for anything stupid. I just need it for an hour or two."

"So why can't you just tell me what you need it for?"

His shoulders sag in annoyance. "Ugh, it's for a couple of the guys. Okay?"

"And you can't do this at your *hockey* house, why?"

"Your place is nicer." He shrugs. "Plus, only a couple of us are going to be there, and we need a clean area." He smiles.

"Fine." I turn to look at Dean and say, "I swear to God, Dean, if my place is destroyed when I get home, your ass is grass."

"Don't worry, your highness." He bows slightly. "Thy house will not be destroyeth."

I roll my eyes. I continue to warm up as Dean shuffles through my duffle bag to grab my keys.

When I gaze back into the mirror to double-check my posture, I notice the man now standing in the doorway. He wasn't there when Dean walked in. He's about six-foot-two, wearing a gray hoodie with black jogger pants while leaning his head against the door frame. The fabric hugged his frame in all the right places, hinting at an underlying strength. His dark brown, tousled hair framed his face, which seemed to carry a subtle smirk. I can't get a clear view of his face because he had his hood on while inside a building like a dumbass, but from here I could see he had sharp, dark features.

"Dean, you know you're not supposed to bring anyone in here!" Madame Christine hates having non-dancers in the studio.

You can wait for your children in the lobby, is what she always said. She felt like our parents were a distraction. We focused on our parents instead of her. Also, it gets crowded with the parents in the room.

It is her most sacred rule. It didn't matter if she's in the dance studio or not; she *always* knows if there is a non-dancer in the studio. The only exception is my brother. Madame Christine loves my family and welcomes them whenever they want to be here. I've been coming to this studio since I was a kid. In a way, she's raised me just as much as my mother has. Especially after Cassie's death. She was there for it all. Another shoulder to cry on if I ever needed it, and I always needed it. Something she's never told anyone else, not even my parents. Which is something I'll forever be grateful for.

"Oh, sorry, Jay." A shiver of discomfort runs down my spine as that stupid nickname echoes in my ears. "He was just riding with me to your place. He's cool. He's on the team."

My brother has been on the hockey team since his freshman year, but I barely know his teammates, and we're juniors now. I only know about the guys he hangs out with on a daily basis. The only reason I know those players is because they came over to my place all the time with Dean.

"He could've waited in your car!" Turning my attention to the tall figure in the doorway, I said, "Look, I'm not trying to be rude. You seem like a cool dude, or whatever. But can you leave?"

"Why is it that when someone starts a sentence with *not to be rude*, everything that follows afterward is always rude?" he remarks.

"Dean! Get him the hell out of here." I snap as irritation brews inside.

He looks over his shoulders, then to Dean, and back to me. "So, we're just pretending like I'm not standing right here? Why don't you tell me yourself?"

I huff, "I just did. Clearly, you have a listening problem."

"Okay, damn Jay, calm down. It's not that deep," Dean intervenes.

"It is when Madam Christine comes in and chews my head off for letting him into the studio. You know she senses that shit," I bark.

Dean chucks the keys off of my lanyard and walks toward the door. "She won't notice. Trust me. That whole energy BS she spills on about doesn't exist. Unless you snitch on yourself." Tell that to Madam Christine.

Dean knows she takes that crap seriously. She walks into the studio and immediately knows someone was in here. Trust me. She *always* knew. "Dean, get the hell out of here. Now!"

"Damn. Okay, we're leaving." He puts his hands up in surrender. He pats the guy on the chest. "Come on, Nick. Let's leave before she chokes us with her tutu."

"We wouldn't want that, now would we?" A sarcastic smile rises on his face.

"Dean!" I scream while chucking an extra pointe shoe at the door.

Dean chuckles one more time before rushing down the stairs with Nick—I think that's the name Dean said—following behind him. Dean always knows how to get under my skin. I guess that's what happens when you're a twin. I should've taken my keys back from him and told him to go screw himself. God, I hate him.

I needed to focus on warming up and running through our routine.

Focus!

I let out a deep breath and went back to focusing on my feet, returning to my zone.

Chapter 2

Nick

"Sorry about my sister, dude. She's not normally that rude. Just when it comes to dancing." Dean snarls as we get back into his car.

I've never met Dean's sister. Actually, I didn't really talk to Dean until this year. Last year, he kept to himself and didn't really socialize with a lot of the guys on the team.

When it comes to conditioning and training, he is always the first one on the ice and the last one off. He puts in the work that no one else does. I'm impressed, to say the least. I graduate this year, so I needed to find a replacement for the captain's position. Dean is my choice. He'll be a senior next year, so it'll only be for a year, but he can do a lot in one year.

If I can condition him, he will be the best fucking captain this school has ever seen. He has the drive and the motivation. He just needs someone to push him in the right direction.

"It's fine." I shrug.

"Seriously, Jay is one of the coolest people you could ever meet," Dean defends.

"What is *Jay* short for?"

He laughs. "Oh, dude, she would kill me if I told you. She hates that nickname, but it's the only reason I still call her it." He sets the car in drive, pulling onto the street.

Color me intrigued. I raise an eyebrow, encouraging him to continue.

He glances at me before turning back to the street. "Okay, but seriously, don't say anything." I nod. It's not like his sister and I are best friends. "So, our parents thought they were having twin boys. They had already picked out names. James and Dean."

My eyebrows furrow. "I don't get it."

He laughs again. "Dude, James Dean. *James and Dean.*" Finally connecting the dots, Dean laughs harder. "Obviously, my mom didn't want to name her James. So, my dad said he would settle for her middle name being James."

"So, what's her full name?" I question.

"Luna James Beitar. I mean, all things considered. She really did luck out. It could have been a lot worse than Luna James."

This whole name ordeal has got to be one of the dumbest things I've ever heard of. Don't get me wrong; it's funny but dumb as hell.

We pull up to the Treasures Grove apartments thirty minutes later. I've come over here a couple of times when I hooked up with girls, but I'm always in and out. I never stay longer than I need to. I don't want to give these girls the wrong impression. I'm down for a quick fuck, but nothing else.

We walk into the main entrance and head straight to the elevators. Dean swipes a key card onto the elevator pad. "What the hell is that?"

"Oh this." He holds up the card. "It's the only way you can use the elevators. You get one when you move in. Jay had one made for me since I come over a lot."

"Well, you can't say she's not in a well-protected building," I remark.

"Yeah, I mean, they have 24-hour security with cameras on every floor. I'd say she's pretty fucking safe. Trust me, I checked."

We make it to the seventeenth floor, and her apartment is the seventh door from the elevator. This girl must have a thing with sevens because her apartment number is 1707. I shake my head as Dean unlocks the door, and we walk in.

Her place is spotless. I can eat a whole meal off her floor. It's a nice apartment. Her wood floors are laminated and tan. To the left of the entrance is her kitchen. The cabinets are an off-white color with black handles. There's a small island in the middle with a black top and an off-white base, with three brown stools around it.

The living room isn't huge, but it isn't small either. There is a gray U-shaped couch with five white and black throw pillows. A rustic trunk coffee table sits in the middle of the room. The room is tied up with a 65" TV mounted on her wall.

I now understand why Dean wanted us to come over here. It's comfortable and low-key. Not really all in your face, which is nice. I know her family isn't super well off, but they do live in the middle to upper class.

I set my backpack on the stool and sit on the couch. "Do you want something to drink?" Dean asks as he heads for the fridge.

"No. I'm good." This couch feels like heaven on earth. I could melt right into it. A groan slips from my lips.

Dean laughs. "Yeah, that's the only reason I came over here." He points to the couch. "Our parents went all out for her first apartment. Especially since I didn't get my own place."

"I'm low-key thinking about robbing her," I joke.

Dean shakes his head. "Anyways, we should probably set up before the guys get here."

"Alright. Just give me five minutes. I didn't sleep well last night." Dean laughs again before heading to another room. I spent the night on the phone with my mom. She is doing mildly better than before. So, I thought I'd give her a call and just talk with her. We ended up speaking until three in the morning, not that I mind.

Forty-five minutes later, the rest of the guys show up. We're supposed to review our films from our past games. We're currently undefeated, standing at 4-0. I would like to finish my college experience as a champion. The only way to do that is to whip my fellow teammates into shape.

"Can someone help me? This shit is heavy as hell," Xander complains, carrying a 4x6 whiteboard. He's definitely lifted more in the gym. So I'm trying to understand why he's complaining.

I walk over and take the white board from him. "Xander, it has wheels." I groan.

He grins. "Yeah, I know. I just didn't want to carry it. Thanks, Captain." He pats me on the shoulder before slumping on the couch.

Dick.

I placed the whiteboard in the middle of the living room. Then chuck a whiteboard marker at Xander's chest. "Stop being so lazy." He just laughs. "Let me get the film, and then we can get started."

We've been studying film for the past three hours. I'm exhausted and starving, so we order pizza. The guys are currently arguing about Xander not blocking enough. Obviously, Xander argues he's the *only* one blocking, and everyone else needs to up their game. Honestly, all of their blocking could be better. There are moments where our offensive men are left open when we shouldn't be, but I don't have the energy to argue with them about it right now.

I check my phone to see when the pizza will arrive, but there's no update. "Hey, do you think your sister will mind if I steal a snack?" I whisper, leaning over to Dean.

"No. Go ahead. If she says something, I'll just say I ate it." He smirks.

I walk to the kitchen and open every cabinet to find something to eat, but there's not much. The cabinets have a couple of dishes, but no food. It's like no one lives here. How does she eat? *What* does she eat?

When I open the fridge, there are only protein shakes, water, and an open bottle of Rosé.

"Looking for something?"

I jump. "Dammit the hell!" I yelp, holding my chest. "You scared the shit out of me."

"Why are you going through my fridge?" She prods, ignoring the near-heart attack she just gave me.

"There's not much to go through." I add, closing the door.

"And yet, here you are." She sets her bag down on the counter. "Why are you in *here* and not in there?"

"I was looking for something to eat."

"Well, considering this isn't your place, you should've brought your own food." Crossing her arms over her chest.

"We ordered pizza, but it's taking too long to get here, and I haven't eaten all day." I tell her, mirroring her stance.

"That sounds like a *you* problem, not a me problem."

"Are you always this snippy?"

"I'm not *snippy*. I just don't like people going through my shit. So if you could kindly go back to your pack of wolves," she says, shooing her hands in the direction of the living room, "that would be great."

I grin cheekily. "Sure thing, *Jay*." I start to walk out of the kitchen. I know I promised Dean I wouldn't say anything, but what the hell? Why not have some fun today?

"What the hell did you just call me?" She asks slowly.

"Huh, oh, I'm sorry, isn't it James?" I watch the blood drain from her face.

"Dean!" She screams, clocking her attention in Dean's direction.

All the guys' heads snap to where we stood. "Oh shit." Dean mumbles before standing and running to Luna. "Hey, Jay. What's up? Is it the mess? I will..."

"You know damn well that's not the problem right now!" Luna scowls, cutting Dean off.

"Dude, what the hell? You said you wouldn't say shit." Dean grits, sending me a *what the fuck is wrong with you* look.

"I know, and I wasn't, but she kept egging me on." I shrug.

"How was I egging you?" Luna asks, crossing her arms over her chest.

"You make it too easy to fuck with you."

She rolls her eyes. "You are by far the most infuriating human I have ever met." You can practically see the fumes blowing out of her ears.

I grab my chest. "Aww, thank you." I say it with extra sarcasm.

She is by far the most infuriating human. I've never met someone so stuck in their own world. Like nothing and no one else matters to them. This morning, one thing was very clear. Luna James is one of the most uptight and controlling people I've ever met.

It's obvious how important dance is to her. That much is clear, but what the hell is her deal? It's like she's the only person in a movie, and everyone else is just an extra. That shit's toxic as fuck.

It pisses me off.

She pisses me off.

Chapter 3

Luna

Who the hell does this guy think he is? I understand he's Dean's captain or whatever, but he is two seconds from getting another pointe shoe to the head. "You guys can leave now."

"Come on, Jay." I glare at Dean, cutting his sentence off. "I mean, *Luna*." He gulps. "We just ordered pizza. Also, we haven't finished our film review. We just need, like, one more hour. Please?"

I want to say no; I really do, but I don't. "You have one hour! I don't care if your pizza never arrives. You're out of here. Got it?"

Dean nods. I grab my bag off the counter and push past Nick, toward my room.

"The word is excuse me," Nick grumbles.

"What was that?" I turn around to face him again.

"You know? That thing you say when you need to get past a person, it's excuse me." He huffs.

Snapping my head to the left, then the right, "Oh, I'm sorry. I didn't realize this was your place. I thought I was it was mine." I roll my eyes. "Therefore, I can do whatever the hell I want in *my* apartment. If you don't like it, there's the door. No one is stopping you."

"Luna, seriously. Chill. Why are you acting like this?" Dean intervenes.

Probably because this dude's being a dick for no reason. He's in my house. Not the other way around. "Look, Dean, if you don't like it, you can all leave."

Dean grabs my arm. "Let me talk to you." He pulls me into my room before speaking again. "I don't know what the hell your problem is, but you need to fucking chill. Seriously. That's my captain out there. He's been helping me with a lot of shit, and I think he wants me to be captain next year. So, I need you to chill out. If I lose the chance to be captain because of you, I will never forgive you, Jay."

My heart sinks as I listen to the words leave his mouth. I would never intentionally cause Dean to lose anything. All he's ever talked about is being in the NHL. Becoming captain would do wonders for him. I don't like this Nick character, but if I have to put up with him for Dean's sake, I will.

"I'm sorry." I look down at the ground like a kid who just got scolded by their parents. "Seriously, I'll chill. I'll stay in here until everyone leaves. Just don't bring him over here anymore. Okay?"

"Deal." He grins softly, then pulls me in for a hug. "Thanks."

"I'm still mad you told that dickwad my middle name," I say into his chest.

He pulls back, resting his hands on my shoulders. "Yeah, sorry about that. I'm going to go back to watching the film with the team. Do you want me to bring you pizza?"

"No. It's fine. I have homework to do anyway," I say, even though I haven't eaten all day, and my stomach is growling for attention. "Dean. Make sure you all clean up after yourselves. I'm neither your mom nor your maid."

"Yes ma'am." With that, Dean walks out.

I walk to my bed and immediately crash. I'm so tired and exhausted from dancing and from helping Gia this morning. I just want to go to sleep. I know I have homework to do, but maybe a couple of minutes of shuteye will do me good.

It's seven o'clock when I wake up. I didn't mean to sleep in so late. I really do need to do my homework. I know it's an excuse I use whenever I don't want to do something, but this time I have a huge essay due before class tomorrow.

I walk into the living room to see that it's damn near spotless. Great, now I don't have to yell at Dean. I really do hate arguing with him.

I continue on into the kitchen when I see a note taped to the fridge.

> *I put two slices of pizza for you in the microwave.*
> *Eat <3*

A smile works its way up my face. It does make me happy when Dean looks out for me. We've been looking out for each other since Cassie passed. So, the constant overbearing protection, although annoying, is somewhat welcome.

I open the microwave to see two slices of pizza, just like the note said. I set the microwave for one minute and pressed start.

I return to my room and grab my phone. I have two missed calls from Gia. "Shit," I mutter under my breath.

I dial her number before she calls the police. What might look like two missed calls to someone else is two months of not hearing from me to Gia. She's also become overbearing and protective. She makes sure I eat, that I party, and basically anything else that being a college student consists of.

She answers after the first ring. "Luna! Are you okay? Are you hurt? Where are you? Are you dying? Do I need to call the police? Hit a random number twice for yes."

I laugh. "Gia, calm down. I'm fine. Sorry, I was taking a nap and my phone was on do not disturb. Sorry, I missed your call."

"What the actual fuck? You missed my call because you were *napping*? Do not put your phone on do not disturb mode. Ever. That's how people end up murdered."

"You need to stop watching *Criminal Minds*." The microwave beeps, and I rush to open it. Pulling the plate out, I take a bite out of the scorching pizza, nearly burning my tongue. "I wanted to take a nap and not be bothered." I say this around the food in my mouth.

"Aww, babes. Well, did you at least sleep well?" she asks, dropping her voice a couple octaves.

"Yes. Yes, I did. Anyway, why did you call?" I take another bite, waiting for her to answer.

"Oh, yeah. Do you want to go to the hockey game tonight?"

I turn to look at the clock on my wall. I can't go to the game tonight. I really need to work on that essay, and I haven't even started. But if I said no, I would never hear the end of it. "What time does it start?"

"9:30."

"That gives me, what, an hour to get ready? I have to shower, do my makeup, and pick out an outfit. Is it even worth it at that point?" I feel the nerves start to climb my throat as I list off things I would need to do to be ready for this game.

"Yes, it is. It's your brother, and I heard he's on the starting lineup. So get moving." Then she hangs up.

I throw the plate of pizza back in the microwave and quickly head to the bathroom to shower. I turn the water on so it's not too hot or too cold. I quickly undress, jump in, and wash all my hotspots twice. I didn't have time to enjoy the water like I normally do.

Which sucks, by the way.

Once I finish with my shower, I race against the clock to figure out what I'm wearing. I'm shuffling through my closet and have no idea what to pick out. Maybe I should've answered the phone earlier, but the sleep was too good.

Finally, I settle on a gray hoodie that says "BSU Hockey" with a pair of ripped blue high-waisted jeans. Pairing it with my white *Airforces*. I wanted to do something to my hair but decided to just brush it into a bun. Rushing back into my room, I then sit at my vanity and apply my concealer under my eyes and some mascara.

I gazed into the mirror one more time, admiring my outfit. It's not the greatest, but it's as good as it's going to get. My brother is in the starting line-up every blue moon. As his twin and biggest supporter, I feel this urge to be there and support him.

There's a knock at my door. I grab my black purse off the coat rack sitting next to my door and run to open it.

"What took you so long to open the door?" Gia pushes past me to enter. Her burgundy locks are in a high ponytail, and she's wearing a black BSU crop top with a red bomber jacket.

"Yes, please come in," I answer sarcastically. "Gia, you said the game starts at 9:30; we need to go."

"I know, but I need to use the bathroom. I'll be quick." As she makes a beeline for the bathroom. I groan loud enough for her to hear. "I heard that."

"That was the point," I call back.

She comes out five minutes later. "Okay. Let's go." She looks at the time on her phone and then stuffs it back into her black bell bottoms.

We arrive at the arena twenty minutes later. There's almost no parking anywhere. We loop around the parking lot for a good five minutes before finally finding one in the far back, with almost a five-minute walk to the stadium. Once again, I ask myself, *Is this even worth it?*

This is exactly why I don't like to do anything at the last minute. Everything needs to be thoroughly planned out. Down to the last detail. What time do we need to arrive? Who's driving? What am I wearing? Even what I'm eating for dinner?

This last-minute planning is just not for me. Gia knows that.

We make it to the front gate and pull out our phones. Gia had me download the ticket on the drive over.

The guy at the gate scans our tickets. "Enjoy the game, ladies." He gives us a quick smile. We rush into the stadium, hoping to find a good seat. Knowing we probably won't be able to.

When we walk into the arena, a breeze of cold air welcomes me and introduces itself to my face. Maybe I should have worn my bomber jacket over this hoodie. Gia had the right idea, but then again, she's been to almost every hockey game. I cross my arms over my chest to warm my body. It's not super cold, but it's cold enough for my teeth to chatter.

"Hey!" Gia calls for my attention. "I see an open spot on the third row." I lift my head slightly for her to lead the way.

As we shuffle through the crowd, I try to find Dean on the ice. He's nowhere to be found. Men from both teams are shuffling, running through what I assume are warm-ups. I don't really know much about hockey. Just enough to make Dean happy.

We finally settled into our seats after shuffling through a field of people. "Can you help me find Dean? I can't see him anywhere," I shout into Gia's ear.

"He's probably still in the locker room," Gia responds.

I continue to scan the rink. No luck. She's probably right, not that I would ever admit that to her. It is not good for her ego.

Another group of men skate onto the ice from the home team's box. I finally locate Dean as he skates toward the neutral zone. Like I said, I don't know much about hockey. I do know that Dean's a forward. So, I know he's the person who tries to shoot the puck into the goal. Which is all that matters to me.

After about ten minutes, all skaters skate off the ice, with the exception of the starting five for each team. Which includes Dean. A smile breaks free on my face as pride swells in my chest. Seeing Dean on the ice makes me happy with satisfaction that he's living out his dream.

He's doing something that most people are too afraid to do—going after what he wants. And what he wants is hockey. Dean was born to be on the ice, and every time he plays, he just proves it.

I watch as Nick—God, I hate him—skates into the middle of the rink for the face-off. I'm guessing he's a forward. I've been to a ton of Dean's games. How have I never noticed this guy? His last name, "Beckett", is bold in black on the back of his jersey, sitting high on his shoulder blades. A name shouldn't be hard to remember, yet I can't seem to find it anywhere in my memory.

The referee drops the puck, and Nick is quick to swipe it to Dean. Dean shuffles toward the goal as the defenders try to ward off the opposing team. He passes the puck back to Nick, who is rallying down to the offensive zone. Nick scrambles around the determined defenseman who is trying to bodycheck him.

I hate to say it, but I'm impressed. The way he moves on ice is like watching an artist paint. It's so eloquent, it's impossible to look away. All of this is second nature to him. It's almost... beautiful.

If he wasn't such an ass.

Nick and Dean work in harmony, like a beautiful symphony. Interchanging the puck between one another. As they close in on the goal. With only a couple of inches between them and the goal, Dean passes the puck back to Nick one more time. Nick preps his stick, pulling back just enough to slap shot the puck into the goal before it even has time to stop at his feet. With that, we're 1–0. Boston Warthogs taking the lead.

We're down to the last period. The Warthogs are leading 5-3. I check my phone for the time. It's currently 10:14. I need to leave if I want to get my essay done before tomorrow.

I tap Gia on the shoulder to get her attention. "Hey, can we leave? I need to write my essay, and it's due at noon tomorrow."

"I thought you said that essay wasn't due until next week." Her eyebrows furrow.

"That's a different class." I huff out a breath and say, "Look, I need to write a three-page essay by noon for my class tomorrow, and I haven't even started. Can we please just go? It's the last quarter, and we already know who's going to win. What more do you need to see?"

"Well, the game is almost over. Can't you wait till the end?" She asks, clearly irritated.

I couldn't. I shouldn't have even been here. I really needed to write this essay. But I wanted to support Dean. He's only put in the starting lineup every now and then. If the roles were reversed, he would be front row at my show.

I never put things off till the last minute, but Gia really needed help studying, and I couldn't say no. Then Dean took over my apartment. Then I fell asleep for longer than I meant to. Now, I'm at a hockey game, and I didn't even really want to come.

I can feel the anxiety start to rise and the panic bubble in my stomach. I really need to leave. I couldn't stay any longer than I already had, but Gia is having fun. She is also my ride home. At this rate, I won't be able to finish before class tomorrow.

I grab onto my chest.

A tightening grip clutches at my chest, each breath becoming a struggle against an invisible weight. My heart, once steadfast, begins to race, its beats echoing in my ears like an erratic drum. The world around me blurs, and an overwhelming sense of impending doom wraps its cold fingers around my consciousness, pulling me into a suffocating abyss.

This can't be happening right now. I try to run through the exercises my therapist gave me, but nothing comes to mind.

Fuck!

I push through the people standing next to me as I try to get to the bathroom. I can hear Gia calling my name, but I can't find it in me to care.

I need air. I need to calm myself.

I push through the first doors I see. Tears start to filter down my face, and my breath grows rapid. The walls are closing in on me, and I can't stop them.

I fall to the ground, holding my chest.

I look around the room, searching for something to focus on to slow my breathing. There's nothing. Silent rivers of emotions escape, tracing a path down my cheeks. I try to scream for help, but the words are caught in my throat. I can't speak. No matter how hard I try to push them out, they're stuck.

Grabbing my hair, I strain to focus on literally anything else. Please. Focus!

Luna focus! Dammit!

"Luna?"

Chapter 4

Nick

The game is almost over. We're up by one. If we keep our heads on, we can leave tonight still undefeated. I race back onto the ice as we come into our last ten minutes.

Vermont doesn't suck per se, but we are better. I nod to Dean as we take our positions for the last face-off. The ref drops the puck, and normally I'm able to swipe it away, but this guy is persistent. He shoulder-checks me and swipes the puck himself.

He's a bigger guy, but I like a challenge.

I race off toward number 31, and I return the shoulder-check he gifted me. He drifts to the right, which gives me just enough space to collect the puck and hit it backward to Dean. Like I said, we're better.

As I turn on my heels, 31 cross-checks me into the boards. I push him back with my stick. "Dude. What the hell is your problem?"

"You should watch where you're going," he retorts, then cross-checks me again before skating to the defensive zone.

I turn to see if the referee caught that. And of course, he chooses this moment to look dazed and confused. "Did you not just see that?" I yell to the ref.

He holds his hand up to my chest. "I'd advise you to back up, 27," he warns.

"You're going to tell me you didn't just see him cross-check me! Are you fucking kidding me?" I didn't really need to yell at him, nor did we need the point. But I hate when a ref doesn't do their fucking job. What's the point of a referee if they're not going to ref?

He blows his whistle. Placing both fists on his hips.

"MISCONDUCT?!" I feel the rush of anger rise from my neck.

"Beckett! Off the ice, now!" Coach howls.

I skate to our bench, where Coach stands. "Coach, you saw that shit, right? 31 cross-checked my ass *twice*."

"Yet you're the one who was penalized. You're out for the rest of the game. Hit the showers," he demands, never meeting my eyes either.

"The rest of the game? Coach, come on. You can't be serious. How is that fair?"

"You're the damn captain, Beckett. You should know better! Hit the damn showers, now!" He ushers to the locker room before turning back to the game.

I huff out a breath and chuck my gloves off. I know I'm the captain, but I'm also human. That fucker should've been penalized for cross-checking me, but he wasn't. Then I'm the one who gets penalized. What kind of bullshit is that?

I snatch my helmet off my head and brush through a crowd of people as they pat me on the back. They all tell me I did a good job, but I don't really feel like I did. I should still be playing, not heading to the showers. I give them the best fake smile I can before I push through the doors of our locker room.

When I open the doors, I see a girl sitting on the floor. Who the hell let a puck bunny in here? They do this quite often. Every now and then, one sneaks her way into the locker room in hopes of fucking one of the players. Normally, we have really good security, and they can fend them off. Somehow, one slipped through. It happens.

I'm about to tell her to leave when I notice she's crying. Not just crying, but her whole body is shaking. I throw my helmet and gloves on the bench next to me and try to get out of my skates as fast as humanly possible. As I kneel closer to her, I see her face. "Luna?" Her name leaves my mouth before I can stop it. What is she doing in here? "Hey, what's going on? What happened?"

She lifts her head, and I've never seen someone look so broken. Her face is bright red, and her breathing is rapid. Tears are streaming down her face. She is sucking in air so fast, and I have no idea what I'm supposed to do.

"I. Can't. Stop. M-Make. It. Stop," she stammers in between breaths.

She's having a panic attack. I don't know what to do. I grab hold of her hands and place them on my face. I think I saw somewhere that contact helps. "You should focus on your touch. I think you're supposed to focus on something, right?"

She doesn't speak. Her breath just keeps rushing forward with no stop in sight. "Luna, focus on me. Okay? You have to slow your breathing." I say slowly. I need to get her to focus on something else. *Anything* else. I push her palms against my face. I'm hoping the hair on my cheeks will feel weird to her and give her something. "You know, I thought you were a puck bunny. Oh, you don't know what a puck bunny is?" I shake my head.

"Some sister you are. Isn't your brother a hockey player?"

Her breaths slowly start to even out.

"A puck bunny is a girl who wants to fuck the hockey team. Yes, the *entire* hockey team. Okay, I'm being dramatic. Not the entire hockey team, but if she can make it through a quarter of the roster, she's golden. Is that rude to say? It probably is."

A small smile edges its way onto her face. "Yep, you're right; I thought you were a puck bunny. Listen, if you want to sleep with a hockey player, all you have to do is ask. There's no need to sneak into the locker room and do all of this. Your brother *is* on the team. I think you have free rein or something like that, right?"

"I don't. Want access," she comments softly as her breath returns to a normal pace.

"I mean, you're the one who snuck in here." I pull her hands from my face, squeezing them in mine. Once her breathing is back to normal, I give her a few seconds to come back to earth. "Are you okay now?" She looks me in the eye. We stay like that for a minute before she snatches her hands out of my hold.

"I'll take that as a yes," I respond sarcastically.

She stands up, fixing her brown curls that rest in a bun, and wipes the tears from her face. "Don't say anything about this to anyone. Especially to my brother, got it?"

"You know, normally people say thank you. But you're not normal, are you?"

"Screw you." With that, she walks out of the locker room, slamming the doors behind her.

What the hell just happened?

We end up winning the game 6-3, keeping our undefeated streak. It kind of pisses me off that I wasn't in the game to help us actually win, but still. We're undefeated, and that's all that matters.

When I get to my house, all I want to do is crash. My body is aching, and my head hurts like hell. It feels like there are a thousand tiny hammers banging against my cranium.

I sit on the bench next to my door and start to take off my shoes when my phone buzzes. It's almost midnight. Who the hell would be calling me this late? I pull out my phone. Overstead Nursing Home flashes across the screen.

Fuck.

"Hello?" My voice shakes.

"Mr. Beckett, I'm sorry to call you so late. I know you had a game tonight, and I wasn't sure when you would be available to talk," a pleasant woman says on the other end.

"Yeah, I'm sorry. I'm available now."

"Well, I just wanted to let you know your mother has been asking about you."

The blood drains from my face. I haven't been to see my mother in a couple of weeks. Even though I talked to her last night. It's not the same as actually going to see her. "Oh," is all I can string together in response.

"Yes. I think she's starting to notice small things, like your absence." I don't respond as the guilt gnaws at me. "I'm sorry, Mr. Beckett. I'm not trying to make you feel guilty. I know you have a busy schedule. With school, hockey, and everything else in your life, I just want you to understand your mom's situation and how precious time is."

I don't need the reminder. I am well aware. "Yes. I know. I'll be there this weekend to see her. Can you prepare a cot? I can spend the weekend there."

"I'm sure she would love that. I'll have the nurses prepare the room for you." I can hear her smile in her words. "Well, I'll let you enjoy your night. Also, congrats on your win!"

"Thank you. Have a good night." I wish for this conversation to be over sooner rather than later.

"Good night, Mr. Beckett. See you this weekend." Then she hangs up the phone.

I suck as a son. I should've gone to see my mom sooner. With hockey and training, I've been distracted. I hate to admit it, but I forgot. Out of all the things for me to forget, I can't believe I forgot her. She's my mom, for crying out loud.

I'll do better.

I need a shower to clear my mind. Technically, I took one in the locker room, but I needed another one after that phone call.

I walk into the bathroom and turn the dial for the shower on to as hot as it gets. I strip my clothes off and step into the waterfall, letting the water drown out all of my shame, rinsing off the guilt, watching it wash down the drain. I love my mom more than anyone on Earth. There's no one on this planet who has been there for me more than her. My dad is great, but my mom is my hero. She's been everything to me. She's like my best friend.

Not remembering her makes me feel like shit. I'll do better. For her, I'll do better.

I shake my head as I pour the body wash onto the towel and lather myself in it. When I finish my shower, my phone chimes again. Wrapping my hips in my towel, I grab it off the counter.

It's a text message from the one person who could ease my stress.

PC :)

Hey handsome, I'm going to be in town this week and wanted to know if you were free?

I might be able to rearrange some things.

If you come over right now

How can I say no to that :) I'll be there in 30

Alright, see you then!

Just like that, my mood elevates. I run around my room, trying to clean up while getting dressed at the same time. I grabbed the first pair of sweats and shirt I find and throw them on. I make my bed and throw all of my dirty clothes into the laundry basket. I'm not normally messy, but it's been a crazy week.

There's a knock on my door thirty minutes later, just like she said. I run to open the door. There stands one of the most beautiful girls I've ever laid eyes on.

Paris Cardone.

As I opened the door, she stood before me—a captivating sight. Her flowing black hair cascaded gently, framing a face with a golden tan that emanated warmth. A lovely grin decorated her lips, instantly brightening the room and taking my breath away in the sight of her unquestionable beauty.

"Are you just going to stand there and gawk at me, or do you plan on letting me in sometime tonight?" She pesters, snapping me back to reality.

"Yeah, sorry. You're just a sight for sore eyes." That was stupid.

"That was corny as hell, Beckett." She laughs as she steps into my house.

"Well, tonight was rough, so you'll have to excuse me for my lack of romance." I say, defending myself.

She laughs again. The one that just warms your soul and defrosts any ice I think I have around it. "Why was it rough? I would think you'd be on cloud nine considering you guys are still undefeated."

"Yeah, well, without my help. I was kicked out of the game before it was over. Then I got a call that I didn't necessarily want to hear." I stop myself from spilling more than necessary. I draw lines for a reason. I don't have time to unload myself onto others, just like I don't have time to have other people unload their stuff onto me. I'm into casual, and that's exactly what I get from Paris. Nothing more and nothing less.

"What call?" she pushes.

"Not important." I grab her waist, pulling her closer to my chest. "This is more important right now."

She smiles. "If you say so, *captain*." She raises to her toes before crashing her lips into mine. I pull her further into my chest as she deepens the kiss, swiping her tongue against my lips, asking for access. I grant it to her without a second thought. Her kiss was a sweet melody on my lips, a delicate blend of warmth and tenderness that lingered like a sugary whisper.

I lean down to lift her by her ass, and she moans into my mouth. I pull back. "God, I've missed you."

She kisses me again. "Me too."

I carry her into my room, laying her on my bed, not breaking the kiss. I can feel myself harden as she squirms underneath my touch. "So, you're staying the night, right?"

"If you keep this up, maybe."

I return my lips to hers, rubbing my hard on against her opening. Making sure my answer is clear.

This is exactly what I needed: a distraction.

Chapter 5

Luna

This night has been anything but fun. After leaving the locker room, I decide to just call an Uber home. I can't stand to be in that arena any longer. I just want to get home, write my essay, and then go to sleep.

I haven't had a panic attack in months. They started after Cassie's death. I've been in therapy for it and everything. I'm sure Jenna will be upset to hear that I forgot all of our techniques. We worked so hard to get them under control. Even if they were to happen, I should be able to work through them. That was the whole point of her teaching me, but everything happened so fast tonight. There was no time to count back from ten or find something to focus on in the room.

Then Nick came in. Of *all* people, it just had to be him. I would have literally taken a serial killer over him. Okay, maybe that's a bit dramatic, but still you get the point.

Now he has something to hold over my head. God, *is* he one of those people?

Just in case he is, I'll avoid him at all costs. Not that I plan on seeing him anytime soon.

I finish the last page of my essay with two hours to spare and no sleep. Now, I have to shower and get ready for class. This is exactly what I wanted to avoid. I didn't want to rush this paper and not have time for sleep. Oh, fucking well, I guess.

I really need to get myself in check. I can feel the myself of the brink of a mental break, and over something so trivial. It wasn't that deep, but my mind wasn't getting that. Grabbing my phone off the side table, I dial my least favorite phone number.

"Luna, what a nice phone call to receive." She answers.

"Hey, Katheryn. I'm sorry for calling so early."

"Don't be. It's nice to hear from you. Especially since I didn't have to track you down." She laughs. "What's going on?"

"What do you mean? Why does something have to be wrong? Can't I just call you just to call you?" I ask sarcastically.

"Luna." She drawls.

"Yeah, yeah. I know, no deflecting.." I sit on the edge of my bed. "I just...I don't know. I don't know what's wrong."

"Okay, so tell me what made you call now."

"I, um, I had a panic attack yesterday."

I hear her shuffling papers around as if she's writing this down. "Okay, can you tell me what set it off?"

"It was everything. I was at a hockey game I didn't want to be at, I had a ton of homework to do, and I just felt like I was suffocating." I confess.

"Luna, have you been doing what I said? Learning to say no when you're uncomfortable. Learning to set your boundaries."

"No." I answer honestly.

"Well, what do you think you would change about last night? Scratch that. What do you think would have prevented *this* panic attack?"

I inhale quietly. "I should've stuck my ground and said no. I didn't want to go, but I also didn't want to let her down, but I should've said no."

"Exactly. I know you want to make others happy, but your happiness is just as important if not more important. At least to yourself. You should always come first. Not everyone else. Does that make sense?"

"Yes."

"Luna, I want you to do something for me. I want you to have a conversation with your friend. Tell her exactly how this situation really made you feel. Be honest. Speak from your heart and tell her how this can be prevented in the future. Also remember, when you're being honest, talk to your friend and not at them. You can be honest without being angry. Can you do that?" Kathryn advises.

I internally roll my eyes. Kathryn knows I can have a short fuse when I can't get my point across. I'm working on it. "Yeah, I can." I agree. "Thank you, Kathryn."

"Of course. Please call more often. Don't be afraid to set an appointment in the future either." I stopped going to Kathryn after I graduated from high school. She told me to keep her number and to continue to come see her when needed, but clearly I haven't.

"Yeah, yeah. Let's not push it." I joke, sort of. "A conversation on the phone is all I can do at the moment."

She laughs softly. "I guess I'll settle for a phone call then. I'm proud of you, Luna."

"For what? I didn't do anything."

"You called me. That's a big step for you."

Pride swells my chest. "Thank you." I huff. "Well, I need to get ready for class."

"Okay, well contact me anytime." I agree to call more, and I hang up.

I take a quick shower and run into my closet to find something to wear. I pick out a pair of black leggings and a gray long sleeve. I put on a pair of socks and rush to slip on my high tops. I look around my living room one more time to make sure I'm not forgetting anything.

It feels like I am. Like something is supposed to happen, but for the life of me, I can't remember.

Screw it.

Grabbing my keys off the counter, I head for the door, making sure to grab my backpack off the chair before reaching for the handle. When I pull it open, there's the last person I was expecting standing right in front of me.

"Hey, teddy bear!" she screeches.

"Paris!" I drop all of my stuff before leaping into her arms. "What are you doing here?"

"What do you mean? It's ladies week. Did you forget?"

"Shit! Sorry. So much has happened this week. It totally went over my head."

"Don't worry about it. Do you want to reschedule?"

"No," I immediately respond. "I need this. Right now, I have class, so you can just stay here and make yourself at home. If you're tired, you can use my bed."

She laughs. "Sure thing. Get to class. I'll see you later." She pats me on the butt before heading for my room.

I grab my stuff off the ground and rush out the door. I'm upset I forgot about Ladies Week. It's the one thing I look forward to every month.

Ladies week is when Paris, Gia, and I spend a week at my apartment together. We watch movies, catch up, and just relax. It's only for a week out of the month because of Paris's busy schedule. But it's kind of a de-stressor for us. Especially after the last couple of days, I say it's perfect timing.

When my class finishes, I run to my car. I couldn't wait to get back home. Dance classes were canceled this week because Madame Christine was taking, I quote, "a much-needed break from all of the disappointment". I know I should feel like shit for essentially failing her, but I needed the break, too. This week has been hell, and I need to re-calibrate my mind.

I reach my car and see Gia leaning against it. I haven't spoken to her since the game. I'm kind of pissed off with how she acted. I could've done the essay earlier, but she totally disregarded me and completely brushed off the fact I needed to go. She didn't care, and that pissed me off. I would have never done that to her.

"What are you doing here?" I grunt.

"I wanted to talk to you," she answers quietly.

"Talk," I push, my tone more irritated than intended.

"Look, Luna, I'm sorry. Although I didn't feel like I should have to sacrifice what I wanted to do for you to complete your homework, I should've been more considerate."

My jaw drops. "Is that an apology?"

"Yes."

"The hell it is, Gia. That was a backhanded apology. You basically said I ruined your fun because I needed to do my *homework*. As if *I* were an inconvenience for *you*. We were in the last period. What would have been so bad about leaving early? We knew who would have won." My voice rises.

"Anything could have happened within the last ten minutes. *You* could have waited. Then you left and didn't even say goodbye or that you were leaving. Just up and left."

I take a deep breath. "Gia, I didn't even want to go to that stupid ass game in the first place! I needed to do my homework. You asked me to go last fucking minute. What the fuck did you expect from me? Also, I didn't just leave. I had a fucking panic attack. I don't have time to explain to you how important school is because you could give two shits about it." I bite my tongue before I say something I will regret.

"How was I supposed to know you had a panic attack? If you didn't want to go to the game, you could have said no. It's not like I held a gun to your head and forced you to come!"

I finally snap. "You never let me say no! Like ever! I tell you I have shit to do, and you ignore me. Then you get onto me about how *I'm not living because I'm so busy.* Not everyone wants to party all damn day and night."

"I just want you to have fun. You literally eat, sleep, breathe, and dance. If it's not dance, it's school. I want you to live life, not just simply live. I love you. I don't want college to pass by, and you have no stories to tell your kids in the future about your college days."

I snicker. "What makes you think I'll have kids?"

"How else will I be a godmother?" She shrugs, and sighs softly. "Seriously, though, I'm sorry. I'll be more considerate of your planner. Even though I *really* hate it." She apologizes, rolling her eyes.

"Thank you. I'll be more considerate of your *fun* time. Not that I will always agree with your timing. Gia, I can't always go out and you can't always force me. If I say I don't want to, please don't make me feel bad about it." I request, reminding myself what Kathryn told me to originally do. Not that she would be happy with the yelling match I ensued.

"I'm sorry, Chica. I know it's a habit, but I'll try to break it. I promise." She gives me a quick hug, sighing.

I hate arguing with Gia. So, I wrap my arms around waist, dropping the fight. "Oh, um, Paris is in town."

"Oh my god! Where is she?" she shouts.

"She's at my place. Want to ride together?" She nods and runs to the passenger side of my car.

We just did a one-eighty, but that's just the kind of friendship Gia and I have. We could argue one minute and act like nothing ever happened the next. I love her too much to let shit get between us. So, I tend to brush off the stupidity because it's just not worth it in the long run. I don't really think there's anything Gia could do that would make me hate her. Not that she's ever tried.

We pull into the parking lot of my apartment building fifteen minutes later. The car isn't even fully parked, and Gia's already racing to the front entrance. To say Gia loves Paris is an understatement. Gia is an only child, so we kind of adopted her into our family. When we were younger, it was us, Cassie, and Paris. Now it's just us and Paris. Our own little makeshift family—it's nice.

"Gia, slow the hell down." I call out. I feel like a mom chasing after an overly excited child.

"*Or* hurry *your* ass up," Gia barks.

I run to the door and pull out my key card. As we walk to the elevator, I grab my mail. There's a yellow, thick envelope. I scrunch my eyebrows as I try to figure out who it's from.

"What's that?" Gia probes.

"I don't know." I shrug.

I stuff the envelope into my purse and swipe my card against the elevator pad, and we step into it, pressing the seventeenth floor. The elevator comes to a stop on my floor, and Gia is jumping in her skin to get off. "Dude, calm down. You're acting like she's a celebrity."

"She might as well be. We rarely get to see her since she became a principal."

Paris became a principal ballerina a couple of years ago. She now lives in New York and works at a dance company. She stays busy. Therefore, we rarely get to see her. Except for one week out of the month. Although, since she became a principal, her visits have been less frequent. I think the last time we saw her was a couple of months ago.

Gia bursts through my doors the minute she reaches them. I've never seen her move so fast.

"Paris!" Gia runs to the living room, jumping on the couch with Paris.

"Gia Mia!" Paris sings.

"Can y'all lower your voices? My neighbors are going to file complaints." I laugh, shaking my head as I close the door behind me and throw my keys on the counter. I walk to my room and take my shoes off before setting them back in their rightful spot in my closet.

When I walk back into the living room, Gia and Paris are already snuggled up with each other.

"So, when did you get into town?" Gia questions.

"Last night," Paris responds.

I came to a screeching halt. "Wait, last night? Why didn't you come over last night, then?"

"Um, I went to see someone else. I ended up staying there." She answers, pulling her long, wavy hair into a bun exposing her long, golden-tanned neck.

"Who?" I push, leaning against the couch.

"Someone."

"Was it a friend's place or a *friend's* place?" Gia pesters as she wags her eyebrows.

Paris stands. "It was a guy's."

"Ohmygod! Tell us more!" Gia pulls her legs under her, clasping her hands beneath her chin in anticipation as Paris paces the living room.

"Okay, but it's nothing serious. I've been seeing this guy since last year. We only text and hang out when I'm in town. He's hot as shit though. And fucks like it's *no one's* business." Her eyes roll to the back of her head.

My interest has officially piqued. "Okay, but *who* is he?"

"I don't want to tell you yet," Paris snips, shutting me down.

"Wait, why?" Gia pries.

"Well, for one, he's on the hockey team." She pauses, looking at me. "So that means you probably know him."

I interrupt, "Unlikely. I don't really know the team like that. I know maybe five players." Which is saying something because my brother has been on the team for two years. How the hell do I only know five freaking players?

"Well, he might be one of those players. Anyway, I kind of want things to get serious between us." Mine and Gia's eyes widen. "Yeah, I know. We live a ways away, but I'm sure we could make it work. I just want to see if he's as serious as me."

"Paris, almost all of the hockey players are hoes. The odds of him wanting something serious are slim to none." I don't mean to knock her down, but it's the truth. Most of the players on the team don't date. They sleep around with a line of girls who want them and never leave room for anyone to get attached.

"Well, damn, tell me how you really feel," Paris says as the hurt coats her words.

"I didn't mean it like that. I just want you to be careful, that's all. Maybe he'll want a relationship with you. I don't know." I shrug, trying to recover.

"Yeah." She shakes her head, "Whatever, enough about me. What about you guys? Any men in *your* life?"

"The only man for me is Dean, but he's clearly off limits."

I roll my eyes at Gia. She knows I hate when she talks about what-ifs when it comes to Dean. I don't even like that she likes him, but she can't help her feelings. As long as she doesn't act on it. I know it sounds messed up, like I'm controlling them. But in reality, I'm trying to keep the peace.

I don't want to see Gia get hurt, but I also don't want to see my brother get hurt either. They're too important to me. I couldn't pick one over the other. Therefore, she can't act on it. Not even just that, though. All three of us have been best friends since we were kids.

If they were to start dating, the whole dynamic would change. They'd always want their alone time and I would have to give it to them because they're a couple. So where does that leave me? They're kind of the only friends I have right now. I've lost one important person in my life, I can't bear to lose another. So I keep my circles small. They less people I have in my life, they less I have to worry about losing.

"Okay, well, what about you, Luna? Any lucky guy?" Paris asks with a hopeful smile on her face.

I shake my head. "Nope. I'm too busy to think about men."

"You could always *make* time if you really wanted to." Paris would know of all people. She's the one balancing a professional ballet career and this mystery guy. For a whole year, nonetheless.

It didn't matter, though. There was no one I wanted to make time for. "No, I'm good." I turn around and walk to the kitchen, dropping the topic. "Do y'all want to order in?" I yell into the living room.

"Yes!" they reply in unison.

After grabbing my phone off the counter, I walk back into the living room. "Oh my god, we should order Tom's," Paris recommends.

Gia and I lock eyes.

Tom's Pizzeria.

It was mine and Cassie's favorite spot to eat after dance class. We went there so often the restaurant knew our order by heart. A large pizza with cream cheese, bacon, pineapple and jalapeños. It's a weird combo, but for some reason we loved it. Cassie had me try one time and I swore it was the nastiest thing I've ever seen, but I could never get enough of it.

I haven't ordered there since her death, nor have I been back to eat. I feel like if I ate there with anyone else, it would be a betrayal to Cassie. I know it's not true, but that's exactly what it would feel like. Everyone knows it's the one place where I'll never eat again. Well, everyone but Paris apparently.

"Um, can we choose something else?" my voice barely above a whisper.

"Oh, come on, please? I haven't had Tom's in months!" Paris pleads.

"I agree with Luna. I just had Tom's yesterday, and I'm not in the mood to eat it two nights in a row." Gia lies right through her teeth. This is why I keep her around.

"Ugh fine. Ooh, I know. Let's get Chinese!" Paris says, finally giving up.

I unlock my phone, entering our order.

I don't tend to talk about Cassie a lot. So, anything that could possibly bring her up, I stray from. It's fine to think about her, but not to talk about her with other people. It's too much. It brings me back into a deep depression I worked too hard to drag myself out of.

I pass the phone to Gia so they can input their orders and walk back into the kitchen to catch my breath. I can feel the anxiety beginning to rise again, so I try to count down from ten. My stomach unfurls at the thought of Cassie and I sitting at our favorite booth at Tom's laughing about Sydney Carlson's nose job that makes her look like the witch from the wicked west.

"*Nine.*" I count in my head as I think about the time Cassie and begged the owner of Tom's to let us work off our bill because Cassie forgot her wallet at home.

He ended up giving us the order for free since we were regulars.

"Eight." The next time we came back we ordered extra food and left a huge tip. I feel the tears prickle behind my lids as I grab hold of my chest.

"Seven. Breathe Luna." I'm okay.

"Six." I inhale. *"Five."* I exhale.

"Four." Inhale. *"Three."* I wipe the tears from my eyes as I take in another deep breath.

"Two." I exhale. *"One."*

"Okay, order placed," Paris shouts, pulling me out of my thoughts.

I take one final breath before walking back into the living room with a bottle of water. "Okay, let's put on a movie while we wait." I huff, and make a mental note to call Kathryn.

Chapter 6

Nick

My government professor assigned us an eight-page essay that's due next Wednesday. I've been re-reading the same question for the last thirty minutes, and I still don't know how to answer it. It's honestly so stupid.

Discuss the American Constitution. Is it rigid or flexible?

Like what?

If I really think about it, the question isn't that hard, but I don't have the brain capacity to care about it. It was my fault for waiting until my senior year to take my gen-eds. I probably learned this shit in high school, and coming into freshman year, this would've been a breeze. I just really hate anything that has to do with history or the government.

Like, why do we need to bother the old men who have already told their story? Can't we make new stories? *You learn history, so you don't repeat it.* At least that's what everyone keeps telling me. But it seems like the same shit is being repeated, just smarter.

So, once again, I ask, Why the hell can't we just leave the shit in the past? Slamming my computer shut, I walk to the kitchen to find something to eat.

There's a knock on my door.

I'm not expecting anyone. I haven't even heard from Paris since she came over a couple nights ago. She left before I could say goodbye or make plans to meet up again while she's in town.

I don't really have feelings for Paris, but I do like her. She's hot, for starters. But that's not even what attracts me to her. Paris has this calming energy about her. I'm sure if I wanted to, I could talk to her about personal stuff, but I've drawn the lines in the sand it's where I want to keep them drawn.

I opened the door, half expecting and hoping it would be her. But when I open it, it's Dean. "What are you doing here?"

"Dude, you asked me to come over?" he replies.

Shit. I forgot he was coming over. We're suppose to come up with new plays. I want to see if he could come up with good ones on his own. As captain, we're always creating new plays for the team. Obviously, Coach gets final say, but as captain we should still be making them. We should be thinking of ways to improve our team at all times. "Oh yeah. Come on in."

I open the door for him to enter. He walks to the couch and sets his bag on the ground, pulling out an array of notebooks. "I've started on some already. You can look them over and tell me if you like them or not."

I grab the book from his outstretched hands and glance over the plays. They're actually good. They're intricate and, honestly, would give the other teams a run for their money. "Dean, these are really good."

He clasps his hands, rubbing them together. "Really?"

I see the worry painted across his face. "Yeah, these plays are damn near perfect."

"Thanks." His shoulders relax. "There are some things I want to fix and run by you."

I hand him back the notebook. "We can do that."

It's been three hours. We've been working on these plays nonstop. We are finally to a point where I feel confident enough to call it a night.

"Oh, yeah. There's this party tonight at the hockey house." Dean says as he starts to head for the door.

My eyebrows dip. "On a Thursday?"

He laughs. "Yeah, dude. You should come." He halts in his step. "Beware, though, my sister is coming. Our family friend is in town, and they're always doing stupid shit when she's in town," he warns.

I haven't spoken to Luna since I saw her in the locker room. I feel this urge of wanting to check if she's okay, but I decide against it. I wonder if she ended up telling Dean about the panic attack. I never promised to not tell him anything, but it's also not my business either.

"Why would I care if she's there?" I question, shrugging my shoulders.

"Just… I know you both have a hard time getting along with each other. I just wanted to warn you in advance." He retorts.

"Alright. Just give me, like, twenty minutes to get ready. Then we should get some food and go." I haven't eaten all day, and I'm fucking starving.

Pulling out my phone, I pull up Paris's contact.

PC :)

Hey, there's a party at the hockey house tonight.

You trying to swing by?

Funny, I was just about to text you about it

Great minds think alike, I guess.

Does that mean you're coming?

Maybe… if you're there, I just might ;)

Say less. I'll see you there

Okay, ooh, you can meet my friend. You'll love her. She's great

I'm sure I will

I throw my phone on my bed and continue to look for something to wear. I settle on the first black t-shirt I find with a pair of washed-out blue jeans. I pair it with my navy-blue bomber jacket.

Walking back to the living room, I see Dean sprawled out on the couch. "You ready?"

He quickly sits up. "Yeah. I'm starving."

I rub my stomach as it starts to growl. Right on queue. "Same. Let's go."

I grab my keys off the hook, and we head out.

We make our way to my car. It's a black 2020 Chevrolet Camaro. I know I'm cliche, but its been my dream car since I was eight. My dad got it the minute it was on sale three years ago. Kind of his "*I'm proud of you* gift". It's the one thing I love more than hockey. Okay, not the *one* thing. Speaking of which.

I quickly pull my phone from my back pocket and shoot a text to the nursing home nurse that's looking over my mother.

Mom's Nurse

> Sorry to text you so late, but can you set out a cot for me for tomorrow?

Her reply is almost instant.

Mom's Nurse

> *Of course, I can. I'll see you tomorrow Mr. Beckett.*

After seeing her text, I pocket my phone before twisting the car keys in my hands. "Where are we going?" I ask, unlocking the doors.

"I honestly couldn't care less. Anywhere that sells food is good with me." Dean laughs.

I shake my head, and I get into the car. I put the car into reverse before pulling out of the driveway. We drive mindlessly for the next fifteen minutes until we finally decide on Taco Bell. My stomach is going to hate me later, but I'm hungry, and it's the first thing we saw.

We quickly ordered our food and pull into a parking space. Why didn't we just eat inside? I don't know.

Music is playing quietly in the background as we eat and sit in an awkward silence. Dean's not much of a talker. Something I've realized within the last couple of weeks of training with him. Not that it really bothers me. Honestly, I kind of prefer it.

"Do you think we'll make it to the championships?" Dean ask, breaking the silence first.

I shrug one shoulder. "I don't know. I hope so."

I sound nonchalant, but this year matters the most. Not only because it's when I could get recruited, but because it's my senior year. It's the last year I can play with the guys. The last year I can lead them to a championship. The last year I can really make an impact on them.

Becoming the hockey captain in my senior year is more than just leading a team; it's a chance to prove myself, not only as a player but as a leader. In this final chapter of my college journey, wearing the captain's C isn't just about scoring goals; it's about navigating the complexities of this team. Making sure every player is on top of their game. That every player knows every play inside and out. Whether we win or lose, it's on me because it means I failed to make sure that everyone knew what the hell they were doing. It's a burden I proudly carry, so they don't have to.

I crumple up my burrito wrapper and throw it back into the bag. "Let's not worry about it tonight. Yeah?"

He nods his head.

I turn the key in the ignition and head to the hockey house.

We sit in silence for the rest of the drive. I can't really think about the championship right now. It would drive me crazy. So, I focus on looking for Paris as soon as we arrive.

I pull into the captain's parking spot. Something I'm grateful for. Parking at the hockey house is next to impossible. I'm not sure who put it here, but I'm not complaining. The lawn is already overflowing with people. You can hear the music blaring from out here. Once I lock my car, we head inside.

When we walk in, the smell of beer and adolescence floods my senses. I'm not really a party kind of guy, but it's senior year.

I tap Dean on the shoulder. "I'm gonna go get a drink." He nods his head in acknowledgment, and I head toward the kitchen.

I stop in my tracks when I see Paris. She's laughing with some girls. She's wearing a blue dress that hugs her waist and her hair sits in a high ponytail, showing off her long neck.. Damn, she's hot.

I should go talk to her, but I decide against it. She looks to be enjoying the conversation she's in. If she really wants to see me, she'll either text me or find me herself. Continuing what I originally came in here to do, I walk to the kitchen for a beer.

When I reach the kitchen, I see Luna. Standing in a peach strapless minidress. Her hair is in a high bun with a couple of curls framing her face. The dim lights shine against her flawless light brown skin. It doesn't look like she's wearing a lot of makeup, and yet, she looks fucking stunning.

I might not like her, but I'm not blind, nor am I dead. I can admit when someone is hot.

I walk to the opposite side of the kitchen island from her. "So, she does get out."

She looks at me through her eyelashes, rolling her golden-brown eyes when she sees my face. "Not that it's any of your business, but I do have a life. I just put other things above getting drunk. Unlike you." She continues to make her drink.

"I don't get drunk," I retort. I don't even really drink, but I don't tell her that.

"Whatever you say." She continues making herself a drink.

I could easily just drop the conversation there, but I don't. "What's that supposed to mean?"

She palms the counter, then gives me her full attention. "You're like every other hockey player here. You glide through relationships like you skate through opponents – fleeting, leaving a trail of broken promises. You wear that jersey like a badge of honor, but all I see is a player who thinks scoring off the rink is the only win that matters. You're not unique; you're just another stereotype, and I refuse to be another name in your playbook."

"First off, I'm nowhere near like that. You don't even know me." I step closer, until the smell of her seeps into my senses. Coconuts and strawberries. "Second, you're assuming I wanted anything to do with you in the first place. Not one time did I mention sleeping with you. Also, you're clumping all of the hockey players together. Isn't your brother on the team?"

"I'm not saying my brother is perfect. He's just not as bad as you and the rest of the men on the team." She sneers, glaring into my soul with those hypnotizing eyes of hers.

I laugh. "Wow. That's really cheap coming from you."

"What does that mean?" She snips.

"You're the one who's stuck in her own world and thinks the world revolves around them. It's like you choreographed your entire life around dance and decided everyone else is just an audience." I step close enough that we're toe-to-toe, and I'm hovering over her. She doesn't back up like I thought she would, instead she squares her shoulders and straightens her spine. "Newsflash – not every guy is a damn cliché, and not every girl is swooning at your solo act. I've got my own game to play, and guess what? It's not centered on scoring in the dance studio or between your sheets."

I push her curls behind her and I see the small shudder in her lips. "Unless, if you just wanted to ride my dick, you could've just asked. No need to get jealous." Trailing my tongue across my bottom lip. "There's plenty to go around."

She pushes out of my embrace before taking the cup off the counter and throwing whatever was in it in my face. "You're a dick, and that's one ride I'll happily avoid." Then she turns on her heels and waltz out of the kitchen.

Maybe I took it a little too far. But hell, the girl is a pain in the fucking ass. I should apologize. I walk out of the kitchen to find her, but no luck. Not with this sea of people. I feel like an asshole, and I smell like shit. The irony isn't lost on me.

I text Paris that we should meet up some other time, and I head home.

I think I've reached my social quota for tonight.

When I arrive back home, I get a text from Paris.

PC :)

Hey I'm coming over

Okay I'm here

I lock my phone and change into something more comfortable. This was not what I had envisioned for the night. Not even a little bit. I had planned to go to the party, maybe have a couple of drinks and end up leaving with Paris. *That* didn't happen. I hang up my jacket, pull out a pair of gray sweats, and shrug them on.

There's a soft knock on the door, and I run to open it.

"That was fast." I open the door for her to enter.

"Well, you left so quickly. I wanted to make sure everything was okay." She says tenderly.

There's this weird feeling that fills my stomach when she says that. Not a good kind either. "Yeah. I'm fine," I say, shrugging off the awkwardness. "Are you hungry or thirsty?"

She shakes her head, smiling. "I did want you to meet my friends. They're kind of great, but I guess you'll never know now."

A smile tugs on my lips. "The shame." I laugh lightly. "One day, I'm sure you'll introduce us." I don't actually want to meet them. Meeting them feels like I'm committing myself to Paris, and that's the last thing I want.

I like how we are now. There's no interlinking of friendships. I don't know her family, and she doesn't know mine. So, when we eventually call things off, it won't be awkward. I don't want a relationship right now. I have way too much on my plate. The last thing I need is a relationship to top it all off.

"Yeah, I'm sure I will." Paris remarks. "For now, I want to get to know *you* better." She wraps her arms around my neck.

God I hope she means physically. I smile tightly. "What do you mean? You *do* know me."

"Not really. Nick, we've been doing whatever this is between us for a year now. And I still don't know much about you."

Fuck. "Paris." I grab her wrists and pull them down from my neck, holding them in front of me. I look at her hands then look at her. "What are you doing?" I ask, softly.

"Nick, what is this?" She releases her hands from my grip and waves them between us.

And there it is. That's what I was afraid of. I thought she was on the same page as me. I thought she didn't want anyone tying her down the same way I don't. I step back from her and sit on the bar stool. "I thought you didn't want any strings."

"I didn't." She shrugs, "But things change. *People* change." She responds as she steps in between my legs, spreading them farther apart.

The air around me is starting to constrict my lungs. "I haven't. Hockey is the most important thing on my mind right now. Nothing and no one else. I'm sorry."

She steps back and gives me her back, resting her hands on her hips. "Wow."

I grab her wrist, twisting her to look at me. "What? You can't say you're shocked. I literally told you this from the jump I didn't want a relationship, and you agreed. This is why this worked so well. You weren't looking for anything, and I wasn't either. What changed?"

She snatches her arm back as if I burnt her. "You think sleeping with someone for a year wouldn't impact my opinions on dating? I *like* you, Nick."

"Fucking hell, Paris. Just stop liking me then. It's not that deep." I groan, standing up from the stool and walk into the kitchen. With her following close behind.

"I can't just *stop* liking you, Nick. That's not how things work." She mutters. "Why won't you even give it a chance? It would work." She reaches for my bicep, turning me around with hopeful eyes. "I mean, I'm in New York the majority of the time, and I'm here once a month. You would have your space, and I would have mine. It would be damn near perfect."

"No!" I crack. "What don't you understand? I don't want a fucking relationship, Paris! So, either we fuck, or you leave. That's it! That will be all you get from me."

She just stands there, silent.

What the hell is my problem? Contrary to belief, I don't get off on upsetting women. I really do like Paris. A lot. Just not like that. I have too much on my plate right now. Maybe if we met in the future, and I was settled in the NHL, we could try. Right now, I just don't want to. I need to focus on my career.

"Fine," she finally says.

I watch as she walks toward my room. I follow behind her. "What are you doing, Paris?" I ask defeated.

"You said either we fuck, or I leave." She starts to unzip her dress. I stand in the doorway, watching as it pools at her feet. "So, get over here and fuck me, Beckett."

I know I shouldn't, but I'm fucked up in the head right now. I should just tell her to go home but with everything that's happened, I don't have it in me to care.

It takes all of five paces for me to grab her face and crush my lips into hers. All of the fire from the conversation fused into our kiss. It's not sweet, nor is it slow. It's passionate and... angry.

She's angry.

What the fuck am I doing? My mom would beat me senseless if she knew I were taking advantage of a woman like this. So, I pull back.

"What are you doing?" she questions, as tears grow in her eyes.

"I can't do this, Paris. You're mad." I step back again, putting space between us.

"For Christ's sake!" She huffs. "First, you want to fuck me. Now you don't. Make up your damn mind."

"Not like this."

"I'm leaving." She picks her dress off the floor.

I grab her arm. "No. Stop. You can still stay here. You can leave in the morning. It's late. Just stay here."

Reluctantly, she agrees. Dropping her dress on the floor, she walks to my bed and throws herself under the covers. I can hear her sniffling. Which makes me feel like an even bigger dick.

I slide into the bed next to her. "Paris?" I whisper.

"Leave me alone," she cries, in between sniffles.

"I'm sorry. I really do like you. I just can't give you what you're asking for."

"Please, Nick, just go to sleep and leave me alone." She shuffles further away from me. I guess this is why they make king size beds.

I tentatively scoot back to my side and try to fall asleep. When I wake up the next morning, she's gone.

Chapter 7

Luna

I've never been so furious in my life. Nick acts like he knows everything about everyone. Like he's God or some shit, and personally, I'm over it. He thinks just because my brother is on the team, that automatically means I want to sleep with every hockey player. Well, I don't.

Honestly, hockey players aren't even close to being my type. Especially because my brother plays. I've never met a person who gets so far beneath my skin you would think they were a part of me, and not in a good way.

I'm over this stupid ass party. I didn't even get to make myself a drink. Well, I made one, but wasted it on that jackass.Why the hell would I do that?

Looking around the room, I try to find Gia and Paris to let them know I'm leaving. There's no reason for me to stay any longer than I already have. I walk through the living room and into the dining room to get to the back door. It just dawned on me how big this house is. I mean, it makes sense since, it houses half of the team.

The living room alone could probably fit two swimming pools, which is probably why they have all the parties here. There's probably about four hundred people in here. Two boys are guarding the swirling staircase that lead upstairs.They look to be about eighteen. They must be freshmen.

Shaking my head, I continue walking down the hallway pushing through couples who are shoving their tongues down each other's throats. I can't even remember the last time I kissed someone.

Fuck my life. I really hate this party.

When I make it outside, I spot Gia and Paris, leaning against a rail that surrounds the house, talking to Dean and some other guys from the team. I tug on Gia's shirt to get her attention. "Hey, I'm going to head home."

Gia frowns, setting her drink on the table. "What? No. Don't go. We just got here an hour ago," she pleads.

"I'm kind of over it. This dude just pissed me off, and I'm not really in a partying mood anymore." I glance over at Paris, who is currently texting someone on her phone. It must be the guy she was telling us about the other day. She said we would meet him tonight, but honestly, I couldn't care less right now.

Paris notices me and walks over. "Hey, is everything okay?" she asks, brushing her long, black waves out of her eyes.

"Yeah. I'm just going to head home." I hug her and Gia before she can argue. "Gia should have a spare key card to get in." I mumble in her ears before pulling away.

"Okay." Paris frowns at Gia. "I really wish you would stay. I'm only here for a week."

I know what she's doing. She's trying to guilt me. I really do want to enjoy the time I have with Paris. It's rare for her to come out here without planning it in advance. So, every moment she's here is special. But she also knows I hate parties, so we can do *literally* anything else. "I know, but tomorrow's Friday. So, we can stay out all night then. Okay? I promise I'll make it up to you two."

They both nod their heads, and with that, I leave.

I could've stayed. I wanted to find some reason to get over Nick's assholery, but I couldn't find one. So, I call an Uber and head home. As soon as I get home, I head straight for the shower, shrugging off the dress before chucking it into the laundry basket. The one day I'm glad I didn't wear any underwear.

I didn't plan on sleeping with anyone, but also, I wouldn't have stopped it if I met someone worth the time. It obviously isn't happening.

I turn on the shower and let the water run until it's hot, then I step in, letting the water cascade down my body, melting all of my annoyance. I pull my hair out of the bun and let the water soak my curls. Just what I needed. When I finish showering, I pull on an oversize t-shirt and tuck myself into bed. Closing my eyes and forgetting tonight ever happened.

I wake up the next morning to complete silence. Which is weird. It's never quiet when Paris is over here. Normally, she has music blaring while she and Gia cook breakfast. Not gonna lie, it aggravates me, but I easily digress when I see a stack of buttermilk pancakes and crispy bacon on a plate for me.

So why the hell was it so quiet? I jump out of bed, pull on a pair of biker shorts, and walk into the living room.

The blow-up mattress that Gia and Paris were using is still rolled up in the corner. Unused. Weird.

Walking back to my room, I grab my phone off the charger. I have no missed calls or texts from either one of them. So, where the hell are they?

I open our group chat to text them.

Me

where are y'all

There's no reply. I start to bite my nails. I can feel the panic rise in my throat. Anything could have happened to them.Maybe they didn't make it home last night because something *did* happen to them. What if they got hurt? What if they were in a car accident? What if they're in the hospital? I can feel my stomach churn at the thoughts. Then my phone buzzes.

Charmings <3
Paris

Sorry I stayed at that guy's house last night I meant to text

Me

You should've told someone before you left Paris

She knows how much anxiety I get when I don't know where they are. We have strict rules when we go out. If you're leaving the group for any reason, you *always* tell someone. If you can't find them, you text it in the group chat. You always keep your location on, too. That way we always know where we are if we don't hear from each other. There's still no word from Gia and her location is off. I would be pissed if I wasn't so worried.

Charmings <3
Paris

> *You're right I'm sorry, teddy bear. Never again, I promise*

Me

> *It's fine as long as you're ok*

Gia Mia

> *Babes I'm so sorry. I got plastered and just stayed at a friends*

What friend? If she was plastered, she should've just come here. That doesn't even make sense. But Gia isn't the type to spend a night with a guy she doesn't know. It takes her a while to even hit a home run with one. So, who did she spend the night with? I know her friends. It's Dean and me. I mean, Gia is a social butterfly, but she doesn't have *friends* friends. Just people she calls her friends. So, I'm really confused right now.

Me

> *umm …ok*

Paris

> *Gia if you got dicked down just say so*

> *no need to lie ;)*

Gia Mia

> *I'm not lying, wth*

> *I stayed at a friend's. I wasn't sober enough to go back to Luna's*

Me

okay

I still didn't believe her, but I didn't know where else she could be. Plus, Gia only gets defensive when she feels backed into a corner. So, I just drop it. I shoot them a text that I'm heading to the dance studio and will see them later.

When I arrive, I head straight for Madam Christine's studio. I chuck my bag across the room and sit on the ground as I pull my pointe shoes on.

I know classes were canceled this week, but I can't go that long without dancing. I'd feel like I was suffocating sitting at home doing nothing but resting. I can't do that. I'm the kind of person who needs to stay busy. If I'm not doing something, I quite literally will lose my mind. So, here I am, on my day off, in the studio.

This winter, we're performing *Serenade.* It's a pretty complex choreo, so I try to get in as much practice as I can. We've only covered the first section, *Sonatina.* We're supposed to start *Waltz* next week. First, I needed to perfect the first section before I even feel ready to move on. Regardless of how I felt, we would move on to the next section because Madam Christine says so. Therefore, I come into the studio on my free time so I can perfect it.

I lace my left shoe's ribbon around my ankle and walk across the room to set the barre in the middle of the room for my warm up. As I rest in the first position, anxiety washes over me again. It's been happening a lot lately. I don't know why. I try to shake it off and refocus. Looking into the mirror, I plie and start our warm-up routine.

I finish with my last grand plie. Taking a last deep breath before walking to find the remote for the stereo, grabbing it from the top shelf, I turn back to the middle of the room. I take the barre and set it back in its place against the mirrors.I take my place on the center floor. Feet together as I stretch my arm to the sky with my palm facing the ceiling. Then press play on the remote before throwing it across the room. Returning to my original stance.

As I start, I close my eyes and allow the music to invade my thoughts, brushing aside any and all outside problems. I focus solely on this choreo right here and right now. The only thing that matters to me in this moment.

The music wraps around me, a rhythmic heartbeat guiding my movements. There's an electric hum in the air, a fusion of anticipation and exhilaration. My body becomes a vessel for emotion. My body becomes. A vessel for emotion, each pirouette and extension a brushstroke in the canvas of expression. A symphony of limbs choreographed by the music's invisible hand. Every leap and twirl is a conversation with the soul, leaving a trail of emotions echoing through the space like a delicate dance of dreams.

I finish running through the entire choreography from start to finish, ending on the opposite end of the room. I inhale a deep breath before I hear a slow clap behind me. I turn to see Madam Christine in the doorway.

"Oh dear, I didn't mean to scare you. It's just... that was so beautiful." She grabs onto her chest as if her heart warms with pride.

"I messed up on my pirouettes," I critique.

"That's what practice is for. Honestly, I thought you did lovely."

It's rare for Madam Christine to hand out compliments, so anytime she does, I better look at it like a rare jewel. I never know when I will hear another one. She doesn't believe in stroking our egos. Her words, not mine.

"Thank you," I respond.

"I'm actually glad you're here. I wanted to talk to you about something." She walks into the room, wrapping her arms around her petite frame. Considering Madam Christine was forty-four, you wouldn't be able to tell. Her hair didn't contain a single fleck of gray hair, instead it was dark auburn. There wasn't a single wrinkle either. Her skin is tight around her face and arms. If anything, she looks like she's in her late twenties, and moves like it, too.

"Okay." I feel the nerves rise again.

"I wanted to formally offer you a principal role in *Serenade*." She smiles.

My mouth falls open. I knew she was currently emailing and talking to people about the principal roles for the show, but I didn't think I would get one, no matter how badly I wanted it.

The principal roles are typically reserved for seniors. It's the chance to showcase their talents with all of the dance companies in the audience. I'm only a junior, so I still had another year before I graduated college. Which means, the chances of me getting an offer are slim to none. But damn did I want one. "Oh my god. Seriously?" I blurt, covering my mouth.

"Yes," she nods. "I would like you to be the Dark Angel. I think it's perfect for you. Your turns are lovely. Plus, I think you have the strongest legs out of almost all of the ladies here."

She wasn't wrong. I worked hard on my legs and my turns. Something I knew I could be proud of. Despite my turns today. I mean my pirouettes were ass, but it's only cause of the bullshit plaguing my mind.

"So would you like it?" she asks.

"Yes!" I shrieked, not missing a beat.

Her face beams with a bright smile. "Well great. Luna, I hope you know you will have to put in extra hours in the studio. You will also have a one-on-one with me every week until the performance."

"That's fine. I'm always in the studio anyway." I shrug.

"Great. Well, we will start next week. Also, if you want to land your pirouettes better, you need to spot yourself. Pick a spot on the wall and don't take your eyes off of it as you turn," she adds.

"Thank you, Madam Christine."

She nods as she walks out of the studio. I move my gaze to the mirror. I feel like crying right now. Having a lead role in the showcase increases my chances of getting asked to join a dance company.

I need to be perfect. Everything *has* to be perfect.

No screw-ups. No slip-ups.

Yeah, I don't feel the pressure *at all*.

Chapter 8

Luna

"We've been waiting on you. Where have you been?" Gia grunts as I enter my apartment.

"I literally told you guys I was going to the studio. What's wrong?" I put my duffle bag on the ground and walk further into the living room. There's something different in the air, like I just walked into the middle of a war zone. "Who died?"

"My love life," Paris interjects with tears streaming down her face.

I run to her side, cradling her hands. "Oh my god. Paris, what happened?"

"I finally told him. The guy." She sniffles. "I told him I wanted more." She sniffles again, shaking her head.

"He didn't. He said he didn't want more, and he never would."

I wrap my arms around her shoulders, consoling her. Paris rarely puts herself out there. I don't know why, but she just doesn't. It doesn't make sense to me because she is hot as shit. Like really hot and so caring. Her heart is as big as Texas. Yes, I'm aware of how outdated that is, but it's true. "He doesn't deserve you, then. If he can't see how amazing you are, then he doesn't deserve you."

She wipes her eyes and runs her hands through her hair. "This is so stupid. Why am I crying over him?" Because no one likes rejection, not even you, but I refrain from actually saying that.

"This is why I don't do men. I can't deal with the emotions that come with them." I shiver in disgust.

"You will one day. You're going to find someone you'd risk it all for. Then you'll feel every single emotion. Trust me."

"No. I cut men off. There hasn't been a single guy to change my mind, and there won't be one now." I give her a soft pat on the shoulder and walk back to the kitchen. Paris and Gia surround themselves with men, but I don't. I mean, I support their endeavors, but I only wanted to focus on dance. That's all that matters to me.

"You say that now. Just wait." She blows out a puff of air. "Anyway, can we talk about something else?" Paris insists.

"Oh yeah, how was your time in the studio?" Gia asks, changing topics.

"It was great. Actually, I have some news." They both give me their full attention. "I was given a principal role for our winter showcase."

"Oh my God!" they screech in unison.

"I know. I can't believe Madam Christine gave it to me. Especially since I'm only a junior. She could've given it to a senior." I shake my head. "Regardless, I need to bust my ass. I really want someone to sign me or even show interest." I really can't screw this up.

Paris stands and walks over until she's right in front of me. "Teddy bear, I'm happy for you. I really am."

"But?" I drawl, knowing there's going to be one. Why can't we just let well be enough? Why is there always a but?

Grabbing my hands, Paris says, "But I want you to make sure you're not stressing yourself in the process. I mean, this is a great opportunity, but you're only twenty, and you're putting *so* much pressure on yourself."

I pull my hands out of her hold. "First off, I'll be twenty-one in a month." Real mature Luna. "Second, you of all people know how much this means to me. *Why* this is so important. I'm not stressing myself out." I lie right through my teeth. "I have to do this."

"I understand you feel like you *have* to do it. But do you *want* to?"

Of course, I do. I love dancing, it's all I know. I mean, I started because of Cassie, but I do love dancing. Dance is my therapy. I don't think I'd even be here right now if it weren't for dance. But also, I dance for Cassie too. I don't see what's so wrong with that. Dancing for someone who never got the chance to. That's what matters too, right?

"Yes. It's what I want to do. Let's not ask stupid questions, yeah? I know what I'm doing, and I know what I want to do. I don't need you second-guessing me." I walk around her to my room, slamming the door behind me. I sit on the edge of my bed, taking a deep breath.

I pick up the picture of Dean, Cassie, and me. Tears start to swell in my eyes. I look up to the ceiling to keep them from falling.

"I promise I'll make you proud, Cassie." I whisper, hoping she can hear me, wherever she is.

I set the picture back on the desk and shuffle under my blankets. I know I should shower, but I just want to crash. Just for a minute. Cassie is always on my mind, but she rarely affects me. Not like she used to. But every now and then, her absence will hit me like a pile of bricks, like I'm finding out she died all over again. This just happens to be one of those moments.

I miss her so much. Having her around to listen to my problems and give me advice on how to handle them. She was always there for me. Six years later, and I'm still feeling the effects of her absence every day.

I wake up and go straight to my bathroom to shower. Sleeping in my sweat is just not the move.

Once I finished, I walk back to my room and put on a pair of tights and a black pullover with my brother's name on it.

Dean's name was plastered on sweaters, hoodies, and jersey's months after joining the team. He gave me one when they shipped him a collection. They were test runs, but they sold out the minute they went on sale. Something I'll never get used to is Dean's popularity.

Walking into the living room, I search for Gia and Paris. I feel like I should apologize for snapping at Paris earlier. I didn't mean to. I know she's just looking out for me. Sometimes I have a bad habit of snapping at people who want the best for me. It's a toxic trait I'm trying to work on. I'm only human.

When I walked into the living room, it was so quiet you could hear a pin drop.

"Paris? Gia?" I call out.

There's no reply. I walk back to my room to grab my phone.

It feels like d*éjà vu.*

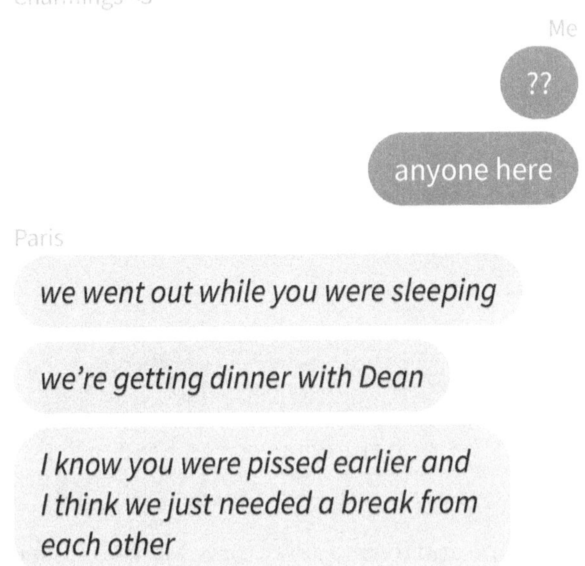

Not that I blamed them, but that hurt. It hurt more than it should have. They went to dinner with my brother without me. That feeling of being forgotten claws at my throat. I understand why they went to dinner without me, but it didn't make it hurt any less.

How was I supposed to feel? Happy?

Regardless, they were right. I shouldn't have snapped like I did. I love them, and I need to realize they say things to look out for me. I don't want to lose them. I can't afford to lose anyone else, but here I am again. Alone in my apartment.

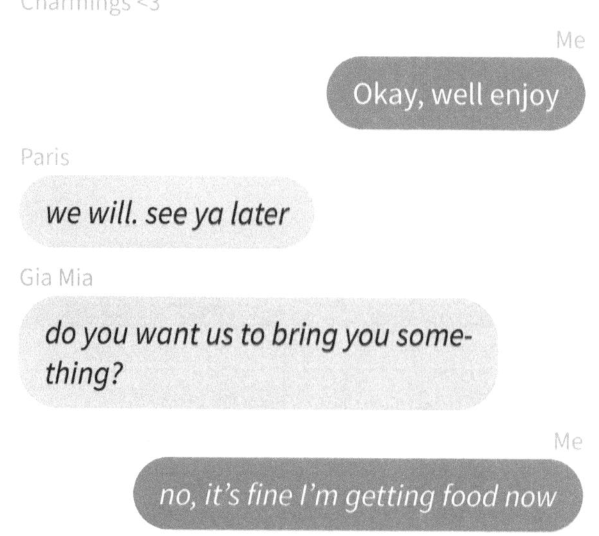

I grab my keys off the counter and head out. I'm not really sure where I'm going, but anywhere is better than staying home and feeling sorry for myself. I hate feeling excluded and unwanted, but it was my own fault for blowing up on Paris. I should've kept my cool. Been more understanding of where she's coming from.

I decide to go to the cafe, which is just ten minutes from my house.

I order a chicken Caesar salad and a lemonade. Picking a table that's bathing in the golden hour sun. As I settle into my seat, the bell above the door rings. I don't pay any attention until the person calls my name.

"Luna?" I look up to see the last person I'd want to see. Nick. "I thought that was you." His cheeky grin plasters his face.

"What do you want, Nick?" He sits in the chair across from me, and a breeze of his cologne brushes my nose. Bergamot and cinnamon. I roll my eyes. "Bold of you to think you could just sit at the same table as me."

He holds both of his hands up in surrender. "Hey, I come in peace." He clears his throat, "I just wanted to apologize for the other night. I was out of line."

"Yeah, no kidding." I thought slut shaming was 90s thing.

"Yeah. What you do or don't do in your free time is none of my business."

"Okay. Are you done?" I turn my attention back to my phone.

"This is the part where you apologize."

I place my phone face down on the table. "What do I need to apologize for?"

He holds up his fingers as he starts to tick off the reasons. "For one, you threw a drink at me." He grins again. "Has no one ever told you to use your words?"

I fight the urge to roll my eyes.

"Two, you said some pretty shitty stuff about our team. Look, I'm not saying some of our players are without fault, but you just assumed all of us are raging dicks, and we're not. I get what I said was fucked up, but you started it."

"You started it? What are we, in third grade?"

"Number seventy-two, your order is ready," the barista calls out my number, saving me from talking to Nick any further.

I quickly grab my food from the counter and start to walk out of the cafe. Nick stands in front of me, with his broad shoulders and rock-hard body blocking my path. "Can you move?"

"I'm still waiting on my apology." He crosses his arms over his chest.

I cross my arm over my chest, mirroring his stance, staring right into his dark green eyes. Not backing down. "No, I don't."

His smile widens, shaking his head. "You're stubborn as hell, you know that? Where are you going?"

"Somewhere you're not." I try to push past him, but he shifts to stop me.

"I'm trying to be friendly," he says, softly.

This time I don't resist rolling my eyes. "I don't want to be friends."

He looks around me as if he's searching for something. "It looks like you could use them. It doesn't seem like you have many. Every time I see you, you're alone." My grip on my bag tightens as his words cut deeper than I think he even intended. "Actually, I don't think I've ever seen you with friends. I mean, besides your brother, but does that even count as a friend? You're related."

"Do you get off on being a dick? Seriously, I would like to know." I finally shove him out of the way.

Honestly, I don't really have friends. Besides Gia and Paris, Paris doesn't really count since she doesn't even live out here. Gia only hangs out with me every now and then.

Gia is a fun and live in the moment kind of person, and I'm not. No matter how hard I try, I'm just not. She wants to change me, but I can't change how I'm wired.

So, when he said I didn't have friends, he wasn't wrong. I just refuse to admit that shit to him. As I exit, a nice warm breeze welcomes me, blowing back the tears trying to make a run for it for the last couple of hours.

It's not long before Nick is right behind me.

I groan loudly. "Do you not have a life? Or is following me your plan for the rest of the night?"

"What if it is?" He grimaces.

"Then find a new one." I start to walk to the light at the end of the street with Nick on my tail.

I stop in my tracks, forcing him to crash right into my back. His hands wrap around my shoulders, and I try to ignore the heat that radiates from his calloused hands. "What will it take for you to leave me the hell alone?"

"What are you eating?" he asks, eyeing the bag in my hand.

I hold it up. "A chicken salad."

"Share with me. I'm starving." He begs, rubbing his stomach with the ugliest pout on his face.

"No. I'm hungry, too. They don't make these salads big." I reply, hiding the bag behind my back.

"Well, then I guess I'm following you the rest of the way. Wherever you're going." He says, extending his arm for me to keep walking.

A deep sigh escapes my mouth. "Fine. You can eat *half* of the salad. Then leave me alone." I hand him the bag.

He takes the bag and starts walking in the opposite direction.

"Where the hell are you going?" I call after him.

"I don't stand and eat. You could follow, or you could just stand there admiring the view of my ass," he shouts over his shoulder.

I resist the laugh that wants to come out. "Wait, dammit." I run to catch up with him.

We continue to walk for what feels like an hour, until we reach a deserted area. "Is this where you kill me?"

He laughs. "No, not tonight. I don't have any of the proper tools I need. Can't have people finding your body now can we." He winks. "It's just a secluded area." He stops walking. "You know, now that I think about it, no one would hear your screams for miles. It would be kind of perfect."

"I know you're joking, but I don't like the way you said that." I keep walking past him until I reach a dead end. "Wow."

Standing in front of me is one of the most beautiful sights I have ever had the pleasure of laying eyes on. It's Boston's skyline. I could see my building from here. The lights of each building glisten like candles on a birthday cake. It's breath-taking. The silence. The sight. Everything.

"Gorgeous right?" Nick asks, sitting on the edge of the rock that faces the view. "I come here to clear my mind. Not many people know about it, though. I guess that's what I like about it."

He looks back up at me and smiles. "You can sit. I'm not going to bite. A lot. Unless that's what you're into."

I scoff. "Disgusting." I sit at the edge of the rock with him, putting enough space between us. "If not many people know about this place, why'd you bring me here?"

He turns to look at me. His eyes stare into mine for a beat. He looks... sincere. "Honestly? You looked lonely."

Chapter 9

Nick

If someone had told me I would be sitting at my favorite place with my least favorite person, I would've laughed in their face. Yet here I am. Sitting at this hidden treasure of a spot with Luna James Beitar.

Fuck me.

When I was walking past the cafe earlier, I wasn't planning on bothering her. I actually planned to keep walking and ignore her. But as I stood at that light, I watched as she sat in that cafe. She looked sad and alone. Like she wanted to cry. No one was around to console her either. I felt...bad. I wanted to do something, but we're not really friends. Still, we're now sitting here staring and admiring Boston's skyline.

Lately, I've been a dick to her, but that's only because I don't like her. Granted, that's not really a good reason to be an ass to someone. Okay, it's not a good reason at all, but she just brings it out of me. Every time I see her, I have this sudden need to piss her off by any means necessary.

Toxic. I know.

But today was different. She looks like she needs a friend. So, here we are. This is me offering an olive branch. We'll see if we can stay cordial for the night.

"How did I look lonely?" She starts to fiddle with the hem of her shirt.

I shrug my shoulders. "I don't know. It was like you had the weight of the world on your shoulders and needed someone's help to lift them off."

"How poetic." She gazes back at the skyline.

"Yeah, I know. I got a couple of hidden talents you don't know about, Jay." I wink.

Sitting this close to her, I realize how fucking beautiful she is. I'm not blind. I've always known she was cute, but staring up close? She's stunning. Her brown skin glows like polished mahogany, kissed by the subtle luminescence of the city. Those golden brown eyes hold a quiet allure, reflecting the myriad hues of the night. As the city skyline twinkles around us, she becomes a constellation of beauty in her own right, each curve a testament to the elegance of her existence. The night lights play upon her features, casting a gentle glow that transforms the ordinary into the extraordinary.

Like a moth to a flame, I want to touch her. But we all know what happens when moths go near a flame. They burn. And something tells me that's exactly what Luna would do to me.

Burn me straight to hell without a second thought.

Her curly hair sits in a messy bun on top of her head, showing off her long neck. Which has a tattoo right under her ear. I've never noticed it before, not that she's ever given me a chance to. I lean over slightly, trying to get a better look. It's one word that starts just behind her ear and goes to the top of her shoulder. All I can make out is the letter C. The rest is in tight calligraphy letters.

"What the hell are you staring at?" Her gaze is still transfixed on the view in front of her.

"Your tattoo. I'm trying to read what it says." I squint harder to piece the letters together, but she turns her head to look at me.

Our eyes clash like the Titanic and the iceberg. Her eyes sparkle with something sad. I want to reach out and hold her hands for comfort. Something tells me that would be a terrible idea.

"It's my sister's name," Luna says, breaking the gaze first, turning back to the view.

I sit back up. "You have a sister?"

"Had." She doesn't explain further.

Had? Meaning she's dead? "I'm guessing you two were close." She doesn't speak, so I do. "I mean, I've never seen Dean with a tattoo of her name. Just you."

"Dean doesn't like tattoos. It doesn't mean he wasn't close with her," she defends.

"What does it say?" I change topics before I say something else to piss her off.

"Cassie."

"Your sister's name?" Duh, smart ass.

"Yeah. Her full name was Cassandra." She starts to play with the hem of her shirt again, something she does when she's nervous or anxious. Or so I've noticed.

So, I decide to change the topic again. "What's your problem with me?"

Her face scrunches. "That was random."

"It's really not. Since the first day I met you, you've done nothing but tell me how much you hate me. Even when I'm trying to be nice. So, clearly, you have a problem with me."

Shrugging her shoulders again, she says, "I just don't like you."

I scoff, "Why? What did I do to you?"

She takes the salad out of my hands. "You're narcissistic, for one. Two, everything that comes out of your mouth is a damn insult or a backhanded compliment. Three," she stares at me. "you're you. Need I say more?"

"Okay, what are we three?" I shake my head.

She shoots a glare with her gorgeous brown eyes. "Those are dumb reasons, and you know it." A grin tugs at my lips. "I don't think you have a real reason not to like me, so you made up some bogus answers."

She stuffs her mouth with a fork filled with salad and chicken. "No, those are definitely reasons. You just don't agree with them. There's a difference."

"Whatever." The silence fills our space once again as she continues to eat. "Are you not going to ask me why I don't like you?"

"I don't care enough." She shrugs.

"Well, I'll tell you anyway." I watch as she rolls her eyes in annoyance. "You're stubborn as hell. You act like you're the only person in the world. You have this *my way or the highway* attitude that's mad fucking annoying. Every time I'm around you, I feel like I'm in the middle of a fucking debate. One I didn't sign up for, nonetheless. It seems like everything with you is a fucking competition. Also, you act like there's nothing more to life besides dancing." I hold my hand up when she opens her mouth to protest. "Which is fine, but does that mean you have to treat everyone around you like shit? You really need to learn to live a little. I get that dance is important, but you act like that's all there is in life. It makes you really negative to be around. You bring the whole vibe down when you enter a room. You're not going to die if you miss one single eight-count."

She stops chewing. "Is that all?"

This was not the point of bringing her up here, but she just brings it out of me. "I think so. Yeah."

She stands up and dusts her pants off. "Well, thank you for this... insightful meal. It's been rather enlightening. And *thank you* for not holding back." She closes the salad bowl and throws it back in the bag. "Seriously. It's really great of you to make these wackass assumptions about me."

I stand up with her. "What was it you said earlier? *You just don't agree with them. There's a difference.*"

"Fuck you." She scoffs, walking away.

"Ah, I lied. There's one more thing I forgot to add to the list." She whips around to look at me. "You can dish it, but you sure as hell can't take it. Got to love that. You're soft as hell, Jay."

"No, I'm not." She stomps like a fucking kid.

"Oh, and childish, apparently. What are you, six?" I ask sarcastically, shoving my hands into the pockets of my jeans.

"Go to fucking hell." She walks off in a huff.

I laugh loud enough for her to hear. "Do you even know how to get back?"

"I'll figure it out," she yells back, chucking her middle finger over her shoulder.

I could easily just let her figure it out, like she said. But I would never hear the end of it from Dean if I let his sister get abducted. Or lost.

Dammit.

I run to catch up with her. "For one, you're going in the wrong direction." I hook my thumb over my shoulder. "That's the way back to where we were."

When I look at her face, it's red, like she's been crying. She gives a light sniffle and wipes her nose. It must be allergies, right? There's no way I made her cry. Right? What I said was the truth. I mean, I could've said it nicer, but still. She's been giving me shit for weeks.

How is it this girl can always talk mad shit to about any person she talks to, but if anything is said to her, she falls apart? It makes no sense. Something else that just annoys the hell out of me. She's so fucking soft. You can't say anything to her without setting her off.

Fuck me, man.

She brushes past me and continues walking. I grab her arm and turn her to face me. "Are you crying?"

"No." She tries to pull her arm out of my hold, but I only squeeze tighter.

I watch as her chest starts to pick up its pace. "Luna, I'm sorry. I really wasn't trying to upset you."

"Can y-you p-please let go?" she tries to speak in be-tween sobs.

"Are you having another panic attack?" I catch her eyes with mine again. And she gives me a soft nod.

Grabbing both of her shoulders, I shuffle her to a tree and force her to sit down. As her breaths start to become more rapid. I see the panic rise in her eyes, and the tears fall from her eyes. Her entire body is shaking as she hyperventilates.

I grab onto her hands again. "Hey. You're okay. Every-thing's okay." I try to calm her, but it's not working. She continues to try to suck in air in quick sips. "What do you need?"

"Please...make...it...stop. Please," she pleads.

Before her, I never saw someone have a panic attack. Last time I saw her have a panic attack, I felt helpless, so I researched what to do. I didn't expect to be there for another one, but I still wanted to know what to do if I was ever in that situation with anyone else.

We need to slow her breathing. She's breathing way too fast. This can't be good for her. Last time, I distracted her, but I don't know what to distract her with. I don't want to piss her off any further. "You need to think about something else. Literally, anything else."

I know it's easier said than done, but I didn't know what to do. I'm not trained for this. Her chest is rising too fast. That I do know. She's not getting enough air. "Hold your breath."

She's not focusing. "Look, I know it might be hard, but it'll help. Hold your breath for me, Luna."

She tries to suck in a gasp of air but can't. "Okay, you can beat my ass later, alright?" I do the one thing I know takes a person's breath away.

I kiss her.

Chapter 10

Luna

He's kissing me. Nick Beckett is kissing me. I'm not even moving. He's doing all of the work. But I don't stop him. I *could* stop him. But I don't. I let his lips mold into mine.

I think I'm still in shock, but there's nothing romantic about this kiss. I'm sitting on cold dirt, against a tree, in the middle of nowhere. Okay, maybe not the middle of nowhere. I think we're about a good thirty minutes from the café we were at. Regardless, I'm having a panic attack over something somebody, who doesn't even mean anything, said to me. Not that he should have any kind of effect on me, but it does. Maybe it's not even about *what* he said, but that it's true.

Still, all I can think about right now is how Nick's lips feel against mine—soft and languid. His lips send a comforting warmth over me, like a warm blanket during a blistering, cold snowstorm. Weirdly, I don't want him to stop. But he does. He opens his eyes and pulls back.

"Why did you do that?" I whisper, as if we are in a crowd of people.

"I, uh, I realized you needed to, uh, hold your breath. It's the only way I knew how to do it. Without killing you, I mean," he replies, his voice matching mine.

"Okay." That's it. That's all I say. No, thank you for helping. No, thank you for literally *stealing* my breath away. Nope, just *okay*.

I mentally slap myself back into reality. I realize I'm still on the ground, and *he's* still holding my face in his hands. My eyes dart to his hands and back up to him.

"Oh, sorry," he apologizes, quickly removing his hands from my face before standing up and offering me his hand.

For once, I take it, brushing the dirt off my ass when I'm fully standing and wiping the tears from my face, because this isn't embarrassing at all.

"What happened?" Nick asks, reminding me of his presence.

"What?" I try to play stupid, but we both know I'm not.

"Why did you have a panic attack? Was it about what I said? I really wasn't trying to offend—"

I cut him off. "Someone's narcissistic. It's not always about you, Nick."

He stares at me with the same sincerity, and I feel like an ass. "No. I'm not offended. I just—you're the second person today to say something about my attitude. I don't mean to be rude and standoffish. I just worry about different things compared to everyone else." I sigh. "I focus on dance while other people focus on school or finding a boyfriend. I don't have that luxury. I need to keep my mind trained on the things that matter most."

This is the second time this week I've had a panic attack. I haven't had them this frequently since I was seventeen. I learned how to keep them under control. I learned to recognize my triggers. Things that set off my anxiety. Maybe I really should book a session with Kathryn.

Realizing we're still in the woods, I say, "We should really get out of here."

"Yeah. Quick question before we do?" Nick stammers.

I gaze into his green eyes. Not just any green, though. Forest green. With golden flecks. Like shining a golden flashlight into the vast forest. It's kind of...hot.

"What?" I snap myself out of the trance I set myself in.

"How, um—" his voice staggers. But I know exactly what he's trying to ask.

"How often do I have them?" I finish his question. "Believe it or not, not often." Until recently. I couldn't even tell him why, though. Even if I wanted to. I don't know what's causing me so much stress.

"I've been around for two of them, though."

"Don't remind me," I murmur under my breath, more to myself than to him. "Look, just forget about it. It's not your problem. It's mine. So, it would be nice if you kept this to yourself. Thanks." I start to walk past him, but his calloused hand grabs onto my bicep.

I look at his hand, then into his eyes again. "You can't just ask me to keep this to myself. There's clearly something wrong. I think you should talk to someone."

I snap out of his hold. "Don't tell me what to do. You're neither my dad nor my boyfriend! Mind your own goddamn business."

"You made it *my* business when you had two of these fucking panic attacks in front of me. Don't get mad at me because you can't admit there's something wrong," he yells.

I scoff. "That's not your job nor your concern."

"Then talk to someone. It's like your addicted to the pain or something."

I open my mouth to say something, but nothing comes out. I have nothing to say. I'm not addicted, but he acts like it's so easy to do. To admit there's something wrong. To say there's this underlying problem you haven't talked about. He doesn't get it. No one does.

If I were to talk to Kathryn, she would pry and pry until she peeled back all my layers just to find the actual problem. And then I would have to face it. Not only face it, but then try to fix it. It might sound easy to everyone else, but it's not. It's the complete opposite.

Talking about my feelings and the things that hurt me makes me feel like a burden. I hate feeling like my emotions make others feel guilty. Then I would have to explain what they did to contribute to my emotions, and that does what? Nothing. Because this is an ongoing cycle.

I say there's a problem, and then they will say that it's me, I'm the problem. So, what's the point of even talking about it anyway? I go to Kathryn and talk about these problems because she listens. She doesn't judge me, but the minute she says I need to talk to the people who have a hand in the problem, I shut down again.

It's stupid, I know. I just can't help it. It's an ongoing cycle.

"I never thought I'd see the day where Luna James Beitar was speechless." He laughs.

"Do *not* use my full name. That is a criminal offense. One I don't take lightly. Also, I'm not speechless. I just don't have anything to say."

His chest rumbles with laughter. "That's the literal definition of being speechless." He sighs, "Look, regardless, you should at least tell your brother. He's your twin after all."

"So, what should I say? Oh, Dean, I've been having panic attacks lately. Also, Nick has been there for the last two I've had. Oh, and by the way, he kissed me." I grit, hoping he feels guilty enough to drop it. "Is that what you want me to say, Nick? You want me to tell my *twin* brother that you made out with me?"

"You know what? Screw it. It's on you. I tried to help." He throws his hands up in surrender. "Oh, and by the way, I didn't *make out* with you. I *kissed* you. Trust me, you'll know the difference."

"You don't understand," I argue, disregarding the last part of that statement.

"Understand what? You should be leaning on your friends and family when something is going on with you?"

"That's all I'll get from them. Pity." I clear the lump from my throat. "They'll say it's because they care about me. They'll claim it's because they're concerned about me. Then, every hour of every day, text me to make sure I'm okay. They'll be worried all the time." I blow out a puff of air. "That might sound all good and dandy, but it's suffocating. The constant berating to make sure I'm okay. Every hour of every day? No one should want that. *I* don't want that. So please, for the love of God, drop it!"

Nick stares at me blankly. I try to read his expression, but I come up with nothing. "Fine." Nick shoves his hands into his pockets. "We should get out of here. It's getting pretty late."

Nick starts to walk back to the cafe, with me directly behind him. We walk in an uncomfortable silence until we reach my car.

There are about a million things running through my mind right now. For one, the fact I just kissed my brother's captain and friend. Two, how this anxiety has been kicking my damn ass. I wish I could say I have a hold on it, but considering I've had two panic attacks within a few weeks of each other, I'd say I don't.

"I won't say anything," Nick finally says, breaking the silence. My brows furrow. "To Dean. I still think you should talk to someone, though. Seriously."

"Whatever. I need to go." I unlock my car and start to open my door. Nick catches the door before I can fully open it.

"I know we're not friends. And I know we don't like each other, but if you want to talk," he offers, scratching his well-trimmed beard.

"*Don't* call you?" I joke, and he just grins. "I'm fine. I don't want your pity."

"The last thing you have is my pity, Jay. I just know what it's like to hold shit in until you combust. It sucks ass." He shrugs. "So, I'm here."

I'm not entirely sure how to feel at this moment. Should I feel touched? Offended? Moved? I don't like Nick, not even a little bit. But he's somewhat of a decent human being. And that's why I say, "Okay."

He pulls the car door wider for me to enter. I mumble a thank you as I get in. "I'll see you later, then?" he asks.

I reach for the door handle. My brother would kill me if he ever found out about what happened tonight. Regardless of *why* Nick kissed me, all he would hear is that Nick kissed me. So, I think it's best I keep my distance. "I guess." As I try to pull it close, he yanks it back open. "What now?"

"Nothing. I just wanted to piss you off. One for the road, ya know." He smirks. I roll my eyes, and he releases the door.A complete jackass. "Good night."

I close the door and turn the keys in the ignition then drive home.

When I arrive home a half hour later, Paris is the only one sitting on the couch. I look around for Gia, but she's nowhere to be found. Weird. I thought they went to get dinner together, so she should be here too, right?

"Hey," Paris calls out. "Can we talk?"

I walk into the living room and sit on the couch next to her. "Yeah."

"Look, I don't like the way we left things earlier. We're not like that. We talk to each other. We don't yell."

"I know. I also know I don't like to be questioned. I know the shit I do is a lot of pressure, but it's *my* pressure. I don't like that every time something good happens to me, you always seem to knock me down. It makes me feel like crap. I want your support. Not your doubt."

"Babe, you have my support. But with my support, you also have my concern. You can't expect me to love you and not worry about your mental health. You can't carry the whole world on your shoulders, no matter who it's for." She grabs my hands, tugging me closer to her. "I know why you're doing all of this, but you don't have to do it just because of her. I want to make sure you're doing it because you *want* to."

"Okay, but you can still worry and support me without questioning my decisions." I retort, pulling myself out of her hold. "I love you, Paris, but you have no right to tell me what I should and shouldn't do. I told you from the jump I would do whatever it took to become a dancer. Why all of a sudden is it a shock that's exactly what I'm doing?"

That's the problem. I've always said I would do *whatever* it took. Why the hell is everyone acting like this is abnormal?If I this were Dean putting all his focus and drive into hockey, no one would second guess him. They would say he's driven and ambitious. But since it's me, everyone thinks I'm taking on too much. I'm so fucking tired of the double standards.

"I'm sorry. I know. I just don't get how you can just put your whole life on hold."

"Paris, I'm not putting my life on hold. God!" I stand and start pacing as the frustration builds up. "What is the difference between you putting in your blood, sweat, and tears to get to where you are and mine? Why, because you didn't have to work as hard as me? Or because I put in more effort to stay focused on dancing rather than focusing on men? Just because you want to put more effort into a guy who doesn't want you doesn't mean I should too." The shock on her face is evident. I know I went too far.

"Wow." She stands up from the couch. "Well, I'm glad you can speak your mind, Luna."

She called me Luna. She never calls me Luna. "No, Paris. I'm sorry I didn't mean that." I apologize. "I'm so sorry."

"I'm going to go ahead and go back to New York. It's clear I have overstayed my welcome." She walks into my room and rolls out her suitcase. "I love you. I hope you know that. I just want you to be happy without sacrificing yourself in the process." She doesn't say anything else and walks out the door.

I know I went to far with the whole guy remark, but how could she judge me for doing exactly what she did? It was Paris who encouraged me to push through the barriers and do what it took to make my dreams a reality. Instead of going after her, I let her leave, giving us the break we probably need.

I want to talk to Gia, but she was nowhere to be found.

Pulling out my phone, I shoot her a text.

What friend is she talking about? This is now the second time she has mentioned staying at a friend's house. Who the hell is she hanging out with? This really has my curiosity beads tingling. Gia doesn't really hang out with anyone.

Besides me.

So who the hell caught her attention? Or what man caught her attention? I feel like she's got a man in her life and just isn't telling me. Which is weird because I would love to see who she's dating. Just because I can't have a love life doesn't mean she can't. Honestly, I live vicariously through her love life. I wish she would just talk to me about it. She never keeps secrets from me. Why is she starting now?

I call one more phone number before calling it a night.

"Well, hello Luna. It's always a nice surprise to receive a phone call from you."

"Yeah, you knew it was coming after our last talk." I sigh. "Kathryn, can I set an appointment with you?"

"Of course, Luna."

Chapter 11

Nick

"**D**ude, get your fucking head in the game!" I yell at Dean.

Normally, we're in sync. Like bread and butter. Tonight, his head is in the fucking clouds. I don't know what the hell his problem is, but he's causing us the game. We've been undefeated this entire season. Now he's unfocused and can't get the puck into the fucking net. Every time I pass him the puck, he either misses the puck or misses the damn goal.

It's the end of the first period. Our score is currently 2-0, with their team in the lead.

We all make our way into the locker room with Coach hot on our tail.

"What the hell are y'all doing out there? Because you're sure as shit not playing hockey," Coach bellows.

Everyone sits in silence as we all try not to think about how fucking bad we're playing tonight. I don't even know what the hell happened. The last couple of games, we've been on fire. Then tonight, it's like they don't remember how to play hockey. Well, not everyone, just one person in particular. Dean.

I walk over to Dean, grab him by the arm, and pull him to the back of the locker room. Once we're where no one can hear us, I shove him against the wall.

"Dude, what the hell?" Dean scoffs.

"That's what I should be asking you. What is going on with you tonight? You're playing like shit. I can't recommend a shitty ass player for captain." I cross my arms over my chest as I wait for his reply.

"It's nothing," he responds as he starts taking his gloves off.

Clearly, it's something. Dude, it's distracting you from playing. What is it?" I push.

He groans. "I just have something I need to tell my sister. I don't really feel guilty about it, but I feel guilty for not telling her. I know she's going to be pissed."

For two people who claim to tell each other everything, they sure do like to keep secrets from each other.

I still think that Luna should tell Dean about her panic attacks, but I haven't brought it up with her again. Not that I've seen her.

She hasn't spoken to me in weeks. Not since we were in the woods. I told her she could if she needed to, but I didn't think she actually would. Stubbornness and all.

"Okay, well, if it's eating you up so much that it's screwing up your game, you need to tell her." I tell him more of a demand than a request.

"It's not that simple. She would literally hate me. She'll never speak to me again." He puffs out a breath of air and crashes onto the bench.

"What is it?" I ask hesitantly. I really shouldn't be getting in the middle, but if it gets his damn head on right, what the hell?

A heavy sigh escapes his mouth before speaking again. "I just did something. Something I promised I would never do. It probably wouldn't matter if it happened once, but I keep doing it. It's like I can't fucking help myself. The main reason I want to tell her is because it's becoming serious. *Too* serious. If the roles were reversed, I would probably be livid with her. Keeping like this to herself."

What the hell does that even mean? "Okay. So, tell her. *After* the game, just tell her, suffer the consequences, and move on." He stares at me like I have something on my face. "You said that she would be pissed. So, either you tell her what the hell you did or shut up and keep it to yourself. Either way, I need you to get your head straight. We all have personal shit going on in our lives. The difference is, we don't let it affect our game. We leave it at the door and keep pushing. Which is what *you* need to do."

He nods his head in agreement. "You're right. I'm sorry, cap. Let's go finish the game."

Was I harsh? Maybe. But there's a time and a place to feel our emotions. This is neither the time nor the place. I don't know what the fuck is going on with Dean, but I need him to get over it.

We walk back to the other side of the locker room with the team. I grab my phone out of my locker to check the time, only to find a message from an unknown number.

Unknown

So, I might have stolen your number from my brother's phone.

I know this is borderline stalkery, but sadly, I need to take you up on that offer of using your ear

oh, this is Luna, by the way

I honestly never thought you would actually ask for help…

color me impressed

yeah, yeah whatever

so are you free

lol I have a game right now, but we can meet up afterwards

oh shit I forgot, yeah afterwards works

bye

oh wait, meet at the cafe that I saw you at a couple weeks ago

lmao okay

Is it weird we were just talking about her and now I have plans to see her later? I think this whole situation is weird. But I don't say anything as I save her number in my phone and chuck it back into my locker. It's time to get our heads back in the game. Hopefully, Dean can get his head out of his ass.

I walk up behind Dean as the team heads back out to the rink. "You get your shit figured out?"

"Yeah, cap. I'm ready." He nods.

"Alright then. Let's get this dub then." I pat his back and rush out of the locker room.

We win 3-2, with Dean scoring two goals and my one assist. Then, in the last period, I scored the last winning goal. It was a close call, and I almost had to beat Dean's ass over it. But he got his shit together and pulled through.

After showering, I quickly dress and pull my phone out of my locker to text Lun *oh, did y'all win?*

I'm supposed to care right?

lmao isn't your brother on the team shouldn't you be watching the games

no, I don't really care for hockey

he knows that

damn that sucks for him

don't get me wrong, I support him and all that

I just couldn't care less

fuuck... well anyways I'll be there soon

okay bye

I chuckle to myself as I pocket my phone. That's all I seem to do when I'm around her. Laugh. Well, besides calming her down from her panic attacks, I mean. Also, it's more laughing at her expense, but that's what makes it so enjoyable. She makes it too easy. It's like she purposefully hangs this fruit in my face and asks me to take it. How can I resist?

Thirty minutes later, I'm parking my car in front of Mama's Cafe. As I walk toward the front door, I see her sitting alone in a booth in the back corner. She's wearing a graphic t-shirt with a black long sleeve undershirt. She's resting her chin on her palm, and she looks...somber. Like her whole world came crashing down on her.

Did Dean tell her? He couldn't have, right? I mean, he showered and immediately left the arena. I was texting her as soon as I was done showering, and she was fine. When would he have time to tell her?

I open the glass door and walk straight to her corner. "It's a bit cloudy over here, no?"

She rolls her eyes. "You're so funny. You should go on tour with that act," she says sarcastically. "Sorry. I have a lot on my mind."

"I'm sorry? Did Luna James Beitar just apologize?" I say, pressing my hand into my chest.

She laughs softly. "No, I did not. That was not an apology. It was a statement. Also, what did I say about using my government name?" She groans.

I shrug lazily. "Can't remember. Anyways, what's up?" I sit in the chair that's directly in front of her. I ignore the fact that this feels a little too intimate. Like a first date.

She starts to pick at her fingernails. "I don't even know where to start."

It's weird. I've never seen her look so vulnerable. Normally, she has a thousand-foot wall up. Today, it's nowhere to be found. "You just start."

"Well, I think my best friend is seeing someone. Not that I would care, but she's keeping it from me. I just don't know why. Every time I bring it up, she either changes the topic or tells me I'm crazy." She sighs, tucking a loose curl behind her ear. "Also, my brother hasn't spoken to me in weeks. I have no idea what the fuck is going on with that. He's been distant, and he's *never* distant. It's starting to seriously freak me out. Then, my friend, who was in town a couple of weeks ago, we got into it. So, she left town early. She hasn't answered any of my texts or calls. I just feel like I'm on the brink of having a mental breakdown." She sits back pulling her legs to her chest.

I stare at Luna for a beat. I don't really know what to say. I don't have an answer for her, nor do I know how to help her. I'm guessing Dean decided not to tell her whatever was bugging him. I can't say anything about something I don't even know about. I just want to help her feel better.

I lean forward, crossing my arms on the table. "Have you ever gone skating?"

She glares into my eyes. "I'm over here spilling my heart out and you want to talk about skating?" She starts packing her stuff up. "I knew this was a bad idea."

I grab on her arm. "No, it's relevant." I stand up. "Let's go skating. I know a place." I grin, my hand still holding her soft arm.

I take the bag off her shoulders and walk back to my car. "You didn't drive right?" I question over my shoulder as she's running to catch up to me.

"No, but where are we going?" she asks, but it comes out breathy.

I laugh. "I just told you. Skating."

I open the passenger and nod my head for her to get in. She grabs her bag out of my hands and shuffles into the car. I gently close the door behind her and run to the driver's side.

Turning the keys in the ignition, Luna speaks. "You're such a cliche."

"What? Why?" My eyebrows furrow.

"A Camaro? Really? You couldn't pick any other car?" She laughs.

"Yeah, whatever. Camaro's are classics. I don't need some fancy ass car when this baby right here does the job for me." I say, caressing the steering wheel.

She just shakes her head, and we drive in silence for the rest of the way. Thirty minutes later we're back at the arena. "We're here." I turn the car off and pull the keys out of the ignition.

"You were literally just here. Don't you get tired of being at the arena?" She exits the car.

"No. It's my happy place." I grin.

She gives me no reaction as we walk to the back entrance of the arena. I pull open the door and usher her in. A shiver rolls over her as she continues on to the stands. "I'll be right back."

When I walk to the locker room, I grab a pair of extra hockey skates from the closet along with mine from my locker. Quickly, I spray them with antibacterial spray. They're our smallest size, so hopefully she can fit in them.

Before walking back out to the rink, I grab a hoodie for her from my locker.

Walking back to the rink, Luna is sitting down staring at her feet. Once again, looking anything but happy. I just need to get her mind off of things.

"Alright. Here we go!" I call out. I throw the hoodie onto her lap. "I brought you the smallest pair we have."

Her face scrunches. "I'm not putting my feet anywhere near those nasty ass athlete-footed infested skates. Also, what is this?"

"Okay, one, no one here has athlete's foot. No one really wears them. They're super small and if you haven't noticed, hockey men have huge feet." I point at the hoodie on her lap. "Two, that is what we like to call a hoodie." I say sarcastically. "Clearly, it's something you're not used to. But I refuse to have you catch pneumonia on my watch. Just put it on." I set the skates down at her ankles. Reluctantly, she pulls the hoodie over her head. Unlacing her shoes, I start to put the skates on her left foot.

As my eyes slide up to her face, I see her chest rapidly rise up and down, and her cheeks have a soft red tint.

"Are you okay?" I halt my hands around her ankle. Her pulse pumps at a rampant speed under my palm.

"Ye-yeah." She clears her throat. "I'm just trying to figure out why you're putting my skates on for me?"

"Have you ever put skates on yourself?" She shakes her head. Then I proceed to take her shoes off her next foot. "Then, just sit there and let me help." I slip the hockey skates on and lace them up.

Giving her knee a quick pat, I stand up. "Okay you're good to go. Just give me a second to put mine on."

She sits there quietly. Staring. I don't know why, but my heart starts to race a little. Maybe it's the anxiety building from the hole she's burning in the side of my face. "Do you like the view? My mom did always tell d me that I was good looking."

Her head quickly snaps to the rink. "No. Shut up. Are you finished?" She asks, shifting in her seat.

I laugh before standing, reaching my hand out for her to grab. I pull her up onto her skates and ease onto the ice. She trails right behind me, gripping my hand tightly.

Luna wasn't kidding when she said she's never skated before. She looks like a brand-new calf learning how to walk as she attempts to find her balance.

"Just hold onto my arms." Her grip tightens around my forearms as she tries to maintain her balance. "I got you. You don't need to cut off my circulation."

"I'm s-sorry," she stammers.

I continue to skate backward around the rink. "I think it's crazy Dean never taught you how to skate."

"I'm not really a fan of it, to be honest. How the hell is a single blade supposed to keep you upright? The science behind it makes no sense." She adds.

I stifle my laugh. "First, its two single blades. Second, you're thinking too much about it. You're just gliding across ice. You're basically using your upper body to give you balance. If you hold your arms out, it'll help."

"I can't."

"Yes, you can." I argue. "Just like this." I pull her arms out to the side and hold them up. My palm in hers.

"It doesn't count if you're holding me up."

"You're right." I start to let go of her arms, but she grips onto my sleeve. "Easy! I'm not going to let you fall." Her eyes lock on mine, a long silence surrounds us. I sigh, "I promise."

I train my eyes on her as she trains hers to her skates. As she looks side to side at the ground, I notice how sharp her features are in contrast to her plump lips. She's so close I could kiss her, again.

Her eyes snap up to mine. "What the hell are you looking at, Beckett?"

"Nothing." I answer, clearing my throat. "Do you think you can skate on your own now?" Trying to change the topic. I try to release her arms, but she reaches farther up mine to tighten her hold. "So, I'll take that as a, no?"

She's closer to me now, with barely any space between us. Fuck. That smell. Strawberries and coconut. It's engraved into my brain now.

"I'm going to say this as fast as I can because it's hard for me to say." She looks back at the ground and takes a deep breath. "Thank you for tonight. I know I'm an ass and can sometimes be a bitch but thank you for taking my mind off of things. I don't really open up to many people nor do I ask for help. So, this means a lot to me."

"No problem." I smile.

"This is the part where you tell me I'm not a bitch or an ass." She chirps.

"Then I would be lying." I laugh and hers follows.

Her eyes are locked on mine again. This time, we're not moving. Like we're stuck in this one moment of time. There's nothing happening around us. It's just us right now.

You know that sensation you get when it's 100 degrees outside and you come inside a building with the air conditioning blasting? The first step in a pleasant breeze. That's what it feels like, looking at Luna.

"Okay, then." I try to look anywhere but her face. "I'd say that's enough skating, yeah?" What am I doing? I shouldn't be finding her attractive. I shouldn't be attracted to her at all. I shouldn't even be here with her alone like this.

But she needed someone.

Still, this is Dean's sister. His *twin* sister. It's wrong.

"Yeah," she agrees, thankfully.

We skate off the ice, and I help her take off her skates. Then I drive her home.

Chapter 12

Luna

When I get home, I no longer feel like there's this crushing weight on my chest. Instead, I'm... happy? Is that weird? Nick of all people helped me feel something other than anxious? It should be, but it's not. I don't feel an ounce of weirdness.

Shaking the thought from my head, I search for my phone in my bag. I sift through every pocket and nothing.

Where the hell is my phone?

Fuck! Did I leave it in Nick's car? Or the arena? I keep digging through my bag, pulling everything out of it. After dumping my entire bag on the ground, I've come to the realization that it's not here. I would call Nick, but I don't have a *damn phone* to call him with. Fuck me!

There's a light knock on my door. I run to open it, hoping and praying it's Nick bringing my phone, but it's Dean.

"Hey," he whispers.

"What's wrong?" He looks like someone just died. God, please don't tell me someone just died.

"Can we talk? Please?"

I pull the door wider to let him in.

"Oh, first, can I borrow your phone?" His brows furrow in confusion. "I left my phone in Nick's car and need him to bring it back."

"Why were you in Nick's car?"

Yeah, I didn't think that through. I can't tell him that I felt so down that the only person I felt like I could turn to is Nick. So, what the hell am I supposed to say?

What do I do instead?

I pivot. "Just cause. It doesn't matter. Can I borrow your phone or not?"

He gives me this suspicious look but doesn't say anything. Then he pulls his phone out of his back pocket. Pulling up Nick's contact, I assume, handing me the phone.

As I start to text Nick, a message pops up from Gia.

hey so tomorrow?

One, why is Gia texting him? Two, what are they doing tomorrow? I look back up at Dean. I could just ask him. But I don't know what the answer would be. My heart twists in my chest at the millions of different scenarios going on in my head.

"What?" he asks.

"Nothing." I reply. Then, I go back to texting Nick.

Dean and Gia have been friends for the same amount of time we have. It shouldn't be weird that they're texting, right? I'm being paranoid. They're friends just like we're friends. I send Nick a message.

Nick Beckett

hey, its Luna I think I left my phone in your car, could you possibly bring it to my place

haha yeah, I'll be over in an hour

I give Dean his phone back. "What did you want to talk about?"

He looks down at his phone. I watch as he reads the message Gia sent him. He shifts on his feet, pushing the phone back into his pocket. Like he's been caught doing something he shouldn't have. "Actually, never mind. It's nothing. Look, I'm actually going to just go."

He tries to walk around me, but I cut him off before he reaches the door. "Wait! Dean, I haven't spoken to you in weeks. Anytime I try to, you just brush me off. What the hell is going on with you? Did I do something?" I sound pitiful, begging my brother to talk to me. I shouldn't have to beg my brother's attention. So, why am I?

"Oh my God! Jay, the world doesn't revolve around you. Everything isn't about you. I have hockey and school to think about. I don't have time to hold your hand through whatever dramatic shit you've got going on right now."

My stomach clenches at his words as they pierce my ears. Dean and I have had our fair share of arguments, but never to the point where he makes me feel like utter shit. Like now.

I step out of his way. "You know what? Just leave Dean. Wouldn't want my *dramatic shit* to get in your way."

His eyes soften. "Jay, I didn't mean it like that. I'm…"

"You meant what you said. So, get the hell out of my house, Dean!" I raise my arm toward the door. He shakes his head and finally leaves.

My eyes well up with tears. Normally, I'd call Gia, but she hasn't responded to any of my texts. Either that, or she keeps her responses to a minimum. Which is probably what frustrates me the most. Why can she text Dean but not me?

There's a knock at my door. When I open it, there's Nick. Standing there with the biggest smile on his face. Normally I would have some stupid remark about how annoying his smile is. But right now, it's taking everything in me to hold back my tears.

"What are you doing here?" I ask.

"Um, you literally just texted me to come over and bring you your phone. I saw your brother downstairs, and he let me up." Shit. That's right. The smile on Nick's face starts to fall. "Are you okay?"

I nod my head. "Um, yeah. Can I have my phone now?" I extend my hand.

He just stands there. "No."

"No?" I don't have time for this.

"No." He echoes. "Luna, you said you wouldn't hold your feelings in anymore. That was our deal."

"I never said that. Can you just give me my damn phone?" I'm not angry at him, but he's not making this situation any better.

As if he can read my mind, he says, "Take it out on me. Your anger? Take it out on me."

"Nick, just give me my damn phone and go the fuck away!" I grit.

"No." He steps into my apartment, shrinking the distance between us.

I take a step back. "I never said you could come in. What the hell is your problem? Why are you being a dick?"

He takes another step. "I'm not being a dick. Jay, tell what's wrong?"

"Don't call me that. And there's nothing wrong. I'm just being dramatic."

"Don't do that. Just tell me what's wrong?" He takes another step.

When I try to take one back, my back hits the wall. I turn around to realize there's nowhere for me to go. I return my gaze to Nick, who is now standing right in front of me. His eyes holding mine. I could talk to him, but I don't want to rely on him. That's the problem now. I've become so reliant on other people. I refuse to add Nick to that list.

"I just want to be alone right now. Nick, please, just give me my phone and leave." My voice cracks. I'm doing everything I can to hold back my tears, but I'm barely holding it together.

"Cry." I shake my head at his demand. I refuse to believe he has that much control over me.

Nick takes his index finger and pushes my chin up. "Luna, let it out." There's a silent beat as we stare into each other's eyes, and before I know it my tears begin to fall.

It's like the dam broke. Every emotion coming to a head. Right now, I'm feeling everything. The crushing pain of being neglected by Gia and Dean. The hurt from Dean's words. The torment from Paris not speaking to me. Right now, I'm feeling everything.

Nick wraps his arms around me and pulls me into his chest, running his palm up and down my back while his other hand caresses my head. "It's okay." He whispers into the crown of my head.

My hands tighten around his waist as I grip onto his shirt, muffling my cries into his chest. I don't know what happened. How did I end up in Nick's arms? I didn't want to, but it's like he's the only person that truly cares about me. But I can't help but feel like I'm finding solace in a stranger.

After standing in his arms for what feels like a lifetime, I pull away and wipe my eyes. Nick rubs his hands along my arms, and guides me to the couch to sit down.

"So, you ready to talk?" Nick sits beside me.

I tell him about Dean and I, and what happened before he got here. The message I saw on his phone. To Dean telling me I'm self-centered. "I'm being stupid. I'm making a big deal out of nothing. Just forget it."

Nick lays his hand on mine. "You're not being stupid. If someone says something that fucks with you, it's not stupid. You're entitled to feel however you want. Stop pushing aside your feelings just so other people can feel comfortable."

"Thanks." I sniffle. "Can I have my phone now?" I know deep down what Nick is saying is right, but I can't think like that. It's not how I'm hardwired. I care too much about other people. So, no. I can't just tell Dean and Gia what there is really fucking with me. So I rather just ignore it.

He chuckles. "Yeah." He shifts in his seat and pulls my phone from his back pocket.

"Oh great." I wipe my face again. "Now my phone is gonna smell like ass."

"My ass smells amazing." He chuckles.

I just roll my eyes. I open my phone to see I have no missed texts or calls from anyone. *Shocker.*

"Do you have Netflix?" Nick kicks his legs up on the trunk in front of him.

"Yeah?" I halt as Nick turns the TV on. "What are you doing? You can leave now."

"Nah, I'm good. You look like you could use the company. Frankly, so could I."

I could easily force him to leave, but that's the problem. I don't want to. It's been nice hanging out with him. Nick has been the one constant in my life recently. He's been... a *friend.*

Weird.

"Fine, but one movie, and then you need to leave," I order, tucking my feet underneath the blanket beside me.

"Deal." He nods.

Three movies later, Nick is passed out on the couch. I should wake him and tell him to go home, but it's late. Plus, he looks peaceful. Standing from the couch, I take the blanket I had and throw it over him, then walk to my room. I quietly close the door behind me.

I turn on the lamp by my bed and open my phone one last time. I decide to send Gia a text.

> hey are you free tomorrow?

> I need someone to talk to :(

hey, sorry no I'm not

is it important?

> no

> forget it

okay, sorry

She texted me. Still, she has no time for me, but she made plans with Dean. I want to text and ask her about it, but I decide against it.

I scroll through my contacts and pause on Paris' name. Clicking the call button, I wait for her to answer. Not that I think she will.

"Hello?" she answers.

"Paris?" I whisper.

"Hey, teddy bear." A warmth fills my chest at the nickname. We're off to a good start.

"I'm so sorry, Paris. I didn't mean what I said." I apologize quickly.

"Hey, no. You were right. I have to respect your grind. I'm sorry I made you feel like I didn't. I do. I guess I just got a little overprotective. But from now on, you have my full support. As long as you're happy and healthy, that's all that matters to me." She pauses, "I love you, teddy bear."

"I love you too, Paris. I missed you so much." A small sigh of relief escapes my lips. It's nice to talk to her again. "So much has happened, and I just really need you right now."

"What's going on?" She pries.

I catch Paris up on all of my life's turmoil. How Dean and Gia have been keeping their distance from me. Including the incident that occurred when he came over earlier. I wait for her answer once I finish, but all I receive is silence. "Paris, are you still there?"

"Yeah. Sorry. I was taking it all in. Um, I really hate to even suggest this, but do you... Never mind." She cuts herself off.

My imagination races with a million different explanations. I had a list of possible reasons why they're ignoring me, but I want to hear what Paris thinks. "Wait what? Do I think what?"

"It's nothing just forget it. I'm sure it'll blow over soon and everything will go back to normal."

I really want to know what she wanted to say, though. There's no point. I would probably drive myself crazy just thinking about it.

"Well, anyways, I'll come out there this weekend. Since I left so early. It can just be a you and me thing." She offers.

"Sounds good. Do you..." I'm cut off by a husky voice calling my name.

"Luna?" I forgot that Nick was in the living room.

"Yeah, I'm back here." I shout back. "Hey, Paris. I gotta go."

"Wait, who's that? Was that a man's voice?" I can practically hear her gushing. "Is *the* Luna James Beitar finally cleaning out the cobwebs?"

"Okay first off, eww. I don't have cobwebs. Second, yes it's a guy, but he's just a friend, and he's barely that." Which is completely false at this point. He was more of a friend that Gia was at the moment.

"Well, have fun with your *friend*." She puts emphasis on friend like I don't know what she's insinuating. "I'll text you when I'm driving into town."

There's a knock on my door. "Come in!" I shout before turning back to my phone. "Okay, I love you. Bye."

I hang up my phone and turn my attention to the sleepy-eyed Nick standing in my doorway. "Sorry, I didn't mean to interrupt you."

"It's fine. I thought you were asleep. Did I wake you?" Although, I wasn't talking that loud.

"No." He grins. "I'm actually not good at sleeping in unfamiliar places."

I lift my eyebrow. "But you were just asleep?"

"Yeah, weird." He shrugs then walks to my dresser. Looking over the pictures resting on them. "Is this your sister?" Pointing at a picture of Cassie and me.

"Yeah. She's stunning. I know." I grin.

"Yeah." He stumbles. "Wait is this, Paris?" He picks up a frame, showing it to me.

I stand from the bed and walk to him. "How do you know Paris?"

"It's complicated." He grimaces.

"Oh my God! *You're* the guy that broke her heart!" She said he was on the team, but I didn't think she meant the fucking captain.

"I did not break her heart." He defends. "We weren't dating. Therefore, I never had her heart." He scoffs brushing off the fact that he knows he broke her heart. She cried for hours. I'm sure he knows this by now. "I told her I didn't want anything serious, and she did. So,

I called it off all together. I didn't want to give her false hope on something that would never happen."

"It's not my business what she does with her sex life." I shrug, hoping for a topic change.

Setting the picture frame back down. "Do you even have a sex life?"

I choke on air.

AIR!!

"How is that any of your business?" I catch my breath again.

He laughs again. For some reason I feel like he's always laughing at me. "It's not. I was just curious. It's just, I don't think I've ever seen you with a guy before."

It's *not* his business. Although, I haven't had sex in months. Not because I didn't have any opportunities, but because I can't. I can't sleep with anyone without losing my focus. That's what sex does to me. There's no sex without strings, no matter how much I want there to be. It's just not. So instead, I restrict everyone from the all access pass. It's better this way.

"I'm not answering that." I walk to the bedroom door. "You can leave now."

He chuckles, rubbing his hand along his trimmed beard. "You were going to let me sleep here before. What changed?"

"You woke up. Goodbye." He shakes his head and walks back into the living room to grab his stuff.

"See you later, Beitar." He grins.

"Ugh. You're so corny. It's not cute, Beckett."

He continues toward the door. "So, you think I'm cute?" He asks over his shoulder.

"Of course that's what you heard. It's not even what I said. I said *not* cute. Keyword, *not*."

He gives me the biggest, cheekiest grin and opens the door. "You didn't say I wasn't either, so..." Then he leaves.

He has got to be the biggest narcissist I have ever met.

Nick

It's Friday. Thank fucking God!

This week was so draining. If it wasn't classes, it was hockey, but it's finally the weekend. So, I can rest. Besides going to practice on Saturday, which isn't really practice, Coach wants us to review our film from the last game. You know, the game where we played like shit because our left-winger was running around like a chicken with his head cut off.

He did return for the second period, ready to play, but it wasn't enough. He should've been ready from the start.

Now the team has to pay for it by watching the film on a Saturday morning. Everyone knows it's Dean's fault, so he's on the outs right now. It won't last as long as he gets his shit together by the next game.

Speaking of the devil, I see Dean walking up the steps to the library, so I run to catch up with him. "Dean!" I call out.

His head snaps in my direction. "Oh shit. What's up, cap?"

We do that little hand-clap-back-slap thing guys do. "I was just about to ask you the same thing." His face scrunches up in confusion. "Did you solve that Luna thing?"

"Oh, it's complicated. Wait, why?" He asks, crossing his arms over his chest.

"If it's going to be a problem, you're not gonna play well in the game. We can't have a repeat of the last one. So, I need you to figure your shit out, Dean. And fast."

I'm not trying to be a hardass, but for some reason that's the only way to get through to these damn play-ers. Unless I'm a dick to them, they won't listen.

"You're right. I'm throwing her a birthday party to make up for being a dick to her the other night. I don't think it'll help that much, but it can't hurt, right?"

Luna's birthday is coming up. This is news to me. I mean, we *just* sort of started being friends, so why would she tell me? Still, I wish she would have.

"When's her birthday?" Why am I asking? Why do I care?

"In two weeks. We normally just get pizza and watch movies together by ourselves, but I've been a real dick to her, so I felt like it was the least I could do."

They're twins. Right. I need to keep that at the forefront of my mind. Not that it matters. I'm never planning on doing anything with her. Honestly, I like being friends with someone who wants nothing from me besides my company. No sex. No special treatment. Nothing. Just someone to talk to.

Luna is like fresh air after being suffocated by a pillow. It's a weird analogy, but it's true. She doesn't care I'm a hockey player, nor is she trying to get in my pants just to walk around campus and say she slept with Nick Beckett. She genuinely just wants my company. A part of me just wants her company too. It's nice to have someone to hang out with who isn't on the team.

I love our team, but they really only want to hang out with me because I have a say in who's the next team captain. I already know who I want. Dean, if he can get his shit together. So, I'm not really looking at anyone else. Therefore, I don't need or want their company.

"Okay. Do you want any help? You know, with the planning or decorations or whatever." Good save, Nick.

"Actually, I know you guys just started hanging out. So, I was wondering if, when the day comes, you can distract her. Also, distract her for, like, the next two weeks. Gia and I are gonna be a little distant from her." He adds, shaking his head. "Gia can't hold a secret to save her life. So, I'm going to do my best to keep her *away* from Luna."

Yeah, because that's what she needs right now. More distance. She thinks they're mad at her. So, more distance will only solidify that for her. Unless I get her mind off of the distance. How the hell am I supposed to do that?

"Yeah, I can do that." Why did I say that, knowing full well, I *can't* do it?

"Thanks, dude. I have to get going. Gia and I are going to check out this venue. See you later, cap." He slaps my shoulder and walks in the opposite direction.

Why did I sign myself up for this? Probably because I'm a masochist.

I walk into Mama's Cafe to buy something to eat. Before this semester, I rarely came here. For some reason, I'm always here now. Like *always*. I come here three times a day. In the morning for coffee. The afternoon for my lunch. Then, just before I go home for another drink. At this point, they know my order by heart.

The truth is, I'm hoping I might run into Luna.

As I step up to the counter, I see long, shiny black waves pulled into a high ponytail. She doesn't have to turn around for me to know exactly who it is. "Paris?"

She turns around. "Nick? Hey." She says awkwardly.

"What are you doing here?" I ask. I haven't spoken to her since I called things off with her. I wanted to reach out because I did like talking with Paris. We were friends, and to lose it all because I didn't want a relationship actually does suck.

"Oh, I'm in town to see my friend." I just remembered Luna telling me she was friends with Paris.

"Ah, Luna." Her brows scrunch together.

"How do you know Luna?" Before I can respond, she speaks again. "Never mind. It doesn't matter. What *does* matter is that you stay the hell away from her."

Where the hell did that come from? "What?"

She turns so she's facing me fully and crosses her arms over her chest. Normally, this much sass and attitude would be a huge turn-on. But all I'm feeling right now is annoyance.

"You heard me. Stay away from her, Nick. I know you like to sleep around, but you can't sleep with her. I won't allow you to. Also, need I mention, she has a twin who's on *your hockey team*?"

I'm aware of that. Why is she acting like this is brand new? I'm aware Luna is off-limits. I never intended for her to be *on-limits*. But for Paris to essentially label me a man-whore bugs the fuck out of me.

I'm no saint, but I respect women. If I want to sleep with someone, I'll sleep with a willing participant who knows they'll get nothing from me after. I wouldn't, no scratch that, I *couldn't* do that to Luna. I don't know why, but I just couldn't.

"Funny how we're slut-shaming, but you slept with me, too," I scoff. "Plus, I never said I wanted to sleep with her. We're *friends*." I sneer.

"Yeah, then one thing will lead to another." She takes a step closer. "I know how your mind works, Nick. Like you said, *I've* slept with you. How do you think we got there?" She huffs. "She wants to concentrate on her career, and all you will do is distract her. You'll sleep with her till you've got your fill, then throw her away like a used jock strap." Someone's deflecting.

What on earth is her fucking problem? I've done nothing to her other than let her know where I stand.

I told her from the start I didn't want a relationship. Is it my fault she wants one now? No, it isn't.

I did the only reasonable thing I could think of: I cut it off. She'd believe I want more if I would have kept sleeping with her. I'd offer her the naive hope that it might change in the future, but it never will. My position on relationships remains unchanged.

Now she's telling me who I can and cannot speak with. I'm not her child.

"Look, I'm not sure what crawled up your ass, died, and turned you bitter, but you need to get out of my face with this bullshit. For starters, you're not my mother. You don't get to tell me what to do." I step into her space until I'm towering above her. "Two, Luna is an adult. She has full capacity to determine what she can and cannot do. Not you. So back the hell off. Get your own life and quit trying to dominate everyone else's."

Giving her no room to speak, I grab my order off the counter and walk out. When I get in my car, I can feel the rage ringing in my ears. Luna is off the table. I have never tried to cross that line. Now, it almost feels like a challenge to make *her* cross it for me.

I pull out my phone to text her.

Luna J

Are you doing anything tonight?

I've never texted Luna first. She's always the one to initiate the conversation. Which I don't mind at all. I don't really have anything to talk to her about. Today was a special occasion.

Paris thinks she knows me. Just because we slept together for a year doesn't mean anything. I knew our relationship wasn't going anywhere. So, I kept her at arm's length and only let her see what I wanted her to see. Nothing less. Nothing more.

There's a buzz from my phone with a text from Luna.

Luna J

why?

you're the only person who can call in favors for a friend to hang out with you in desperate times of need? :(

I thought so

but I guess I can free myself up

meet you at Mama's?

no, I'll pick you up

ummm okay...

I'll see you at 8

She sends me a thumbs up, and I chuck the phone into the passenger seat. I'm not even sure what we're going to do tonight, but I'll think of something.

Eight comes around faster than expected, and I still have no idea what the hell we're doing. Yet here I am sitting in front of her apartment building, waiting for her to come outside. I texted her two minutes ago, telling her I was here. She said she was coming down, but she was still nowhere in sight.

As I prepare to shoot her another text, I catch a glimpse of her running down the walkway to my car. She's wearing a white cropped hoodie that shows the black tights hugging her small waist. Her hair is pulled into a tight bun with a few stray curls framing her face.

She's wearing the most basic outfit, and I find her to be so fucking stunning.

Why?

Before I can answer the question, she opens the passenger door to let herself in. "Hey, weirdo," she says. As she slumps into her seat, a wind of coconuts and strawberries invades my nose, making my cock twitch, not that I'm complaining. I've grown accustomed to it now.

"You ready?" I ask as I try to distract myself from how turned on, I'm getting by the way she smells. The. Way. She. Smells. Is. Turning. Me. On.

What the fuck is wrong with me? I'm just going to let that sink in for a second. Actually, I better not. One thing I wouldn't be able to explain is a hard-on with only her in my car.

"Yeah. Where are we going? I mean, you didn't even..." She's cut off by the ringing from my phone.

We both look down at my phone which is sitting in cup holder. My heart sinks when I see the name flashing across the screen.

Overstead Nursing Home.

I quickly pick up the phone and hit answer. "Hello?"

"Mr. Beckett, sorry to bother you. I just thought you would like to know your mother..." I cut her off.

"Is she okay? Did something happen?" I see Luna looking at me from the corner of my eye.

"Oh no, she's perfectly fine. Actually, she's more than fine! She's lucid, sir." I feel the blood drain from my face. I can't even remember the last time my mother was lucid.

"I'm on my way. I'll be there in forty-five minutes." I say before hanging up. I know the odds of her still being lucid by time I get there are slim, but I need to risk it either way.

"Hey, we can do this some other night." Luna grabs onto the door, but I place the car in drive and pull off.

"No, it's fine." There was no time for Luna to leave. It wouldn't sit well with me just making her get out of the car and letting her go back to doing whatever the hell she was doing. So, I'll bring her along. Not that that's a good idea. I've never told anyone about my mom. Not even my closest friends know about her. "Can you keep a secret?"

"Depends? Why?" She rests further into her seat and buckles herself in.

"Where we're going, you can't tell anyone about it. I mean no one, Luna. Not Dean. Not Gia. Not even Paris. I don't care how close y'all are. You can't tell anyone."

"I won't. I promise." Holding out her pinky, I pull to a stop at a red light.

I raise an eyebrow in confusion. "What the hell is that?"

"It's a pinky, dummy." She reaches for my hand that's resting on the steering wheel and pushes all of my fingers down except for my pinky. "You loop it. Then seal it with your thumb." She presses her thumb into mine. "For an extra seal, you kiss it." Then she leans in to press a soft kiss to her thumb.

As I watch her kiss her thumb, my heart comes to a standstill. Like someone hit pause on our movie, and I'm stuck in this exact moment until someone hits play again. I don't want anyone to hit play. I want to stay right here. She has the prettiest smile on her face. Its wide enough to show her pearly white teeth that glisten against her gorgeous, golden-brown skin. It's comforting.

She's comforting me. "You're turn." She pushes our linked hands to my mouth.

I tighten my pinky around hers, pulling it to my lips. Our eyes stay locked as my lips stay centered on my thumb. This is the most intimate I've ever been with my hand that didn't include other parts of my body.

I watch as a red hue brushes across her cheek. It's barely noticeable, but it's there. One thing that doesn't get past me is how her breath gets caught in her throat.

Interesting.

Chapter 14

Nick

The last thing I wanted to do was come to my mom's nursing home. I wouldn't even really call it a nursing home. It's more of an around-the-clock care facility. They do a damn good job at it too. She's not even old enough to be considered for a nursing home. My mother just has a sickening disease that needs to be monitored 24/7. With my dad being on the road ninety percent of the time and me in college, neither of us have time to give her the care she needs, which I hate.

I want to take care of her more than anything, but I can't. Instead, I'll do the next best thing. I'll earn enough money so I can move her into a house with me and a nurse. That way, whenever I come home, I'll always have access to her. She'll be with family, not in a home filled with strangers. My dad could also come and stay with her when he's in town, too, so it's a win-win situation. I would see my dad and mom.

We're standing in the common room, waiting for the nurse to escort me to my mother's room. I know where her room is, but apparently, they have new rules that say they have to take us to their rooms now. Smart, but still irritating.

"Sorry for the wait, Mr. Beckett." A nurse walks up, holding a clipboard.

"Is...is she still..." The words get stuck in my throat.

"Lucid?" She smiles. "She is. Follow me, sir."

I stand, but I don't move. My feet are cemented to the ground. It feels like I'm pulling them to move, but I'm not.

If I'm being honest, I'm scared. What if she doesn't recognize me? What if she hates me for not visiting more often? There are a million things that could happen. My heart is racing, and sweat drips down my face.

Before my mind can wander any further, I feel a hand wrap around mine. When I look up, it's Luna. Her eyes softened with warmth, and a gentle smile plays on her lips as she looks up at me, conveying a genuine sense of care. "What are you doing?"

"I'm trying this thing where I'm nice to those who are nice to me. It feels weird, so take it while you can, Beckett." Her hand tightens around mine. "Let's go."

She tugs on my hand as we follow the nurse into my mom's room. I can hear my heartbeat pound in my ears and my heart in my throat. "Mom?"

As she turns her head, I'm met with her watery eyes. "Oh my god. Nicky? Oh my god! Honey, come here!"

My feet move slowly as I make my way to her. She pulls me into a firm hug. "Hi, Mom," I whisper into her neck.

The tears seep from my eyelids as I wrap my arms around her, breathing in her scent. She smells like a flower shop, like she did when I was a kid. Anytime I was going through something hard, I would just hug her and be enraptured by her. Her smell. Her love. *Her.*

"Oh Nicky. I've missed you so much." She pulls back. "Look at you. You've gotten so tall. What are you, six-two?"

"Six-three actually." I smile down at her as she looks at me.

"Wow. My little Nicky isn't so little anymore." She sighs sweetly. "So, tell me what's new? You're in what, college now? You should be almost done by now, right?" She stops and looks at Luna. "Oh my god! I'm so sorry,

I didn't even introduce myself. Hi, I'm Jenna Beckett. Nick's mom. You must be his girlfriend." She extends her hand.

I nearly choke on my saliva. Luna's just laughing. "Mom! No. She's just a friend."

"We use that term very loosely, though. I'm Luna, by the way," Luna intercedes.

"Well, Luna. It's very nice to meet you." As she grabs Luna's hand, she pulls her into her space. "Can I request something of you?" Luna nods. "Please take care of my Nicky. He won't admit it, but he carries the world on his shoulders. And he has a hard time trusting anyone as he does it."

"Mom." I grit my teeth.

"Don't *Mom* me. I don't know how much time I have left, so I'm not sugarcoating anything. Anyways." Turning her attention back to Luna. "You're clearly someone he trusts."

"What makes you think that?" Luna questions.

My mom looks at me, smiles, then looks back at Luna. "He brought you here. I love Nicky, but I know I can be a burden to him. He never brings anyone to meet me. I haven't met a single friend of his. Not that I would remember it."

I sigh deeply. "Mom, you're not a burden, nor am I ashamed of you. I just keep my personal life personal," I defend.

"Whatever. You love me too much to admit it, but I know I am. To you and your father." Tears swell in her eyes. "I wish I didn't have this stupid disease, but I do. So, please look after him. He looks after everyone else, but who's looking after him? He's my only pride and joy and my biggest accomplishment. I just want him to be happy."

I try to speak so Luna doesn't have to, but she speaks first. "I'll do my best. I promise."

It's the last thing I expect to leave her mouth, but it does. My mom slowly releases Luna's hands. She starts to look around the room, like she's lost.

She's no longer lucid.

"Mom?" I call out, hoping I'm wrong.

"I'm sorry. You look just like my son." Her smile returning to her face.

"Well, if he looks like me, he must be handsome." I joke, trying to lighten the mood.

I know she won't remember even a lick of this conversation, but it doesn't matter. Every time I come to see her, I just joke with her. It feels like nothing's changed. It makes her smile, and it's all I need from her.

"Well, we have to go, but I'll come back another time." I kiss her cheek and nod toward the door for Luna to follow. We walk in silence back to the car.

I miss her. To see the smile on her face again is like being paralyzed and relearning how to walk. Simple but fulfilling. It's as though everything has returned to normal. I know she's still sick, but just seeing her makes me happy. When she's not lucid, she grins, but her lucid smile is more authentic. She knows why she's smiling and understands what's happening around her. Despite it, I want her to be happy at all times.

It means she knows who I am and understands what I'm saying. If I make a joke, she knows what I'm referring to. So, yeah. Her lucid smile is better than her non-lucid smile.

As I look to the ground, a smile creeps its way onto my face without warning.

"You must be happy." Luna nudges.

"Yeah. I am. I'm sorry our plans changed. It's not what I had planned for the night." Which isn't a full lie because I didn't have anything planned for the night. I had kind of hoped to drive around until something sparked our interest.

She shrugs. "I don't think anything would have topped this anyway. Thanks for letting me come."

"It wasn't much of a choice." I dig for the keys in my back pocket and unlock the car. "If I didn't bring you, I probably would've been too late to see her."

"Ahh. Selfish intent. There's the Nick Beckett we all know and loath." I open the passenger's door to let her in. "Well, I haven't eaten. So, I need food." She adds.

"As you wish, your highness." She rolls her eyes and jumps into the car.

I pull into the first diner I find. I've never been here, so I have no idea how good or bad the food is here. Given that it's so packed, I'm gonna guess it's a good place.

A hostess welcomes us at the podium near the door. "How many are in your party tonight?"

"Just two." She nods as we follow her to a booth in the far corner. As I look around, I realize how much of a mistake it was to come here. Everything is romantic. The lights are dimmed to a soft golden yellow. The tables are set with a single flower in the middle in a vase. This is a place I would take someone if we were going on a first date.

This is *not* a date.

Before the panic can set in, Luna orders a drink. I guess there's no turning around now.

"Sorry," I spout out.

"What for?" Confusion washes over her face.

"I didn't realize how intimate this place was. I just pulled into the first one I saw."

She laughs. "I honestly don't care. It has food, so it's good with me." She continues to look over the menu.

I should be looking over the menu as well, but I can't keep my eyes off of her. It also has nothing to do with her beauty. It's everything else. She walked into that nursing home today and comforted me the entire time. She was kind and loving toward my mom, too. Luna promised my mom she would take care of me as if she intended to keep me in her life. I know it's not true, but she had no obligation to do so and still she did.

I've always been afraid of introducing my mom to my friends. Not because I'm ashamed of her, despite what she thinks, I just worry what they would say. I don't need the pity. I love my mom, and I'm here for her in every way possible. I don't want people to treat me any different, with the longing stares or the soft eyes just because my mom is sick.

Luna treats me exactly the same. Still sassy as hell. Even in front of my mom, she was giving me grief. I guess if anyone understands not wanting to be treated differently because of an illness, it's Luna.

So, all I see when I sit in front of her is her compassion. Compassion is not a sufficient enough term. One thing

I *can't* say about her is she isn't caring. Luna's heart was big, and I loved that I got to see it in action. To enjoy even a fraction of it.

"Thank you," I blurt out.

Her head slowly lifts with confusion brushed across her face. "For what?"

"My mom. You, um, don't have to worry about that promise you made her."

"What promise?"

"To look out for me. I know you only said it to make her feel better." I know what I'm doing. I want her to tell me she means it. That she actually wants to be my friend. *Please say it. Tell me it's not a lie and you fully intend on keeping that promise.*

"I think I'm setting myself up for some bad karma if I lie to an elder. I'm not crazy." She grins. "I didn't lie to her. You've been kind enough to help me. I *guess* I could return the favor." She returns to her menu.

They could probably hear my heartbeat across the street with how loud its beating. I've never had this feeling before. The feeling of wanting someone to stay around me. To never leave me. That's what I'm feeling right now.

The thought of her being Dean's sister crosses my mind. But that's slowly starting to fade as a reason not to try. Everyday she's in my presence, she slowly nips at the reason to stay away from her. I should be cautious and stay away, but I can't. Not when she says things like that.

Chapter 15

Luna

I'm so full. I ate so much I feel like my stomach would explode if I take another breath. I really should get home though. Paris texted me ten minutes ago, asking where I am. She's probably worried sick about me. When I left, I told her I would only be out for like an hour.

It's been four.

Nick is currently driving me home, I think. Knowing him, we'll probably make a detour somewhere else first. We get off the highway, and he misses his turn to my house.

Like I said.

I sit up in my seat. "Where are you abducting me to now?"

"You are here of your own volition. So, just sit back and enjoy the ride," he comments.

Yeah, I don't like the sound of that. He sounds just like a serial killer before they lure their prey to their death. Well, if this is it, at least my stomach is full. At least I won't die hungry.

I lay my head against the window and let my eyes close. There's no use in me fighting him to take me home. I know it would be pointless anyway. Also, I didn't really want to go home. It's nice being out. Being around Nick is becoming less and less stressful lately. When I see him now, I don't get this sudden urge to strangle him anymore. Now, I just feel like slapping him. Progress.

We drive for what feels like hours. When I open my eyes, we're parked in Grenice Memorial Park's parking lot. The lights cascade down the jogger's path in a way that makes me feel like he's really walking me to my death.

"Is this the part where you murder me so no one finds out about your secrets?"

His chest rumbles with laughter. "What the hell is your deal with murderers?"

I shrug before letting them fall back down. "I couldn't tell you. I guess if I'm always aware of possibly being murdered, I'll always be alert."

"Yeah, okay. Get out, my dear *victim*," he says before opening the door and exiting.

I follow suit and hop out. He locks the door behind me and nods his head for me to follow him. "No seriously. What are we doing here?"

"You've never been on a night stroll?" he questions.

"No, not particularly. I don't go anywhere at night by myself. Not unless I plan on dying that night."

"Well, good thing you're not alone. Come on." Shoving his hands into his pockets, he continues to walk.

I hear a noise behind me, so I quickly run by his side. When I reach him, he looks down at me and starts to laugh again. "Shut up."

As we continue to walk and the fear has officially subsided, I take in my surroundings. It's actually peaceful. The silence. There's only a handful of people out here. Normally, it's super busy, especially in the parks, with kids running and screaming and adults holding on to their last shred of sanity.

Right now, there's none of that. It's quiet. There are no kids. No screaming. The night sky is clear, with a full moon shining over the pond in the middle of the park. I watch as the water ripples, with the ducks sitting in the middle.

"How often do you come here?" I ask.

"Anytime I need to think." Nick responds.

"What do you need to think about tonight?"

He stops walking. "Honestly?"

"Yeah. I wouldn't have asked if I didn't want honesty." I stand in front of him.

Before he answers, he looks at the pond and takes a deep breath. "Luna…" He's cut off by the sound of my name echoing through the air. "You've got to be fucking kidding me."

I look at him before following the voice that just screamed my name like I was dying. "Paris? How did you know where I was?"

"I have your location, remember?" Yeah, and I'm currently regretting that. "What happened to just being gone for an hour?" She looks at Nick. "What the hell did I tell you?" Oh yeah, they know each other.

I still feel like I'm missing something. Looking at Nick, he looks like he just stepped in a pile of gum and can't get it off. If I didn't know the history between them, I would think they've always hated each other. Wait, what did she mean by that? What did she tell Nick? "What do you mean? What are you talking about?"

"Nothing," Nick interrupts. "Paris, what the hell are you doing here?"

"I figured you were behind her being out this long. Despite me telling you to keep it in your pants," She scoffs. "You never fucking listen. Does Dean know you're out with his little sister?"

I intervene, "Um, one, please stop talking about me like I'm not standing right here. Two, Dean doesn't control me." Although I think he would actually have something to say about this,. "Three, who cares? We weren't doing anything. We were talking."

"It's never *just* talking with Nick," Paris snips.

"You think I'm that easy? Really?" Both of their heads snap to me.

"That's not what I mean, teddy bear." Maybe, but it's what she was insinuating. I know about Nick's reputation. I know he's a man whore, but I would never sleep with him.

For one, he's my brother's friend. Two, there's no telling what he caught from all of those puck bunnies. So, yeah. I'll pass. "Whatever. Look, I'm going to go home. You guys can keep having this little pissing contest you're having. Let me know when you're done making decisions about *my* life." I glance at Nick. "Thank you for dinner."

Then I walk in the opposite direction to Paris' car. I should call an Uber, but I'm trying to save money. I expect one of them to come after me, but they don't. When I turn around, I see they're arguing again. I've never seen Nick angry. Not that I've known him for long, but this is the first time I've actually seen him mad. Even from this distance, I can see that thick vein in his forehead about to pop.

Paris is doing that to him. Maybe it was a good idea that he called it off between them. The air between them seems toxic as hell. How did Paris ever claim to have feelings for him when she's looking at him like that? Everything about them seems like some romance novel. You know those enemies-to-lovers tropes. That's the vibe it's giving. Like at any second, they're going to start hate-fucking.

But what is she saying that would cause that reaction from him? Is it narcissistic to wonder if it's about me? I really shouldn't be even staring at them like this. It seems kind of personal.

As I pull my phone out of my back pocket, I hear a slap. The sound ricochets in the deafening silence. My eyes snap back up to see Nick holding his cheek. Even from all the way over here, I can see he's containing his anger.

What the fuck just happened?

Should I walk over there? I don't want to get in the middle, but her slapping him isn't right. I'm not one for violence. I should say something, right? Before I have time to react or do something, Paris is walking my way, leaving Nick standing there in silence, holding his face. I'm stunned. I should really say something.

"Let's go!" Paris shouts.

"What the hell just happened?" I throw my head toward Nick.

"Nothing he didn't deserve." Paris swings the door open. "Get in. Let's go," she demands.

"Paris. No one deserves to be slapped. I don't care what they do. What the hell is wrong with you?" I don't care how angry I get with Nick, I'll never put my hands on him. Now I might throw a couple of drinks in his face. But to put my hands on him? I could never.

My mom used to always say if a woman is bad enough to put her hands on a man, she's bad enough to get hands put back on her, although I doubt Nick would ever do such a thing. I still couldn't just stand here and condone her actions.

"So, you're taking his side now? You don't even know what he said." She fumes.

"It doesn't matter. How would you feel if he turned around and slapped the dogshit out of you? You would be pissed." I turn back to her and start to walk to Nick.

"He just wants to get between your legs!" My feet come to an abrupt halt. "Once he does, he'll be done with you. You're a conquest to him. Nothing more, nothing less. He'll never want more from you, Luna. Trust me, I know."

I halt in my steps. "Go home, Paris. I don't mean back to my apartment either. Go back to New York. I don't need or want you here anymore."

I thought we were past the bullshit. We had this whole conversation about how we hurt each other and would never do it again. I can't keep doing this with her. She always knows what to say to piss me off or to hurt me. I can't keep going back to her to fix it, either.

With that, I make my way to Nick again. He's still standing there. As if he were frozen in his position. I reach up and pull his hands down from his cheek. A red handprint is plastered on his face like a fresh tattoo.

"Hopefully, it won't bruise." I drag my eyes to his. "Are you okay?"

"Yeah. I, uh, I don't even know what happened." His words are filled with hurt. I still can't believe she slapped him. I wanted to ask what happened, but something told me he wouldn't tell me. Not that he's required to, but still. He was clearly hurt, and the little narcissistic voice in my head keeps telling me it's my fault.

"It doesn't matter. We should probably get you home. Yeah?" I dig in his front pockets for his keys. Our eyes connect, and there's this palpable tension between us that I'm not sure I can even explain, so I look away. "I'll drive."

I cup my hands into his and pull him to his car. We walk in silence as I pull him behind me. When we reach his car, I quickly unlock it to let him in.

"Get in," I demand.

"I don't let anyone drive my car." He tries to reach for the keys, but I swoop my arms behind my back.

"I can drive." I say softly. He reaches for the keys again, and I throw my hands in the opposite direction. "I can do this all night."

"Luna, just give me the damn keys." He holds his palms out, waiting.

"No." I quickly shove the keys into my bra. Why did I do that? It was completely unnecessary.

"You think a couple of boobs would stop me from grabbing my keys?" He takes a step closer. So I take one back. We continue this dance until my back hits the driver's side door. "If anything, it's motivation. So either give me my keys, or I'll take them from you."

He dips his head to eye level with me. "I don't mind touching your boobs. Do you? Give me the keys, or I'm going in, Jay."

I gulp. "Careful. You're treading the line of assault, Mr. Beckett." My voice softens before speaking again. "Just let me drive you home. I promise to be careful with your car."

I watch as his eyes ease as he searches mine. "Please. Be careful."

He takes a step back and walks to the other side of the car.

I take a moment to slow my heart. Why am I reacting this way? I shake the question away and hop into the car. When I'm situated, I make the mistake of looking at Nick. He's reclined back in his seat, looking blankly at the roof. His emotions were clear as day on his face. Frustrated and... sad. I wonder why, though. Why should he feel sad for Paris slapping *him*?

My heart aches for him. He was just in a good mood after seeing his mom. Then Paris comes along and ruins his entire night.

Is this weird? Me, sitting here, staring. Like I have nothing better to do? It's definitely weird.

"Are you gonna keep staring at me or are you going to take me home? Either is fine with me." He adds, still staring at the roof.

I quickly turn to the wheel and turn the keys in the ignition before putting the car in drive and pulling off.

Chapter 16

Luna

"Luna, you're turns have gotten so much better." Madam Christine compliments. She's been working with me on choreography for the last couple of weeks. The first week or two, she was going in on me about my turns. She said I wasn't spotting myself, but I swore I was.

"Thank you," I say while trying to catch my breath.

"Okay, let's take it from the beginning. Shall we?" She walks to the edge of the studio to give me space to start.

My first entrance is in the *Elegy*. I'm supposed to come from the wings, so we've been practicing as if we're on stage. I take position on the edge of the floor and give a firm nod to her, signaling I'm ready.

Madam Christine hits play on the remote, and I begin. I start with my first chassé and let my body do the rest. As I continue to move through the space, my body eases. With every movement, I melt more and more into the music, letting it course through my blood and rid me of all of my thoughts, allowing the music to control me and not my mind.

Dancing to me is a drug. Something I will always come back for, wanting more. The world falls to the wayside, and I'm the sole person here. My anxiety no longer exists. The pain and hurt no longer exist.

"Point your toes, Luna!" Madam Christine notes over the music.

I try to take the note without losing my balance or my place. I extend my legs into the air, going the extra mile to make sure I point my toes.

"Better." She crosses her arms over her chest and starts to pace back and forth while keeping her eyes trained on me.

Continuing through the choreo, I take my first turn into a rond de jambe. Then, sauté with a sissonne. Then execute another turn. Once I land, I lean down as I extend my arms to cross at my feet. Then I rise back up to arch my body backward, finishing my opening combo.

I stand, resting my hands on my waist and catching my breath. Pride swells in my chest. This was the first time I've run through the entire combo without stumbling or making grave mistakes. Normally I fuck up on the turn, but I spotted myself and made it through. So yeah, I'm proud.

"Every time I see you dance, it reminds me why I started teaching." Madam Christine walks into the space with me.

"Thank you. I've been practicing." I smile.

"Well, it shows. I'll leave you to continue by yourself. We'll start your second solo part on Wednesday." I nod in agreement as she grabs her stuff from the chair and heads out. "Also, Luna?"

My head swivels. "Yes?"

"Happy birthday, sweetheart." She smiles.

"Thank you." I turn back to the mirror. I jump up and down like a little kid. I'm just so damn happy with how well this went. This was exactly what I needed. Something good.

I turn to the wall that houses the barres and run to grab one. I set it in the middle of the room. Using it to balance myself, I extend my legs and slowly lift them in the air, making sure to point them. I need to practice pointing my toes, so I might as well start now.

Dropping and lifting my legs, I continue to practice my points. Inhaling on the lift and exhaling as I drop my leg. Before I lift my leg again, there's a knock on the door frame. I look over in the mirror to see Nick leaning against it.

I'm having a weird case of deja vu.

I turn back to the mirror and continue with what I was doing. "What are you doing here, stalker?"

"Ouch." Grabbing his chest as if he's wounded. "Stalker is a strong word. I just figured this is where you would be."

I let my leg fall. "Sounds like stalking *to me.*" I turn, facing him, spreading my arms across the barre as I stare at him. "So, you're here, why?"

Standing up straight. "Right. Are you busy?" I look around the studio, raising my brows. "Right. Ha. So, no?"

"Get on with your point, Beckett." I grit as the annoyance starts to bubble.

"I need someone to get lunch with. Want to join?" He couldn't get lunch by himself?

Things have been weird between Nick and me since he took me to see his mom. We haven't spoken to each other for, like, two weeks. It was a little weird, to be honest. Not the fact that we didn't speak, but the fact that I *missed* talking to him.

It was nice to have someone to go to. We would text every now and then, but not have a real conversation.

Dean and Gia still haven't spoken to me. I don't know what I'm supposed to do. I try to call and text them, but most of the time they reply with a one-word answer or ignore me altogether. It's frustrating. I don't know what I did to upset them, but today of all days.

It's mine and Dean's birthday. So, I kind of expected a happy birthday call or even a damn text.

Every year, Gia would show up at my house in the morning with a stack of pancakes and birthday candles. She didn't today. I didn't receive a text message or a shout-out on Instagram. Not even a quick phone call. Neither of them said anything to me. The only person who remembered my birthday was Madam Christine.

Did I call Dean and say happy birthday? No, but at least I texted him. I didn't even receive a thank-you text from him. Nothing.

Screw it. I have nothing to do and no one to celebrate my birthday with. So, I guess getting lunch with Nick isn't the worst thing I can do today. "What the hell? Why not." I pick up the barre and place it back against the wall with the others. "Just give me a second to get my stuff."

He nods his head. "I'll be outside." Then he heads downstairs.

I quickly pull my sweats back on and throw on my sweater. Then I head outside. When I make it outside, Nick is standing in front of his car, holding a single balloon in his hands.

I bite back my smile. "What's that?"

"A little birdie told me it was your birthday." He hands me the balloon.

"So, you got me a balloon? What am I, twelve?" I laugh. Despite what I said, I actually love it. It's stupid, but it's all I've received today. "Thank you, Nicky."

Ever since his mom shared that little nickname of his, I can't help but call him Nicky. It's cute. I mainly do it to taunt him, though. Not that it works.

"That's better. Come on, we've got a reservation." He unlocks the car and opens the passenger's door.

"Oh, he's a gentleman? Who knew?"

He laughs and shakes his head before closing the door behind me. The day was starting to look up again. "I hope you have a change of clothes," Nick says.

"Why would I have a change of clothes? After the studio, I planned on going home and showering. Wait!"

I didn't want to go to a restaurant all sweaty and smelly. "Can we go to my apartment first? I need to shower and change."

He looks at his phone and lets out an irritated sigh. "Can you be quick?"

"No," I said honestly. "Beauty takes time."

Another hearty laugh leaves his mouth. "Okay, fine. I'll let it slide today because it's your birthday."

He takes a right at the light and heads straight for my apartment.

It's just lunch, and yet it feels like everything to me. The only person who remembered my birthday is Nick. We're not even close, and yet he remembered. I didn't even tell him. Wait. *I* didn't tell him. So, who did?

"Quick question."

"Shoot." He keeps his eyes on the road.

"Who told you about my birthday? I don't remember telling you."

"Uh, I don't remember. I do remember putting it in my calendar, though." He put my birthday in his calendar?

"Why?"

"So, I wouldn't forget it," he says nonchalantly. A small twist grips my stomach.

So, someone told him about my birthday. Then he put it in his calendar. Just so he wouldn't forget it? Weird. Considering he's taking me to lunch, does it really matter who told him about it?

We arrive at my apartment. I let Nick come up with me. I didn't want him sitting in his car for hours waiting on me. When we make it to my apartment, I tell him to make himself at home, and I run to shower.

My showers normally take an hour, but I didn't want to keep him waiting. So, I quickly lather, rinse, and repeat. Stepping out, I wrap the towel around my body. I run to my closet and pick out a white crop top, ripped blue jeans, and a brown cardigan. Throwing the clothes on, I pair them with my brown high-top Converses.

Running back to my bathroom, I pull my hair out of my bun. I let my hair fall to my shoulders. I grab the gel from the cabinet and scoop a hefty amount into my hands, running my hands through my hair before scrunching it upward.

For my makeup, I do my eyebrows and add some concealer under my eyes. I grab my gold hoop earrings and loop them through my ears. I take a final look in the mirror. Satisfied with my outfit, I walk back into the living room with Nick.

Nick stands up from the couch. "Damn, took you..." His words trail off when his eyes land on me. I feel the heat of his gaze as he takes me in. Goosebumps trail up my arms and warmth rises in my neck. Why is my body acting like this?

Quit it.

"Why are you looking at me like that?" I cross my arms over my chest, suddenly feeling self-conscious.

"Sorry. I-I've just never seen you with your hair down."

I start to put my hair back into a bun. "Oh, should I put it back up?"

He quickly grabs my hands and pulls them back down. "Don't you dare." My heart damn near lurches out of my chest. I look down at his hands and back up to him. "You look beautiful. Leave it down."

Generally, I would have some smart-ass comeback, but right now...nothing. His hands are still wrapped around mine, and its sending a pulsing current through my body. Firing up every nerve in my body. This small action should have no effect on me, but it does.

Those words are on a loop in my head. *You look beautiful. Leave it down.* Six words. That's all it took to leave me speechless.

I pull my hand back and walk to grab my purse. "We should go then," I utter, clearing my throat.

"Alright. Let's go. We missed our reservation, but I know the owner so they should be able to squeeze us in."

He made a reservation. Why? "I'm sorry. I didn't know you made a reservation." I thought we were just going out to a diner to eat, like we always do.

"Don't be. Like you said, beauty takes time." He looks me up and down and another set of goosebumps break out across my arms.

I hold the door open for him to walk out, then lock it behind me. With every step we take closer to his car, my heart races even faster. I don't like not knowing what we're doing. Not knowing where we're going or what the exact plans are for the day. But with Nick, that's always the case. It's always a mini adventure with him.

He opens the passenger door and ushers me in. Why is he being so nice? His niceness is freaking me the hell out.

"So can you tell me where we're going?" I ask, rubbing my hands up and down my thighs.

"Somewhere with food. That's all you need to know." He says nothing else as he starts the car and pulls off.

We arrive at this Italian restaurant, Romano's. I love Italian food. It's my favorite. I never told him that though. So, maybe he just likes Italian food, too. There's no reason to let this go to my head, or worse, my heart. Yeah, that would definitely be worse.

We walk to the front door, but before I can open the it, Nick runs in front of me and grabs the handle. His free hand finds my lower back, and he gently pushes me inside. A small shudder runs through me, and goosebumps explode down my arms. I thank whatever god can hear me that I wore a cardigan today.

Nick removes his hand to talk to the hostess. "Reservation for Beckett."

"One second, sir." He scrolls through the tablet searching for his name. "Ah, found it. Right this way." I thought he said we lost our reservation.

We follow him through the restaurant, passing couples laughing and conversing softly. We always seem to find ourselves in an intimate setting whenever we go out together. This time, I'm convinced it was intentional. There's no way he chose the most romantic place and not think about it before hand.

There's soft music playing in the background. The restaurant adorned with low-hanging, soft lights casting a warm glow over black are red décor. The ambiance is intimate, with sleek black tables adorned with crimson accents. The walls are draped in rich, dark tones, creating an atmosphere that exudes romance and sophistication. Looking around the place, I find it hard to believe I could even afford anything in here.

As if Nick can read my mind, he speaks up. "Don't worry, I'm buying."

"Good, because it looks too expensive for me." I laugh anxiously.

"I find that hard to believe. Didn't you say your parents were rich?" Nick pulls out the chair as I sit down.

"Key word, *my parents*. Even so, my parents aren't *that* rich. They're just comfortable." Nick opens his mouth to speak, I hold up my hand cutting him off. "I know you're going to say, *that's what rich people say*. But I'm serious. They make enough money to support their families. The remainder is stored in a savings account. Not enough for trust funds, but enough that if something drastic were to happen they would have something to fall back on." I pause. "Wait. Why are we discussing my parents' bank account again?"

"We weren't. You were the one who decided to go on a tangent about how much money your parents do or don't make. It was entertaining." He shrugs. "It didn't seem right to cut you off." He smiles, splaying the napkin in his lap.

"So can we talk about something else now." I take a sip of water.

"How old are you now?"

I choke on the water, spitting it right out. Instead of helping me, he just laughs. Everyone starts to stare at us with concern.

"What is wrong with you?" I wipe my mouth with the napkin before setting it back in my lap. "You're not supposed to ask a woman how old she is. Didn't your mom teach you that?"

"Yes, she did, but I wanted to see your reaction. I'd say it was worth it."

"I'm twenty-one. How old are you?" I rest my chin on my hands.

"Twenty-three."

"Ahh, so you're old." I swore he was only a year older, given that he's a senior and I'm a junior.

"I'm not old. I did however start college a year late." Welp that answers that question.

"Why?"

"I took time off to be with my mom. It was a bad year for her. I just wanted to be with her." Shit. I forgot about his mom.

"Can I ask…When did your mom get sick?" I start to pick at my fingernails, awaiting his reply.

"Um, my senior year of high school," he says, clearing his throat. "She has Alzheimer. We started noticing little things about her. She would forget where her keys were when they were in her hands. Then forget where she parked her car. We thought it was just normal shit, nothing to serious. Then she started to forget things that mattered. Like her anniversary or that she had a pie in the oven. In all of the time she's been married to my dad, she never not once forgot their anniversary. So, we got worried."

Nick softly scratches his beard. "When we took her to the hospital, they told us she had early-onset Alzheimer. They told us she needed around the clock help." He shrugs. "So, I stayed with her at home after graduating high school. When my dad came back from his last work trip, he told me he wanted me to go to school. It's what my mother would want. So, I came to school, and he checked her into that facility. Despite how much I didn't want to, it made the most sense."

"What does your dad do?"

"Honestly, I couldn't tell you." He laughs lightly. "I just know he makes a shit ton of money."

"So, *you're* the rich one?" I joke, trying to lighten the mood.

"What was that you said, *my parents' are rich not me*?" He mocks. "But yeah, he is. He works hard. Or at least he tries to."

"What do you mean?"

"He's madly in love with my mom. He hates being away from her for too long. Even before she got sick, and now that she is sick, he feels worse about it. He visits her every Saturday, like clockwork. It doesn't matter how busy he is or where he's at. He comes home just to visit her."

Listening to Nick speak about his parents makes my heart swell. To hear he gave up an entire year just to be with his mother is sweet. I can't even begin to imagine what that was like. Wondering if she would be okay. Putting your future plans on hold for someone you loved more than anything. It's admirable.

Although my mother and I don't always see eye to eye, I couldn't even imagine losing her. Either of my parents. I've always been a daddy's girl, but to even the thought of losing one of my parents could shatter me to pieces.

It's clear that Nick's mom is his entire world, just like Cassie was mine. The only difference, he still gets to see her whenever he wants to. Although she doesn't always recognize him, it's still something. I think I'll always be envious of that. "I love how dedicated you are to her. Your mom," I add. Before he can respond, the waiter comes back to take our order.

"I'll have the shrimp scampi. What would you like?" Nick hands the menu to the waiter.

"I'll have the baked cheese ravioli. Thank you." I order, handing the menu back to the waiter.

"Can I get either of you a drink while you wait?" the waiter asks.

Nick nods for me to order. "Can you bring out your best Moscato? Please and thank you."

The waiter gives a curt nod and walks off.

"You're drink of choice is Moscato?" I'm glad he doesn't mention how it's only three in the afternoon. But it's my birthday, so I feel like those rules don't apply today.

"Yes. Is there something wrong with that?" I cross my arms over my chest.

"Nothing at all. Just thought you were more of a red wine kind of girl." Nick grins.

What about me makes him think I like red wine? I absolutely hate red wine. Solely because I think it's a cliche. Almost everybody and their mom likes red wine. So, I don't. I know that liking Moscato is also a cliche, but it's one I can live with. Yes, I know. I'm a walking contradiction.

I tend to stray from things that everyone likes or things I know are stereotypes. Like watermelon, there's nothing wrong with it, but since people automatically think all black people like watermelon, I don't. Fuck the patriarchy and all of that good stuff. "So, what's after lunch?"

"Dessert?" I roll my eyes at his sarcasm. "There's one more thing I had planned. Unless you're *busy*."

"Can't say that I am." I shrug.

Rubbing his hands together mischievously, he says, "Good. Then you're mine for the day."

My heart leaps into my throat at his words. *His for the day*.

Chapter 17

Nick

"You okay?" I ask, handing Luna a cup of water.

She grabs it and takes an enormous gulp. "Yeah. Why wouldn't I be?"

I resist smirking. "No reason." *Except for the fact you're bright red.*

She stands. "I need to use the restroom." She spots the bathrooms before making a beeline for them.

She's cute when she's nervous. I saw the way her hands twisted in her lap. Something I notice she does when she's anxious. Either she starts to twist her fingers or she plays with the hem of her shirt. It's something I should remember in case she has a panic attack.

It's a cue; I should probably change the topic of conversation.

My phone buzzes in my pocket. I pull it out to see it's a text from Dean.

Yeah, me taking Luna out was all planned. Well, sort of. I knew that I wanted to celebrate her birthday with her, but Dean also had a surprise party planned for her. So, when he asked me to keep her busy, I didn't mind. I had only planned to take her to lunch, but why not spend the day with her instead?

When I picked her up from the studio, she didn't seem that upset. Until she saw the balloon. Although she was happy about it, it was probably a reminder that no one else remembered. Reading Luna is something I've become fluent in. Picking up little things about the faces she makes or her body language in general. I can tell she's upset when her eyebrows pull back just a smidge. She tries to cover it up with a smile, but it never works. Or, when she's excited but tries to act cool, she bites the inside of her bottom lip.

Gia and Dean are planning something for her, so that's why they haven't talked to her. But still, it clearly hurts like hell.

So, I made sure to hit all the stops for her. Taking her to this fancy ass restaurant. One that's going to cost me an arm and *two* legs. But it's worth it. Her smile has been beaming the entire afternoon. We talked about some heavy shit, but she's clearly interested in the topic. If she wasn't, she wouldn't have asked so many questions.

It's been nice talking to her about my mom. Which is weird because I don't talk about my mom to anyone. No matter how close I get to people, it's just not a topic I like to bring up. But with Luna, it's easy. It's almost too easy. It kind of scares me how comfortable I am with her. Like I'm waiting for the other shoe to drop.

I shake my head, tossing the thought away, and look back at my phone to check for updates from Dean.

Dean

hey so we're setting up the place now

the food should be here in like 4 hours

DJ is coming at 8

So don't come here until 9

got it

Keeping her busy won't be that hard. I really did have a lot for us to do today. It's three right now. That gives me roughly six hours. Enough time. A couple minutes later, Luna comes back to the table.

This is the first time I've seen Luna's hair down. All it does is emphasize how beautiful she is, just like I thought it would. I look down at the napkin in my lap to hide my stupid grin.

"What are you smiling about?" Luna interrupts.

"Nothing. Where were you?" I try to change the subject.

"I told you, the bathroom." She sets the napkin back on her lap.

A waiter comes to the table with our food. It's a different one from earlier. "Sorry for the wait. Your waiter from earlier had to leave. So, I'll be your…" His voice trails off when he looks at Luna. Why the hell is he looking at her like that? With this gleam in his eye like he just found his lost lover. "Luna?"

I look at Luna and back at him. How does he know Luna? When she looks up at him, her eyes pop wide. I've never seen Luna so excited to see someone. Not even me. Something about that makes my skin crawl.

"Dylan!" She jumps from her seat, nearly knocking the table over, and lunges her arms around his neck. "Oh my god. I've missed you."

She misses him? What the fuck is going on? How did he know Luna? That weird feeling expands in my chest as I clutch my hands together in my lap. I try to resist how badly I want to break his arms off for even touching her. I know *she* hugged *him*, but she didn't know any better.

I look back at him to really take him in, and honestly, I'm not impressed. I've seen better-looking men. I mean, he has a sleeve of tattoos on his arms with dark curls resting on his head. He's like what, six-foot-one. Ha! I'm six-foot-three. I smirk to myself.

He does have a chiseled jawline and looks like he could be on the cover of Vogue magazine. Okay, who am I kidding? He's hot okay. I'm not gay or anything, but I can acknowledge a good-looking man when I see one. Whatever.

She pulls back, thank God. "What are you doing here?" Her hands still resting on his shoulders.

"I work here." He looks at me then back at her. "I'm sorry I didn't mean to interrupt your date."

I try to intervene, but she beats me to the punch. "Oh, we're not on a date. He's just a friend."

A friend! We needed to update that status to at least *best* friend.

"Oh shit, it's your birthday. Happy birthday!" He blurts.

He remembered her birthday? How close *were* they?

She pushes her hair behind her head shyly. "Thank you."

"Well, I'll let you enjoy your food. Don't leave without saying goodbye," he demands before walking back to the kitchen.

Luna sits back in her chair, and I have a million questions to ask. But I'll start simple. "Who was that?"

She piles a fork full of ravioli. "My ex." Then shoves the fork in her mouth.

I didn't know Luna *had* exes. I've never even seen her go on dates. She never even talks about guys. At least not in a romantic way. She only ever talks about how men are assholes and man whores. Well, she mainly calls me an asshole and man whore. Besides the point. She's *dated* someone?

"When did y'all break up?" I stir the noodles onto my fork as I try not to sound jealous. Which I'm not. Nick Beckett *doesn't* get jealous.

"From the start of college to the second semester of freshmen year. I needed to focus on dance, and he was a distraction." She continues to eat.

So, she didn't want to break up with him. She *needed* to. He's the one who got away. That's why she was so happy to see him again. Why does it feel like my heart just shattered into tiny shards which are now stabbing my diaphragm, making it next to impossible to breathe? Why do I feel like this?

I don't like Luna. I mean I like her, just not like that. She's one of my closest friends. When did that even happen? I guess spending so much time with one person will do that. Maybe that's what it is. I don't want to have to share her with anyone. If she were to go back to him, she would split all of her time from me to him. Not to mention, dance.

"Do you want to get back with him?" I ask hesitantly, not really wanting to hear the answer.

"No."

A sigh of relief escapes my lips.

"I've closed that chapter in my life. Plus, I don't have time for dating."

Good. She doesn't need to date anyway. Just dance and school.

After finishing our food, I stand and walk to the another waiter to pay. As I'm paying, I look over my shoulder to find Luna talking to Dylan again. Wait! Are they exchanging numbers? What the hell, Luna? I thought she didn't have time for dating.

She gives him a quick hug before walking toward me. "Thank you for lunch. It was good."

"What was that?" I snip.

"What?" She turns to follow where my eyes are pointing. "Oh, that. Dylan wants to catch up later. So, I gave him my number and told him to text me when he's free."

"I thought you said you didn't want to be in a relationship?" I cross my arms like a child throwing a tantrum.

She looks me up and down. "I don't. He didn't ask me on a date. He asked to catch up. I haven't seen him in a while. So I said sure." She mimics my stance, crossing her arms over her chest. "What's your problem?"

"I don't have a problem. I'm just saying, make sure *he* knows that." With that, I turn around and walk out the building, leaving her behind.

She races after me and grabs on my arm, tugging me backward. "Nick, what's wrong? Why are you acting like some jealous boyfriend? We're just friends. So, I need you to dial back the jealousy factor to zero."

Once again, I'm *not* jealous. That word doesn't even live in my vocabulary. "I'm not. I'm just looking out for you."

"I can look out for myself. Please, don't ruin this day for me," she pleads.

I take in her warm golden-brown eyes and realize how childish I'm being. It's her birthday. She's supposed to be enjoying today. I take a deep breath and wrap her hands in mine. "Alright. Let's go. We have plans."

When we reach my car, I hold the door open and let her get in first. I pull out my phone to see if I have any missed texts from Dean, but there's none. So, I open my map and pull up the directions to the fair. What are the odds the Boston State Fair is the same weekend as her birthday?

Once I get directions, I hop into the car and off we go.

"Where are we going now?" Luna pats her legs like an anxious child.

"Someplace fun." I respond, taking in her beautiful smile as her dimple deepens in her cheeks. Her smile could light up an entire town. Once again, I'm reminded of how happy I am to be in this girl's presence. Not just happy, but the luckiest man ever.

Chapter 18

Nick

We arrive at the fair an hour later. Luna's so fucking excited that she's damn near out of her seat. Okay, who slipped her the drugs? "Yo, chill out, Jay. Have you never been to the fair before?" I laugh.

"NO!" I put the car in park. "I've always wanted to go, but no one else did. My brother thinks the food is too expensive. Gia got really sick the last time she went, so now she's traumatized. Or so she says," she adds. "So, no one wants to take me. I mean, I could've gone by myself, but where's the fun in that?"

I laugh. "Well, good thing I put it on our list then." My chest warms at the thought, I'm the first to bring Luna to the fair. "Come on."

She jumps out of the car before I can even finish my sentence. "Hurry your ass up," she orders as she starts to head for the ticket gate. I could tell her I already have our tickets, but what would be the point? She wouldn't hear me. She's happier than she was when she saw Dylan.

Ha. Beat that, Dylan!

I run to catch up with her. I walk right next to her and lean my head down until I'm right by her ear. "Why are you in line?" I whisper before walking to the entrance.

Her eyes widen, and she follows. "You bought tickets already?"

I flash her my phone with our tickets on them. She lets out a loud squeal. Everyone's head turns to us, and I apologize on her behalf. "Jay, you gotta calm down." I laugh.

We walk to the guy holding a scanner. I show him my phone, and he scans both tickets before letting us in. I head straight for the Tilt-a-Whirl. It's my favorite ride. The ride turns you around in circles while it tilts side to side. It makes me queasy, but it's a fucking head rush.

"Two tickets." The worker holds his hands out.

Fuck. I forgot to get tickets. "Sorry." I apologize before grabbing Luna's hand and walking back to the front to buy tickets.

As we wait in line, I realize I'm still holding Luna's hand. She's too mesmerized by the fair to even notice or care. I run my thumb in circular motions as I try to imprint the way her skin feels against mine. She's soft and warm. Her hand feels like it was made for mine.

People start to push through as they try to get by, and Luna is standing right in the middle. So, I pull her into me until we're chest to chest. My heart feels like it's going to leap out of my throat. She's flush against me, and I get a nice inhale of her strawberry and coconut fragrance. Fuck, I will never get tired of that smell.

Her opposite hand flies to my chest. "What are you doing?"

"You were in people's way." I grin. *Nice save, Beckett.*

"Oh." She pushes off of me but doesn't let go of my hand. Does she even realize I'm still holding it? Probably not.

We finally make it to the front of the line. "Can I get seventy-five tickets, please?"

"Seventy-five?" Luna's eyes widen.

"Yeah. You better use every last one of them, too." I reluctantly let go of her hand and reach for my wallet in my pocket. I pay for the tickets and hand them to Luna. "Don't lose them."

"That's a big responsibility." She gulps.

"Yeah. Can you handle it?" I smirk.

"Yes." Pulling them to her chest. "I will guard them with my life." She smiles, then turns to look around. "What should we do first?"

"Tilt-a-Whirl." I grab her hand again. I didn't need to, but mine kind of missed the warmth of hers.

She shoves the tickets into her purse. Instead of me leading her, she leads me, pulling my arm toward the ride.

"Two tickets. Each," the worker calls out again, holding his hand out.

Luna takes out four tickets and offers them to him. The worker raises the rope and allows us to board. We make our way to the two open stalls in the middle.

I pull the lever down to secure her in her spot. "No running away now, Jay."

She rolls her eyes. "I never said I wanted to, Beckett."

My heart stalls for a second before restarting again. I clear my throat before placing my back against the padded wall. Pulling the lever over myself, trying to ignore the way this girl just gave me all the feels.

The worker starts to walk around the ride, making sure everyone is secure. Then he walks back off to the podium with all of the controls. He yells, "Enjoy." Then presses start.

The ride starts to spin in a circle. I turn my head to look at Luna again. Her face is beaming. She's glued to the padded wall, but she's laughing so hard. She's radiant. Her smile is radiant. I have that weird feeling again. The feeling where I want to protect that smile at all costs. The feeling where I want to be the cause of its appearance. I want to be the person who turns her into this ball of laughter she is right now.

She turns to look at me, and her smile widens. I didn't know it could get any bigger, and yet it did. She covers her mouth to muffle herself. I reach over and pull her hand down, holding it firm in mine.

"Don't hide. Your smile is beautiful!" She just shakes her head and laughs harder. It didn't matter that she didn't say anything, as long as she keeps smiling.

The ride starts to slow down. The lever lifts, releasing us from our spots. I start to pull Luna to the exit, but she pulls me back to grab her purse off the floor.

Turning back to me, she says, "Okay, now I'm ready."

I smile and squeeze her hand. I expected her to pull her hand back, but she doesn't. It stays firm inside mine. Maybe that's our new normal? Her hands in mine? Seems about right. "Let's go."

We've been at the fair for two hours, spent sixty-eight tickets, and won three stuffed animals. I knew Luna was competitive, but I never knew she was this competitive. We were playing the ring toss, and she damn near missed every single throw. When she said we weren't leaving that game until she won, she meant it.

She did end up winning on the thirteenth try. Beggars can't be choosers. I almost paid the guy to just give her the damn bear. She slapped my hand and told me it wasn't the same. She wanted to win on her own. It was kind of hot seeing her all fired up. Who am I kidding? It was *definitely* hot.

Currently, we're riding the Ferris wheel. We had cotton candy and two turkey legs, so we didn't really feel like moving. It was only an hour and a half left before I needed to bring her to the party. So, I figured we could use the rest of our tickets here. Looping the Ferris wheel until they kick us off.

"Thank you," Luna interrupts.

"For what?" I lean deeper into my seat.

"For today. You're the only person who remembered my birthday." My chest tightens at the lie. I know other people remembered, and I wanted to tell her, but it would ruin the surprise.

"Well, I cheated. I put it in my calendar. So, technically, my calendar remembered."

She giggles. Like real-life giggles. Another sexy thing she does. "Whatever. I don't care. You still took time out of your day to celebrate it with me. So, thank you."

I nod my head. "I liked spending the day with you."

Her cheeks redden again. She quickly turns her head to look at the skyline as we watch the sunset. "It's beautiful. This view."

Keeping my eyes trained on her. "It's the most breathtaking view I've ever seen."

The wheel comes to a stop. I quickly hand the guy six more tickets. Then he closes the door again.

Luna claps her hands. "Let's play a game."

"What game?" I sit taller in my seat.

"Um. How about twenty questions?" She wiggles her eyebrows.

"Okay. You first."

"You can't skip." I nod my head in agreement. "If you could fly anywhere else right this second, where would you go?"

"Nowhere." She scrunches her eyebrows together. "I like where I am, currently. What is your biggest fear?"

She taps her fingers to her chin as she thinks of an answer. "Being alone, I guess." She'll never be alone as long as I'm in her life. I won't allow it. "Okay, my turn. If you weren't playing hockey, what would you be?"

"Easy, a groupie." I spread my arms on the back of the seat.

"A groupie?" She laughs. "For whom?"

"You." Her laugh immediately stops. The air cackles between us in our silence.

"Why?"

"I've seen you dance. Well, I've caught glimpses. Its mesmerizing. The way you move, it's like being in a trance just watching." I rest my arms on my thighs and lean forward. "That was two questions, so I get to ask two."

She rolls her eyes. Something I've grown to love actually. "Fine. Go."

"What do you want for your birthday?"

She leans forward, resting her arms on her thighs, mimicking me. "My birthday is over." Her eyebrows furrow.

"Not until midnight. So, answer the question."

"Nothing. I'm not really a materialistic person."

"I didn't say it had to be an object. It could be anything."

Her eyes soften. She looks down at her feet. "You know they forgot my birthday? Gia and Dean," she sighs. "Dean's my twin, and he forgot my birthday. Gia always celebrates my birthday with me, but she didn't today. Neither one of them remembered. I think that hurt more than anything. So, if I could ask for one thing, I would wish for everything to go back to how it was before."

"They didn't forget your birthday." She snaps her eyes to mine. I know it's supposed to be a surprise, but this is killing me. Seeing her this sad. "They're planning a surprise party for you. That's what they're doing right now. Dean said he had to keep Gia away from you because apparently, she can't keep a secret to save her life. That's why they've been so distant. So later when we arrive, can you act surprised?"

Her eyes well with tears. "They're planning a party?"

"That was supposed to make you happy." I move to sit next to her. "Why are you crying?"

"I am happy. I'm sorry. I just thought they hated me. I didn't know why or what I did. Even though I absolutely hate parties." She wipes her eyes. "You're terrible at keeping secrets.

I laugh. "I didn't want to see you upset anymore. I figured it was worth it."

She shakes her head. "Thank you. Anyways." She let out a loud breath. "What's your next question?"

I stare into her eyes. Scrounging up every piece of courage I need to ask her this question. "How set in stone is your no dating rule?" I watch as her breath catches in her throat.

It was a spur of the moment question. After spending the day with her at the fair, I couldn't help it. Seeing her with Dylan sparked something inside of me. I didn't know I was capable of jealousy. Then I saw her interact with another guy who could make her smile. I didn't want to share her with anyone. I kept saying it wasn't jealousy, but it was.

It's true, I don't do relationships. That still stands. I don't do relationships unless it's with Luna. She's the exception *and* the rule. The only person I would date. I don't know if she's the only person I would feel that way about, but for now, she is.

I want to be the reason Luna laughs. I want to hold her when she cries. I want to be the person she texts when something exciting happens in her life. So, if that means being in a relationship with her, then screw it. I'll be in a relationship with her.

I watch her lips fall open. Its taking everything in me not to kiss them. Her chest starts to pick up its pace.

Fuck it.

I lean in slowly, giving her enough time to push me away. I don't want to rush this. I don't want to scare her off either. A part of me expects her to push me away, even slap me. The other half is begging she'll kiss me first.

I watch her eyes close, giving me the green light. As I lean in closer, my hands softly caresses her cheek. Then I pull her into me, when the wheel comes to a halt, snapping us back into reality.

Are you fucking kidding me right now?

The door opens. I shuffle to find more tickets, but Luna is already getting off. Shit.

I scramble out of my seat and chase her down. "Luna!" I call out when I spot her racing toward the exit. When I reach her, I grab her arm and turn her to look at me. "What happened?"

"This!" Waving her hands between us. "It can't happen. You're my brother's *captain*, Nick. I can't do that to him." She wipes her tears from her face.

I forgot Dean was even in the equation. She's right though. Dean was a vital player on my team, and I can't do anything to jeopardize that. So, I couldn't be with Luna. No matter how badly I wanted to be. I couldn't. She's his sister too. Even if *I* wanted to throw all caution to the wind, *she* wouldn't. "You're right. I'm sorry." I drop her arm and take a step back.

"Just forget it happened. We should leave." She continues walking to the car. What a way to end the day's escapades.

We drive in silence for the next hour to the party. The one I spoiled. I mean I knew I would. I pull into this abandoned building. It's completely dark. Giving very much haunted house vibes. I take my phone out to let Dean know we're here.

"You ready?" I look at Luna as she's staring at the building. Then we exit the car.

"Wait." She grabs on the hem of my shirt. "Nick, please don't stop talking to me now."

I watch the hurt paint her face like a blank canvas. I would never do that to her. As much as I want her, I'd rather have her as a friend then nothing at all. "You can't get rid of me that easily Jay."

I pull her in for a hug, praying it melts any of her worries away. "Like you said. We'll just forget it happened." Even though *nothing* did, in fact, happen.

She nods in agreement, and we start to walk again. When I pull the door open for her, she thanks me and continues to walk in. When I chuck the lights on, everyone jumps up screaming, "Surprise!"

She jumps as if she has no idea what was happening. Either she's really good at acting or she is genuinely scared. It doesn't matter when a smile as big as the crescent moon radiates across her face.

Dean and Gia both come out and hug her.

"Sorry we were being assholes. We just *really* wanted this to be perfect for you." Dean releases her.

"How long did y'all plan this for?" she laughs awkwardly. "It's fine. You guys, this is perfect. Thank you. But Dean, it's your birthday too." Of course, Luna would be worried about her brother's birthday.

"Yeah, I know. This party is for the both of us. You're just the only one surprised about it."

Luna shakes her head.

"I'm sorry, babes. Dean swore me to secrecy. Forgive me?" Gia pleads, rubbing her hands under her chin.

"Of course. I've just missed you two. Thank you. For all of this." She pulls them in for another hug.

Her eyes trail to mine. She mouths a thank you. I nod my head and turn around and try to lose myself in the crowd. I need to get away from her. I know I said it was fine, but it's not. I want, no *need*, to kiss Luna like people need to breathe. She shouldn't have this much effect on me. I didn't even realize I had feelings for her. When did it even happen?

Was it today or had I always had feelings for her? It didn't matter because as long as she was Dean's twin, she was off limits. I need alcohol and I need it *now*. I walk to the bar and order a shot of anything strong. While I'm waiting, I feel a hand rub up my arms. I turn to see it's some brunette girl. Puck bunny.

"Nick, I missed you. Where have you been?" She smells like tequila and desperation. Two things I hate. I lift my head to see Luna still talking with Dean and Gia. My stomach churns at how much I want this girl to be her instead.

I turn to the bar grab the shot and chug it. Bourbon. I welcome the burn as it runs down my throat. "Wanna dance?" I shout.

I don't wait for a reply as I grab her hands and maneuver my way onto the floor. They say the best way to get over someone is to get under someone else. So, that's what I'm doing tonight.

We make our way to the middle of the floor, and the brunette wastes no time. She turns her body pushing her ass on my front. She pulls my hands and rests them on her hips, and sways them from side to side. Any other day, this would make my dick twitch. Tonight, the only thing it's doing is reminding me how she isn't Luna.

What the fuck is wrong with me? Nothing has ever happened between Luna and I, and yet here I am, gawking and wanting a girl I can never have. Why does she have this much power over me?

I need to get away from this girl. I harshly push her off of me.

"What the fuck, Beckett?" she grunts.

I should apologize, but I don't care enough. I walk to the bathroom. Only to find that there's a long ass line. "You've got to be kidding me."

I turn around. There's got to be another bathroom in this place. I walk down the halls, opening every door I see. Each one is occupied by some horny ass couple.

Must be fucking nice.

I creak open another door but stop before fully opening it. Blinking my eyes three times to make sure I'm seeing what I'm actually seeing. My eyes *must* be deceiving me. They wouldn't do this here. Not at her damn birthday party. The anger starts to boil in my chest.

"Nick?" I close the door quickly and quietly.

"Luna?" Fuck me. She couldn't have picked worse timing.

"What are you doing, weirdo?"

I look at the door and back at her. "Nothing. What are you doing? Enjoying your party?"

"Yeah, actually. I'm not even a party person, but I guess since Dean and Gia threw it..."

I resist the urge to roll my eyes.

"Have you seen them?"

I shake my head. "Can't say that I have." I hate lying to her. I shouldn't lie to her. But does it count if I'm protecting her? I don't think it does, right?

Fuck!

Her eyebrows scrunch in suspicion. "Why are you standing like that?"

I look down at my legs crossed at the ankles as I lean on the door, praying to any god out there she doesn't ask to go into this room.

"Why not?" I laugh nervously.

She looks at the door behind me. "What's in there?" Are you kidding me? *God, I thought we were cool.*

I look at the handle and back at her. I can't lie to her, but I can't tell her the truth. It's her birthday. It's her *fucking* birthday. "You don't wanna know."

"See now I do." She sets her cup on the floor. Standing back up, she orders, "Let me see."

I shake my head.

"Nick, let me see."

I stand up straight. "Luna," I warn firmly. Her eyes stare into mine. "I want you to have a good birthday. If you open this door, you won't. Please just turn around and go back to the party."

I'm doing this for her. This can't happen on her birthday. When she walked into the party, she was happy again. The smile that took over her face was something I tattooed in my brain. I want her to keep that smile and stay happy. If she opens this door, she'll be heartbroken. Her entire world will burn to ashes.

She looks at the door and back at me, as her smile falters. "Nick, what's behind the door."

"I can't lie to you. So please don't make me answer that." I want to pick her up and take her anywhere else. I wanted her to have one good day. One fucking day. Is that too much to ask? Apparently, it is.

"Nick. Open the door. Now."

Reluctantly, I turn around to the door and slowly push it open. Luna's eyes trail from mine to Dean fucking Gia.

All the blood drains from her face. "WHAT. THE. FUCK."

# Chapter 19

Luna

“Luna!” Dean scrambles to pull his pants back up.

My body vibrates with anger.

Today started off like crap. I thought the two most important people in my life had forgotten my birthday. I thought no one had remembered except my parents. Then Nick came and took me out. He made my day better. He made me feel seen and important.

Then I find out that Dean and Gia have been planning this surprise party for me this entire time. I thought we were on the right track to getting back to where we were. Dean and Gia threw me a fucking party. Although they knew I didn't like parties, I didn't mind this one. I didn't mind because *they* threw it for me. I thought they were doing this for me. This was us turning over a new leaf and moving past the bullshit.

I was *so* wrong.

When I opened the door, I saw nothing but Dean, balls deep into my best friend. This must be a fucking joke. Where are the fucking cameras? Because there's no way that my brother was fucking my best friend. On my birthday, no less. At my damn party!

"What the hell are you doing?!" I yell over the music.

"Luna, it's not..." I cut Gia off.

"Don't you dare try to tell me this isn't what it looks like. Because that's *exactly* what it looks like." I can feel the tears prickle behind my eyes.

The two people I trust the most betrayed me in the worst way. I push the tears back. I refuse to cry in front of them. I refuse to give them satisfaction. They don't deserve to see me cry, no matter how badly I want to.

"You just couldn't help yourself, could you?" I try to sound stern and angry, but it comes out in a whisper.

"Luna!" Gia pleads, tears streaming down her face. "I'm so fucking sorry. I know it's wrong. But you know I've been in love with him for years."

"I don't give a damn, Gia. We had a deal. You promised me you wouldn't. *You* promised. Honestly, I expect nothing less from you. You don't care about anyone but your damn self. What, your life is so boring, you just spread your legs for anyone who gives you just the slightest bit of attention."

Dean wraps his arms around Gia as she sobs. "Jay, chill! You're going too far."

"Oh, really? I don't think I've gone far enough." Watching him wrap his arm around her makes my skin crawl. I'm his twin sister, and instead of being worried about how I felt about the situation, he'd rather care about her. He chose her over me. For some reason, that hurt more than them fucking each other. "This entire time, you've made it seem like I was the problem! Let me guess. You couldn't get some other poor girl to sleep with you, so you sleep with my best friend?"

"What the hell is wrong with you, Luna?" Dean steps near me.

"What's wrong with *me*?" I echo. "No, what the hell is wrong with you? You're supposed to be my brother. My fucking twin for crying out loud. Instead of setting boundaries between you two, you fuck her. Damn how I feel, huh?"

"You know what? Fuck this," Dean snaps. "Yes. Damn your fucking feelings, Luna. You act like the fucking world revolves around you when it doesn't. Gia isn't a piece of property you can just claim. She's a human fucking being! Should I have kept it from you? Probably not. But you act like you own her or something. You don't!"

What does he mean by keeping it from me?

I stumble backward as all of the pieces start to fall into place. They didn't throw this party because it was my birthday. They threw it because they felt guilty. They've been fucking each other for weeks. That's why they haven't been talking to me. That's why they've been ignoring me.

I feel like I'm going to hurl. Tears swell behind my eyes. The hurt and betrayal swirl in my stomach like a dryer on tumble. "This is why you've been ignoring me." My voice drops to a whisper as the realization broke on their faces. They've been caught, and neither of them look apologetic. Just sorry they were caught.

I scoff, shaking my head to the ground. "I'm such a fucking idiot. How long, Dean?" He looks at Gia and back at me. The pressure in my chest tightens.

"HOW LONG?" I shout.

"Since the party at the hockey house when Paris arrived." His words rush out as if they were his final words.

When I thought Gia was lying about her whereabouts, she was. She wasn't at some random friend's house; she was at Dean's. Gia started sleeping with Dean then. I'm so stupid for not seeing it sooner. It should have clicked before that. Both of them we're ignoring me at the same time. That should have been the first sign.

"Wow." I look at the wall, staring at nothing as everything unravels. The revelation pierced through me like a sudden storm, leaving me engulfed in a whirlwind of hurt and betrayal. The trust I'd placed in both of them now felt shattered, the weight of the secret pressing heavily on my heart.

It was a mixture of disbelief and sadness, a sense of abandonment from those I held closest. The ache of knowing they hadn't listened to me when I asked them not to go there only intensified the betrayal, leaving me grappling with unexpected waves of pain and confusion.

All of the anger and hurt turn to pure rage in that instant.

Without thinking, I clutch my hand into a fist and reach back before connecting it to Dean's face.

I feel a crack, not knowing if it's from me or him.

"Luna!" Gia screams before grabbing Dean's face. "What the hell?"

"You two deserve each other. I hope you both rot in fucking hell." I spit.

"Luna don't…" Dean tries to speak while holding his face.

"Don't what? You made me think I was crazy. I wasn't."

He stands straight again. "We're family."

"Were. We were family." I shake my head as the tears threaten to fall. "If you were family, you wouldn't have kept this secret from me. We don't lie to each other, Dean. What happened to it being you and me, Dean?"

"Come on, you don't mean that, Jay. I didn't think it would be that big of a deal. We just wanted to see what this was before we said something."

I sniff. "If it wasn't a big deal, why did you keep it from me?" Dean looks at Gia and back at me, speechless. "That's what I thought." I turn on my heels and push past Nick, exiting the building and walking back outside.

"Hey, are you okay?" Nick rubs my back as we exit the building.

I shake my head as my emotions wash over me like a high tide.

Nick wraps his arms around me like a weighted blanket and draws me into his chest. The tears start falling like a never-ending cascade as I cry in his arms. It's like a thousand shards of glass burst through my chest.

How do we come back from this? How do I forgive them for this?

The answer is that I can't. There is no coming back from this. No matter how much I wanted to put the pieces back together, they were too small to even attempt to find their proper place.

I pull back from Nick and wipe my eyes.

"Can you just take me home?" I ask, feeling the exhaustion wash over me.

"No." He grabs my hand. "You shouldn't be alone right now. You can stay at my place tonight." I open my mouth to tell him how bad of an idea that is, but he cuts me off. "Don't worry, I have an extra room. I won't do anything you don't want me to."

Then he pulls me to his car.

Why should I care anymore? Dean betrayed me. But sleeping with Nick isn't any better than Dean sleeping with Gia. I would be doing exactly what I'm pissed at Dean for.

I also can't do that to Nick. I would just be using him to get even with Dean. Nick's too nice to use like that. He deserves better than that. So, I'll just crash as soon as I get to his place. Maybe when I wake up, this will all be a dream. Not a dream, but a nightmare. But at least it wouldn't be real.

An hour later, we're pulling into Nick's driveway. He inputs a code that opens his gate. It's nice. His driveway is a gray cobblestone. There are golden lights that line up his driveway to his front door. The exterior of the house has a monochromatic color palette. It's shaped weirdly, with an outward box at the top that slightly hovers over the garage. The house is all glass windows and doors. It's small, yet so big.

He said that his family is well off, but he didn't give them enough credit. You could probably fit a family of six in this house. Okay, that's an exaggeration. You could probably fit a family of four, but still. It's huge.

"You live alone?" I open the door and step out of the car.

"Yeah." He laughs anxiously. Locking the door behind him. "Come on. It's warm inside. At least, it should be."

I follow him up the cobblestone path that leads directly to the front door, which features a glass door. The doors have black trimming with a gold door handle.

After unlocking the door, he pulls it open for me to enter first.

I walk in slowly to fully take in how stunning his house is. The marbled floor beneath my feet is sparkling clean. I could see my reflection in it. Everything in his house was black and white. The couch, the counter, *everything.* The space was an open floor plan. It was nice. In his living room, he had a long, black L-shaped couch.

I make my way to his couch and throw myself on it like a throw pillow. I throw my head back and look up at the ceiling. Letting my mind run through the different events from tonight. What am I supposed to do now?

I know I told him he was no longer my brother, but I can't just cut him out of my life. I love him. We could get past this, right? Just not anytime soon, obviously. No matter how much he hurt me, a part of me desperately wanted to keep him in my life. I had already lost one sibling. Could I really afford to lose another one?

Nick sits beside me. "What are you thinking about?"

"How today turned out to be the shittiest birthday." I keep my eyes trained on the ceiling. I totally forgot it was even my birthday, to be honest. With everything that happened, it feels like just another shitty day.

Nick brushes my hair behind my ears. "I thought I did a pretty good job. Fancy ass lunch. The fair."

"Yeah, well, you shouldn't have let me open that door." I push his hand aside. I sit up, crisscrossing my legs as I start to play with the hem of my cardigan.

I know he means well and is just trying to cheer me up, but it isn't working. His touching me wasn't helping. If anything, it was making it worse. All it made me think about was how he was Dean's. Not mine. He could never be mine, either.

I might get little flutters when Nick talks to me, but my conscience always reminds me that he's Dean's captain. No matter how much I hate Dean right now, I would never disrespect him like that.

Nick mimics my movements and sits up. "I can't tell you what to do. I tried. Plus, I could never lie to you."

"Why?" It's not that hard to lie. Especially if you're trying to protect that person's feelings. Would I have been mad? Probably, but what was the alternative? I would've been thankful in the long run. It's stupid to be mad at someone just because they *can't* lie to you.

"You know why." He slides closer to me. He's so close, I feel his body heat meshing with mine.

"I don't. Just tell me." I should move away from him, but I don't. I stay firm in my position. I know what he's doing. I was smart, though. I wouldn't let anything happen between us. Especially tonight.

"Jay." He reaches for my face and cups my cheeks. "I think I'm starting to have feelings for you. No, that's a lie. I *actively* have feelings for you."

My heart comes to a screeching halt. "Nick, don't do that." Shaking my head, I push his hands away from my face again. I stand and start to walk to the door.

"Do what? Have feelings for you?" He shouts after me and follows.

"Yeah. It's a mistake. I'm not the girl guys should have feelings for." I stop and turn to face him. "Like you said, I'm all about me. I have to focus on my dancing. I also have to focus on school. I have no room to focus on anyone else. And if you couldn't tell, every day of my life is filled with drama."

No matter how confused I am about my feelings for Nick, dating him wouldn't be right. I couldn't date him and focus. It didn't work before, and it wouldn't work now. All dating me would do is make him hate me. I would be too focused on dancing, leaving no room to spend time with him. That was the problem with Dylan. He felt like I never had time for him. He was right. I didn't. He would make plans for us, but I would have to be in the studio perfecting something. He just couldn't understand that, so I broke up with him.

Not that he gave me much of an option. He said I had to choose what was more important to me. Him or dance? In reality, he was asking me to choose him over my sister. I never told Dylan about Cassie, and at this point, I'm glad I didn't. If he couldn't understand how important dance was to me, he wouldn't get to know *why* it was so important.

Maybe if I told him about Cassie, he would understand, but it doesn't matter. The minute he gave me that ultimatum, our relationship was over. Seeing him at that restaurant only solidified that. When I saw him, I didn't feel anything. I mean, I missed him, but not our relationship. I just missed his friendship. We were friends before we dated. Then, after we broke up, we never spoke again. I couldn't have that happen with Nick.

I liked having Nick as a friend, no matter how much that kills me to say. He's been the one constant in my life recently. Especially after tonight, he's all I really have in my life. I didn't want to ruin that. I *couldn't* ruin that.

When I snap myself out of my head, I realize he's gotten closer. Making it hard for me to breathe or think.

My mistake is I glance down at his lips, bringing to my attention the fact that I have kissed them in the past. Even if it was just to put an end to my panic attack. Every once in a while, I find it satisfying to reminisce about how gentle they are. How his lips, when they were on mine for just six seconds, caused my insides to melt. Imagine what they might be able to do if they had more time at their command.

My gaze wanders, but I make myself return it to his. They've become darker, brimming with want and an emotion I can't quite put my finger on. I need to think long-term about the repercussions this would have.

"Nick," I say as sternly as possible, but it comes out more like a whisper. "We can't."

He steps into me, wrapping his hand around the back of my neck. "Why not? I know how demanding you are, Luna. I know you are one of the most high-maintenance people I have ever met." He inhales before speaking again. "But here's the thing, Jay. So am I. I have a mother to take care of. I have school. I also have hockey. I under-stand having aspirations. I get that you're busy because, guess what? So am I. So, don't give me that bullshit about you being too busy. What's really holding you back?"

You're my brother's captain, for starters.

I couldn't do that to Dean. No matter how beautiful the fruit sitting in front of me is, it's forbidden. We all know how it turned out for Eve when she took that bite. It seemed feasible at the time, but the ramifications of her actions were her undoing.

Nick will not be *my* undoing.

"Stop thinking." He draws me closer to his chest. When I try to free myself, his hold on my waist just grows tighter. My body just draws to him like two magnets. I want to pull away, but I'm stuck. My insides are churning as his hands rest on my waist. The goosebumps rising along my body does nothing to help me either.

I'm aware of just how much my body reacts to Nick. His touch lights me up like a fireworks show on the Fourth of July. I'm not stupid, but I couldn't. He was my brother's captain. It was a line I couldn't cross. It's the only thing being repeated in my head.

"We can't do this," I whisper, as if I'm trying to convince myself more than trying to convince him. "I can't do that to Dean. Nick, I'm sorry."

"It's better if we ask for forgiveness rather than permission," he rasps, rubbing his thumb along my cheek and letting his hand glide its way to my neck as his thumb sweeps along my throat. My eyes close at his touch. The air begins to thicken, making it hard to breathe. I let his touch vibrate every atom in my body, sending shock waves up my spine.

I should stop. *We* should stop. "Nick," I plead, but he doesn't stop.

He slowly leans forward. My stomach tightens as his lips drag along my neck, leaving phantom kisses in their wake. A moan edges its way up my throat, but I push it down. My body craves him. I shouldn't give in, right?

He continues to walk his kisses higher up on my neck. "You want me as bad as I want you." It wasn't a question. Like he already knows.

I do. God *knows* I do. Being near him is like a drug. Something I need at all hours of the day, but once again, that's the problem.

"Fuck the reasons. What do you want, Luna?" he whispers into my ear as his other hand runs down my front, finding the waistband of my jeans. Warmth pools in my stomach.

"We can't, Nick." I'm holding on by a *very* loose thread, breaking with every breath of his that sweeps across my neck. The tips of his fingers slowly glide up my spine, knocking my head back and giving him better access to my neck. Dammit.

I feel his grin on my neck before his hand grips my ass, lifting me in the air before setting me on the counter. I take a deep gulp as his eyes clash with mine. The fire between us is enough to light an inferno. I need to put it out, but I can't even move.

His stare holds me as a willing hostage at this point. My fight has slowly dissipated. I've given in to him. I can't fight it anymore; my body has a mind of its own, and the longer my mind fights, the harder it is to resist him. Nick's calloused hands run along my waist, goose-bumps causing me to shiver beneath his touch.

Nick leans down until our noses touch. As his breath tickles my skin, he says, "I'll ask again. This time, don't you dare lie to me." He demands in a raspy voice I've never heard before. "What do you want, Luna Moon?"

I inhale sharply. For once, I want something for my-self that has nothing to do with someone else's hap-piness. Rules be dammed. "You. Nick." Reaching up, I run my tremoring hands along his jaw. Feeling the hairs from his beard prickle against my palm. "I want you, Nick."

Chapter 20

Luna

Before the words even fully leave my mouth, Nick's lips crash into mine. Everything comes to a muffled pause. I've been kissed before, but never like this. He's kissing me like he needs me to live. Like I'm the last oxygen tank on this sinking ship, and he'll do whatever it takes to survive.

I feel *him* everywhere at once, my body hyper-aware of his. The way he makes me feel against him is unfathomable. My body comes alive as he molds himself to me. He bites down on my lip softly, parting my lips and slipping in his tongue. As he continues to explore my mouth, he ignites a fire in me that I didn't even know existed.

My hands run up his cheek, bringing his face closer to mine. He deepens the kiss. I feel like I've been waiting a lifetime for this moment. This moment with him. A shiver runs up my spine as his hands roam my body. A mischievous grin emerges on his face. Fuck if it wasn't the hottest grin I've ever seen. He reaches behind his head and pulls his shirt off with just his thumb and index finger.

Heat pools between my legs at how sexy he is. I reach up to run my fingers along his tanned, chiseled chest. Nick's body is probably the hottest body I have ever seen. He's so fucking built. No one should be this gorgeous.

"Like what you see?"

I nod my head slowly as I bite my lip, holding back the whimper's urge to let itself out. I've never been so attracted to a man as I am right now.

He pushes my thighs apart and steps between them. His lips find my neck again as he starts to suck on it. A small moan escapes my lips. He kisses my neck and continues trailing kisses down my chest. His hands find their way up my shirt. My back arches into his touch as he grips my breasts and massages each one methodically while kissing my abdomen. A moan grows thick in my throat as I grip his thick hair for stability.

Grabbing the hem of my shirt, which is more of a bra at this point, he pulls it over my head. Then he quickly snaps the clasps of my bra with one tug, setting my breasts free.

A growl grows in his chest. The feral sound makes me clamp my knees together. Immediately, he pulls my legs apart. "Don't do that. I want to see all of you." He groans before sinking his lips into my breasts and inhaling them one at a time. I moan again as I start rocking my chest into his mouth. I love the way his mouth feels on me.

This is nice and all, but I want more. I *need* more.

Releasing his hair, I push on his shoulder to back him up. Confusion emerges on his face.

"Are you okay?" He rubs his hands gently along my thigh.

I shake my head. Then I reach for the button on my jeans and start to slowly push them down. "You're going too slow."

"Yes ma'am." Fuck me.

He helps pull my pants off and toss them aside. Finding my lips again, he picks me up by my bare thighs. My legs instinctively wrap around his waist as he carries me to the couch, throwing me down with a thump.

He sinks to his knees as he slowly spreads my thighs apart. He keeps his eyes locked on mine, almost daring me to look away. He starts at my ankle, then slowly runs kisses up my leg. Until he reaches my inner thighs. His teeth tugs at the flesh. I bite back my moan.

He's playing with me. He wants me to beg for it. I know it, but I won't.

"Fuck, you smell good." My stomach tightens as his tongue starts to edge closer to my lips. Then he reaches for my lace thongs and pushes them to the side. I start to rock into his face as I try to get his lips to meet mine. I could feel his breath along my clit.

"I'm going to enjoy this." He smirks.

His tongue finally finds my clit, and my back instantly arches to the ceiling. As he drags his tongue up and down, pulling me into him by my hips. My hands find his nape to hold onto him as I continue to rock in his mouth. He's eating me like a starving prisoner. A prisoner who's been locked up for years, and this is his first taste of freedom.

He slips in one finger, and everything in me tightens as I hold on to him and try not to finish. He continues to pound in my opening with such fierceness. The pressure is almost too much.

"Fuck!" I cry. It feels like he's ramming his fist into me, but he's not. Good doesn't even begin to describe what he's making me feel right now. My body starts to push away from him, but he just tightens his grip on my hips, pinning me to his face.

He stops. "Wrong." He pushes his fingers into me again. "Try again," he said, thrusting his fingers right into my g-spot.

My throaty moan fills the room as he slips in another finger. "Luna? You know what I want to hear. Say it."

"Say what?" I try to ask calmly, but it comes out throatier and raspier. I just want him to tell me. I can feel myself on the edge, waiting to be tipped over.

"Say my name," he demands as he enters a third finger.

"Fuck. Please!" I beg.

"Close. Almost there. You don't get to come until you do." He pulls his fingers all the way out before shoving them back in. Roughly. Then again. *And again.*

"Nick! Please!" I plead, wanting him to just finish already. I grip onto his shoulders as he hovers over me.

"That's better." He shoves his finger in my pussy while his thumb massages my clit. Sending me into blinding bliss. All I see are stars exploding.

As I come down from my high. He's right there again, kissing me.

I taste myself on his lips, and although I should be disgusted, I'm not. All I'm thinking about is kissing him. He kisses me until my lips are sweltering and bruised.

Finally, breaking the kiss, he stands up. Where I see his dick pushing on his zipper, begging to be set free.

He gathers me in his arms and carries me to his room, setting me on his king-size bed that feels like I'm sitting on clouds. I think he's going to undress himself, but he doesn't. Walking into the bathroom, I hear water running.

Wait, that's it? That's all we're doing?

He walks back into the room, picking me up once again, carrying me into the bathroom, and setting me in the tub.

"You're not going to fuck me?" I sputter out like a kid desperate for their parents' attention.

He laughs. "Not tonight. Another night. I just want to take care of you tonight. It's your birthday, after all. Is that okay?"

Butterflies explode in my stomach. I sink lower in the tub, letting the bubbles cover my body. They smell like strawberries and coconut, just like my body wash. Weird.

I wonder if he's done this for other girls, but that's a question for another night.

I nod my head, answering his question. "But you have to join me," I add.

In a split second, his jeans are on the ground. My eyes widen when I see his dick. I'm so happy he didn't fuck me. There's no way that would fit. Who the does this guy think he is?

Is he on steroids, or is he just naturally that blessed? I wouldn't even call it a blessing; it's more of a curse if you ask the women he's fucked. Why do they keep coming back? Do their vaginas not hurt?

When I look back up at him, he's smiling. "What?"

"You're just. Um." I hold my hands up and spread them to show that he's big, hoping he gets it.

"Big?" He laughs.

"Yeah. Where did you think you were putting that?" I ask, splashing my hands back underwater.

He laughs harder, shaking his head and ignoring my question. "Sit up."

I do as he says. He steps into the tub one leg at a time and rests them on either side before sliding down behind me.

He must have expected moments like this. His tub is big enough for two people, maybe even three. "Did you plan on having women over when you moved in?"

He pulls me by my shoulders until I'm flush against him. "No. Why?"

"This is just... A big tub for one person." I wave my hands at the tub.

He shakes his hand, and I can feel his smile as he rest his cheeks on my head. "No, I just like space in tubs when I'm bathing. It's easier to relax in."

"Oh." His fingers start to run up and down my arm, and it send shivers through me. Everything about this feels normal. Like we've done this multiple times before.

We sit in silence for a while before he speaks again. "Can I be honest, though?"

I nod my head for him to continue.

"You're the first girl I've wanted to do this for."

I turn my head to look into his eyes to see if he's lying. The water sloshes as my back rests against the side of the tub. "Why?"

He shrugs his shoulders. "Honestly, I don't know. You're different. I know that's not the most romantic thing to say, but it's the truth. I've never introduced my mother to anyone. I've never even told anyone about my mom. But with you, it's easy. I feel like I can tell you anything. I mean you're still a big pain in my ass, but I guess I've just grown accustomed to it. I find it hot rather than annoying now."

I feel the tears trying to prickle through, but I turn around before they do. I can't cry anymore tonight.

When I don't say anything, he continues talking. "I know you don't date, but neither do I. And here I am wanting to date you. So, what are we going to do about that, *Jay*?"

My heart leaps at the nickname. When Dean gave it to me, I absolutely hated it. But, when Nick says it, all it does is send my heart into hyper drive.

I wanted to focus on dancing. I wanted no distractions, but here I am distracted. This big part of me finds no problem with it, though. Is that bad?

Before I can overthink it, I turn around and look at him again. "No."

"No?" Nick echoes.

I know I should at least try, but I can't. Everything in me is telling me to focus on dance and school. I have no room for Nick. No matter how desperately I want to try, I can't.

"I'm sorry. Nick, I can't." Before I finish my sentence, Nick stands and exits the tub.

Wrapping the towel around his waist. "I think you should leave."

My mouth drops. He couldn't be serious. "What?"

"Look, Luna. I'm not into these little mind games you apparently like to play. One second, you're giving me all of the signs you're into me. The next thing I know, you have walls the size of China. I don't have time for it. So, you should just go." Then he turns on his heels and walks out.

I stand in the tub and grab another towel. As I follow after him. "You're fucking kidding me, right?" He turns to face me. "What, because I won't be in a relationship with you, you're kicking me out? What happened to *you shouldn't be alone.* You're so full of shit."

Of all people, I thought that Nick would understand me. But who the hell was I kidding? There's only one person in this world I could count on, and that's my damn self.

Those feelings I had for him disappears within seconds.

"I wanted to make you feel better. But apparently, you're too wrapped up in your own world to see that. What the hell does it take for you to see that there's someone who actually cares about you?"

Is that what he thinks he's doing? Caring about me? If this is how he cares for me, I don't want it. He's literally throwing my ass out on the streets, all because I didn't want to start a relationship. I know I've made the right decision now. He clearly doesn't understand how important my career is.

"You don't care about me, Nick. Stop fooling yourself," I scoff. I grab my clothes off the floor and start to pull them on. "If you cared, you wouldn't be kicking me out right now."

"I do care, but I care about myself more. I'm not playing your fucking mind games, Luna. Either you be honest with yourself about how you feel about me or leave." He takes a step toward me. "I'm not making this shit up in my head. I know you feel something between us. So why won't you give us a try?"

I groan. "Oh, my fucking gosh. Nick, get it through that thick ass skull of yours. I don't want a fucking relationship! When will you start being honest with *yourself and say* that the only reason you want me is because you *can't* have me?!"

"Oh, get over yourself, Luna. You're not that fucking special," he retorts.

With that, I slide my shoes on and walk out the door, making sure to slam it behind me. I call an Uber to come pick me up.

I'd have to say there's no way any birthday will be able to ever top this one.

Chapter 21

Nick

"**N**ick!" Someone calls as I skate onto the ice. My head should be prepping for the game right now, but all I can think about is how I hate the way I ended my conversation with Luna.

I mean, should I have kicked her out of my house at 2:00 in the morning? No, probably not. But that girl just gets under my fucking skin. I should have made her stay and talk it out with me. Instead, I let her call a damn Uber and go home.

What the fuck is wrong with me? But what was I supposed to do? She doesn't want a relationship, and I do. I feel like this is the universe paying me back for what I did to Paris. That's what it feels like, because this is some kind of weird déjà vu.

"Nick!" I turn to see Dean skating up to me. He's the last person I want to see right now. "Dude, what the hell? I've been calling your name for the last five minutes."

"My bad. What's up?" I ask while practicing with the puck, tossing it on either side of my stick.

"I saw you take Luna home last night. Was she okay?"

I scrunch my eyebrows.

This dude is not seriously asking me this right now. "What do you think?"

He shakes his head. "I think she's being a little dramatic. I mean, I'm just having sex with her. I'm not even dating her. Also, it's not even that deep. Why is she tripping?"

I have this sudden urge to knock this dude on his ass. What does he mean by she's tripping? Not only is he sleeping with her best friend, but he's been ignoring her. Made her feel like her feelings didn't matter. Ostracized her for what, some damn pussy?

The fact that he doesn't even see the problem with this makes it that much worse.

I shake my head and skate off to the opposite end of the rink to get a couple of laps in. As I make my rounds, I notice a curly head sitting in the front row.

There's no way. She wouldn't have come.

I come to an abrupt halt as ice showers against the Plexiglas.

"Hi," she says softly.

I pull my helmet off to get a good look at her and make sure I'm not just seeing things. "What are you doing here?"

"I came to apologize. So, listen closely, because I won't say it twice."

A small grin grows on my face.

"I respect you for setting boundaries for yourself. Although I stand by my dating stance, I shouldn't have said what I said. You were the only person who actually celebrated my birthday with me. I appreciated it. I shouldn't have acted the way I did, and I'm sorry."

"I'm sorry. I didn't get that last part. The music is a little loud. Can you say that again?" I push my ear toward her to get her to say it a little louder. Even though I heard her loud and clear. The music wasn't that loud.

She rolls her eyes. "I told you I would only say it once. So, if you didn't hear it, that's on you." She shrugs.

"Fine. I'm sorry, too. I shouldn't have said all that shit either."

"All of what shit? The part where you said I'm not special? Or the part about me being self-centered?" She raises an eyebrow.

Fuck, if she didn't look hot right now. "Yeah, that part,"

She laughs. Like really laughs. The laugh that comes deep from your diaphragm. "Are you staying for the game?"

"I told you. I don't like hockey like that."

"Okay, and? Just stay for one game. Please, for me?" I plead with my best puppy-dog eyes. I look like a damn dumb ass, but I really don't care.

"Ugh, fine. Don't expect it to happen often." I watch as the smile fades from her face.

Without turning around, I can already tell why. Rather, who.

Dean.

Sure enough, when I turn around, I see Dean standing across the arena talking to Gia. I've actually never seen Gia come to any of the games. I'm sure she's been here before, but I don't really pay attention. Did they figure that since Luna knows it just doesn't matter anymore?

I turn to see Luna, staring at them like she just saw a ghost. "Hey." Her head snaps to me. "You don't have to stay if you don't want to. I forgot about Dean, and I didn't expect her to be here." As much as I really want her to stay for me, I wouldn't put her through watching her best friend and brother flirt the entire game. That's torture.

"No, it's fine. I said I would stay, so I'm going to stay." She clears her throat. "Don't lose, yeah?"

"Tell me how you're feeling."

She plucks at the hem of her hoodie."What do you mean?"

"Jay, talk to me."

"I'm fine, Beckett." She sighs. "I promise."

I glance at Dean and Gia before looking back at her. "If you feel like this is too much, don't feel like you have to stay for me. If you feel like your chest is too heavy or you can't breathe, head to the locker room. I'll rush off the ice and meet you there, okay?"

A giggle slips from her lips. "You're not leaving the middle of the game for *my* panic attack. These games are too important to you."

"You're more important, Jay." A red hue brushes across her cheeks. "I will leave this game instantly if you start to have a panic attack."

"You're sweet, but I swear I'll be okay." I glare. "But if I do, I will rush to the locker room." Then she turns around to find her seat in the second row.

I skate back to the box, and Dean follows suit.

"Why is Luna here?" Please tell me he's not serious right now.

"Why is Gia here?"

"What? Dude, did you invite my sister?" He snarls. "What's going on between you two anyway?"

My blood starts to boil. The way this man gives zero fucks for his sister drives me fucking insane.

"First off, no, I didn't invite her here. But I didn't tell her to go home either. You don't want her here; you tell her that because I'm not." The urge to punch him was getting stronger with every second I was in his presence. "Second, there's nothing going on between us. If there was, it would be none of your business."

"What is your problem, dude? I thought you were on my side." Before I can answer, the coach blows his whistle.

"Alright y'all. We are currently undefeated, and I would like to leave tonight with that streak. Let's not ruin that, or so help me, God, I will make your lives hell!" Coach shouts.

"Yes, coach!" We all chant.

"Alright, get out there and make me proud, boys!" Coach claps.

Then the starting lineup skates out onto the ice.

Which includes Dean. I can hear Gia screaming at the top of her lungs. I look over to see Luna standing on her feet, softly clapping her hands. Her smile is tight, but she gives me a thumbs up. This is going to be a long fucking night.

We're down to our last period, and the score is tied. Coach obviously isn't happy. I'm trying to get around these guys, but they're pissing me off. They keep trying to body-check me. Clearly, they suck at it, but does that deter them? No.

Also, I'm doing my best to only pass the puck to Dean when absolutely necessary. Is that smart? Also, no, but he doesn't deserve the spotlight tonight.

He shouldn't have brought Gia here out in the open like this. Even if he didn't think Luna would be here. Common decency means giving the whole situation some time to cool down.

I'm starting to second-guess him as captain. I mean, if he would make dumb ass decisions like this in his personal life, there is no telling what the hell he would do for the captain position.

Every chance I get, I look for Luna in the stands. I always find her smiling at me or rolling her eyes. But every now and then, I catch her staring at Gia, and I can just see the hurt in her eyes. I know she wants to forgive them and let it go, but she shouldn't. Especially considering they give zero fucks about how she's feeling.

Forcing myself to focus on the last ten minutes of the game, I watch the puck as it glides across the ice to me. There's a player coming right at me as I try to get the puck to the other side.

As I skate down the rink, I realize the only open player is Dean. Well, hell.

Reluctantly, I shoot the puck to Dean, but before I even shoot it to him, the player knocks me into the boards.

Now, I'm pissed the fuck off. He wants a fight. He'll get one.

"What the fuck is your problem?" I push him.

"You were hogging the puck too long." He shrugs. "This is hockey; do not keep away." Then he shoves me back.

I notice Luna is standing now. I force my fury back down. I can't afford to show out.

The guy follows my eye line to Luna and looks back at me. "Now that's a piece of ass I'd want a bite out of."

Fuck the rules.

I pull on my helmet and tackle the guy to the ground. It quickly becomes a tussle to see who can end up on top. Then his helmet is knocked off, so I punch him square in the face and keep punching until my teammates pull me off.

"Beckett! Off the damn ice now!" Coach yells.

The referee blows his whistle. Then he tells the coach that I'm disqualified from the rest of this game and the next game. Adding a five-minute penalty in the box.

I make my way to the box, and the coach is right on my tail, yelling multiple expletives in my ear. "Coach, I'm sorry." That's all I can say, even though I'm not.

That fucker deserved it. I would do it again too.

"You're out for the next two games, Beckett!" Coach yells as he turns around and makes his way back to the team.

"Coach, you can't be serious." I stand.

He quickly spins around, pointing his finger in my face. "You're the damn team captain! You should know better. What the hell is your problem? Get your shit together!"

"Coach, you don't even know what happened!" I've never raised my voice to Coach. But it wasn't right. Kicking me out of two games.

"I don't give a damn what happened! What part of being a team captain do you not understand? Dean will be stepping in as acting captain for the next two games."

"You can't be serious! Coach! Not fucking Dean!" There was no way Dean was coming out on top after everything.

"You want to make it three games, Beckett! Keep running that mouth of yours! I dare you!" Then he turns and heads back to the team.

I slam back onto the bench. This couldn't be happening right now.

I pull my gloves off and rub my hands over my face, wincing when I rub across the cut on my lip. I didn't even realize the dude had gotten a hit in. What the fuck was I thinking? I don't do shit like this. I don't fight, especially in a hockey game, but when he said that about Luna, I couldn't help it.

After my time is up, Coach tells me to just head to the showers since he can't even look at me. Walking into the locker room, I slam my gloves into my locker and shut it with my fist, then I sink onto the bench.

I hear the door open. "Coach, I got it, okay? I don't need another speech."

"Good thing I wasn't going to give one." I turn to see Luna leaning on the locker, staring at me.

"I'm sorry, Luna; I thought you were Coach." I sigh.

"What's your punishment? I saw you and the coach having a screaming match. I mean, I've seen Coach mad, but I've never seen him *that* mad."

Same. "I'm out for the next two games."

"Tsk. Tsk. Tsk. Do better, Beckett." I know she's joking, but it was sincerely pissing me off.

"Are you in here for a reason or just pissing me off further?" I stand as I pull the jersey over my head.

"Damn, what crawled up your ass and died?" She crosses her arms over her chest.

"Jay, I just got sidelined for the next two fucking games! What do you think crawled up my ass and died?" I open the locker before throwing my jersey in.

"Then why did you get into a fight? You knew there would be consequences. You're not that stupid."

"What the hell is that supposed to mean?"

"It means you have common fucking sense, Nick. Use it. Don't get pissy at me because of your damn actions."

"It started *because* of you!" I yell.

"How did it start because of me? I didn't even do anything. I wasn't even on the ice." She straightens her stance.

"The dude was checking you out and said he wanted to fuck you." After taking off all of my gear, I'm finally standing in nothing but my hockey pants and shin pads.

She laughs. "Are you kidding me? Do you know how many people have made snide comments about wanting to sleep with me? I'm used to it. Honestly, I'm not even sure why you're pissed. Nick, you're not my boyfriend. Nor have *you* slept with me."

I scoff. "So you're saying I should've just let the shit slide?"

"Yes. Nick, this is your career. You need to be smarter. You can't just start fights over some BS." She takes a step toward me. "I appreciate what you were trying to do, but I don't need you to defend me. You shouldn't be risking your career for me. I mean, I wouldn't risk mine for you."

Even though she was an ass about it, she was right. I shouldn't have done it. I knew I would be benched. Yet, I didn't care. Now that I'm reaping the repercussions, I'm pissed. I needed to think more about my actions.

I smirk. "When did you get so wise?"

She shrugs. "I've always been smart. Now, if you hurry up, I might have stuff at my house for the nasty cut. Also, ice for the huge ass bruise on your back."

I reach for my back as if I can see it and try to feel the bruise. She laughs as she walks out of the locker room.

"I'll be waiting outside," she calls.

I just shake my head as I continue to undress, then head for a quick shower.

Chapter 22

Nick

After the game ended—we won—Coach yelled some more. I finally apologized for starting the fight. Thanks to Luna knocking some sense into me, I'm also allowed to go to the games as the captain. I still can't play, but Dean won't be acting as the interim captain. I'd say that's a fucking win.

When I walk outside, the lot is empty except for Luna, who is lying on the hood of my car, mindlessly scrolling through her phone.

I stop walking just to admire the view. I really owed this girl for tonight. If not for her, I would have been stuck at home while Dean moved in as captain. Obviously, it wouldn't be permanent, but it would piss me off royally.

She turns her head to me, smiling. "Finally. Damn, you took forever. Come on, old man."

"What do you mean, old man? I'm not old."

She scoffs. "Nick, you're a whole two years older than me."

"So, what's your point?" I didn't realize our age difference. Not that it was a problem. I don't really mind it. It's only two years.

"That makes you old, sir." She slides off the hood and steps in front of the driver's door. "Oh, do you want me to get the door for you, sir?" she asks, reaching for the door handle.

I push her out of the way. "Oh, you got jokes, huh?"

She raises her hands up in surrender. "Hey, I was always told to respect my elders."

She starts to step backward, but I grab her by the waist, pulling her back to me. A loud squeal slips past her lips. Lifting her in the air, I lay her back on the hood. I placed my hands on either side of her head, trapping her in between my arms.

"Say it to my face," I challenge her. Nothing turns me on more than her defiance.

"I said, old man." She enunciates slowly, letting me feel every word as if it were honey dripping from her lips.

Then I crash my lips into hers, inhaling her scent. Coconuts and strawberries—a scent I've engraved into my brain. A scent I will never tire of.

She pulls me in by my waist until I'm practically lying on her. I feel my dick twitch with need. I want her. I know I can't have her, but that just makes me want her more.

Kissing her is like my drug. I understand addicts now. One taste of her, and it's all I want, all of the time. She's a fresh breath of air, and I'm inhaling her in like I forgot how to breathe.

I shouldn't even be kissing her right now. Just yesterday, she told me she didn't want a relationship. Right now, that's all I want from her.

I want to text her every night and ask her how her day was. Wake up every morning and tell her how beautiful she is. I want to be the one person on Earth who can make her smile. The one person she wants to be around.

I want that to be me, but that's not what she wants.

I don't want to give up on her, but she needs to be honest with herself too. I know she feels something between us. But I refuse to get rejected twice. So, the next time, she'll be the one to say she wants me.

I pull back, leaning my forehead against hers. "I thought you were supposed to be fixing my cuts and bruises."

"You're the one who got distracted." She inhales sharply, with a small chuckle to follow.

"Mhm." I moan. I step back, giving her space. "Let's go then."

She smiles as she jumps off the hood and heads to the passenger door.

This was going to be a long night.

We make it to her apartment. I walk in, and I have no idea what to expect. Luna's up is down, and her down is up. I'm standing firm in what I said, though. I'm not making another move on her unless she makes it first.

She didn't need to fix my cut. It's something I could do myself, but she invited me over. So, I'll see where it goes.

The puck is in her court now. Contrary to what happened earlier, I just couldn't help myself. She was standing right in front of me, and I'd be damned if I just let the moment slip past me without acting on it.

"Give me a second while I get the first aid kit," she bellows before heading to her bathroom. I walk into her living room and make myself comfortable on the couch.

When she walks out, she's holding a blue container. Then she sits down next to me. Resting the box on my thigh, she pulls out an antibacterial cream and a q-tip. Then she squeezes a small amount onto the tip and starts to rub it across the cut on my bottom lip.

"Do you do this often?"

Her eyebrows furrow in confusion.

"Help wounded men?"

She giggles. "No. I'm a dancer. I always have blisters and scabs on my feet. I had to learn to treat them myself after..." Her voice trails off, and she pulls the Q-tip back to the cream to apply more.

"After what?" I normally don't push, but I wanted to know everything about this girl.

"After my sister died," she returned to applying the cream. "She would always clean my wounds and wrap them. Then, after she died, I had to teach myself."

"You don't talk about her much."

"Yeah, I know. I think about her, though. Like all of the time." I watch sadness paint her face.

I've never lost someone close to me, so I can't even imagine what it's like. Or what she feels. Not only that, but I'm an only child, so losing a sibling is something I'll never have to worry about.

I want to comfort her, but I don't know how. "Tell me about her."

Her hand stops mid-air as she stares into my eyes. I expected to see pain or sadness. Instead, they look as if she's waited for someone to ask that question for years.

She brings her hands into her lap before speaking. "She was perfect. Everyone says that about people they love, but Cassie *really* was perfect. She never did anything wrong. Always colored inside the lines and never strayed. She's the one who got me into dance. I wanted to hang out with her more. I thought she would get annoyed with me, but instead she asked our mom if she could sign me up for dance classes." She shuffles in her seat.

"That became our new normal: school, dinner, and ballet classes. Cassie never made me feel like a burden. She would spend extra time after class and go over what we learned. When I first started out, I struggled a lot. So, to catch me up to speed, she would stay late and work on the choreography or the warm-ups. Cassie was my best friend. I know it's weird to say that your sibling is your best friend. But she was. I looked up to her. When I was younger, I wanted to be just like her."

I stare at her as I watch tears collect in her eyes. I reach for her hands and rest them on my leg. "She's the reason you dance, isn't she?" She nods her head. "My mom is the reason I play hockey."

"What do you mean?" she asks, wiping her eyes with her shoulder.

"When I was younger, my mom took me to my first hockey game. There was something so exhilarating about watching them play. The adrenaline I had I couldn't put it into words. I knew I loved hockey from that day forward. Then, my mom said that she would pay good money to see me on the ice. I'd never even thought of playing hockey, to be honest. Not before that day, but I love my mom. No, I worship her. So, if it would make her happy to see me on the ice, then that's what I would do."

"So, you started playing hockey after that game?" I nod.

"My dad was always so worried about me getting hurt, but my mom kept telling him I would be fine. She would say that boys were meant to get hurt. It teaches us to be strong and to get up and keep trying."

Luna laughs. "It's funny how the roles were reversed. Normally, it's the mom worrying about the kid and the dad pushing the kid into the sport."

I shake my head as a small grin grows on my face. "Yeah, our family was weird that way. We always did the opposite of everyone else. My dad liked to say it's what makes our family better than others."

"I see where you get your narcissism from." She laughs and pulls her hands from mine, then closes the first aid kit.

"Why do you dance?"

"What do you mean? I just told you why," she answers from the bathroom.

"No, you didn't. I get why you got *into* dancing, but why do you continue to dance? I mean, normally, after someone loses someone, they don't find pleasure in that activity anymore. It loses its meaning." Luna exits the bathroom with a confused look on her face.

"That was very psychological of you."

"Well, I'm a psych major."

"You are not." Her mouth is wide open now. "Wait, seriously?"

I laugh. "Why is that so hard to believe?"

"I don't know. I just don't see you as a psych major. I see you majoring in something that has to do with the physical body, not the mind."

I roll my eyes. "Anyway, stop deflecting. What's the reason you keep dancing?"

She lets out a loud sigh, then comes back to the couch. "Cassie wanted to be a prima ballerina. Which is like the top of the food chain when it comes to ballet. When she died, obviously that couldn't happen."

She takes another deep breath before she continues. "The day she died, she was getting bagels and smoothies for us. She got hit because she was texting me." She holds her hands up to stop me from talking. "I know it's not really my fault, but I can't help feeling like it is. No matter how much I talk with my therapist about it. It just feels like if I hadn't made her feel guilty for being late to pick me up, she would have come straight home. So, I told myself if she couldn't fulfill her dreams, I would do it for her."

"That's why it's so important for you to stay focused. With no distractions." I say it, not really needing her to confirm. I understand her now. She wanted to make up for her sister's death. Even if it wasn't actually her fault, she felt like it was. So, she's dancing to make up for it the best way she knows how.

I don't really think it's healthy, but I understand it.

"I'm sorry, Nick." She starts to pick at the hem of her shirt.

I grab her hands and pull them back into my lap. "Don't apologize. You have nothing to be sorry about." Before I can say anything else, my phone buzzes. "Sorry, one second."

I pull my phone out of my pocket; it's a notification that someone is at my door. When I see who's standing in front of the camera, I can feel the anger rise in my ears. "Sorry, Jay. I gotta go." Standing from my seat, I shove my phone back in my pocket. "Thank you for coming to my aid tonight and for sharing with me."

"Are you okay?" she asks.

"Yeah, I just have to handle something. I'll text you, okay?"

She nods, and I head for the door.

When I make it to the elevator, I pull my phone out and hit the call button. "What the hell are you doing at my house?"

"We need to talk," Paris says.

"No, we really don't."

"Nick! Please, I need to talk to you. Can you just get home, please?" My heart tightens at her plea.

"I'm on my way." Then I hang up. I didn't know what the hell was going on, but I don't like the way she sounds.

When I arrive at home, Paris is on my doorstep with her face in her hands. She looks like she's been crying. What the hell is going on? As much as I didn't want to talk to this woman, she was sad, and I couldn't just ignore that. "Paris," I call out.

"Nick." She stands and runs into my arms.

I slowly raise my arms and wrap them around her. Holding Paris in my arms felt weird. There were no lingering feelings for her or even a hint of attraction. It almost felt like I was betraying Luna somehow. Shaking the thoughts away, I push Paris off me. "What are you doing here, Paris?"

"I'm sorry for just showing up, but I needed to see you. I felt like shit. The last time I was here, I treated you and Luna like crap." That's an understatement. "I love Luna, and I know you would never make a move on her. I just got so angry because you ended things with me, and next thing I knew, you were talking to her. My mind just went crazy, and I'm sorry."

"Is there a point to you driving out here?"

"Nick, can we just go back to how things were? I know you don't want a relationship. At this point, I don't either. It's too much for me to handle right now. I just miss being able to text you and have someone to come to when I'm in town. I miss us. So, if you just want sex, then so do I. So, what do you say?"

I appreciate Paris' apology, but the damage was done. She slapped me, and she's right. She treated Luna, and I like crap. I just can't look at her the same way anymore. Plus, I really like Luna, and even though she doesn't want a relationship right now, that doesn't mean she won't in the future. If I started this up with Paris again, I would lose any chance with Luna.

"Paris-" She cuts me off with her lips. My body stiffens. I should push her off, but I can't get my body to move.

"Oh, sorry. I didn't mean to interrupt." I hear a voice behind me, and I immediately push Paris off. Without turning around, I knew exactly who it was.

I swear, this girl has the shittiest timing in the world.

"Luna, wait." I start to walk after her, but she runs to her car.

"Why is she even here?" Paris asks.

I ignore her and run after Luna. When I catch up with her, I grab her by the arm and turn her toward me. "Luna, wait!"

"No, it's fine. I didn't know you and Paris were a thing again. I shouldn't have even come here." She tries to pull her arm away, but I tighten my grip.

"Are you jealous?"

"No! I'm stupid, is what I am."

"You have no right to be angry with me. You didn't want a relationship, remember? You didn't want me!" I can hear my voice getting louder, but her being angry with me makes no sense to me. I've done nothing but tell her how I want to be with her. She has no right to get upset.

"You were just kissing me, and now you're kissing her! What the hell am I supposed to feel? Thrilled?"

"You shouldn't feel anything! You didn't want me. You can't pretend that all of a sudden you've been betrayed. You haven't." I should tell her it meant nothing. That Paris kissed me and not the other way around, but I don't.

"Nick, let go! I'm done!" She tries to pull her arm away again, but is still unsuccessful.

"No." I pull her into me. "What do you want, Luna?" I whisper. "Do you want me? Or is it that you don't want me, but you also don't want anyone else to have me? Is that it? Is this another one of your games?"

I sigh. "Luna, just tell me what you want. I can't keep playing this push and pull with you."

She wants me as badly as I want her. Why can't she just admit it? I know the circumstances surrounding her sister, but it still shouldn't stop her from giving us a chance.

"Okay, I couldn't care less where you get your dick wet." I know she's trying to sound intimidating, but she just sounds hurt. "And I'm not playing a game with you. You're the one who can't make up your mind.You say one thing to me, turn around in that same breath, and make out with Paris. So who's really playing the push and pull game here?"

"I just want you." Releasing her arm, I cup her cheeks between my hands. "What part of that do you not understand? I don't want Paris. I don't want some random girl either. I just want you. I don't do relationships, and yet I'm here asking for one from you. I'm not going to ask again, though. If you want me, you need to tell me."

"I don't want a relationship, Nick." I let go of her face, ready to give up. But she grabs my wrist before they drop to my side. "But I don't want you to see anyone else. You're right; I don't want to see you kissing someone else. I know that's really messed up, but it's true. I don't want you with anyone else. I just can't handle being in a relationship right now. I have too much on my mind and too much I need to do."

"So, where does that leave us?" I ask hesitantly. This is the most vulnerable time she's been with me. I'm afraid if I push her too much, she'll go back to not wanting anything from me.

"I don't know." She takes a step toward me. "I'm not a jealous person, Nick. I never get jealous, but when it comes to you, that's all I know. So, do with that information as you wish."

"I didn't kiss Paris; she kissed me. She came over, asking to go back to the way things were. I was about to tell her no, but then she kissed me. That's when you showed up."

"You don't want her back?" Her brows knit together, creating delicate furrows on her forehead, as her eyes held a distant gaze, which held a distant gaze of concern and worry.

"No, I don't," I answer, hoping it reassures her. I let go of her arms and take a step back. "The puck is in your court, Jay."

She takes a deep breath, like she's mustering up all the strength she needs to speak. "I don't want to be your girlfriend. But I also don't want you to sleep with anyone but me."

My heart leaps into my chest. This isn't exactly what I want, but it's a start. "I can do that." I smile. "But the same goes for you. I don't want you sleeping with anyone but me." She nods her head in agreement.

I grab her by the wrist and pull her into my body again. A small giggle escapes her. "I'm all yours, Beitar."

Then I lean in and kiss her. We mold together like a jigsaw puzzle. Like this was meant to be from the start.

Chapter 23

Luna

I originally came over here to check on him. When he left my apartment, he looked angry and upset. I just wanted to make sure he was okay.

I wasn't prepared to see him kiss Paris. Something inside lit up like a forest fire. I have never been the jealous type, but watching him and Paris kiss set everything in me aflame. A part of me really wanted to somehow run them down with my car.

He was right, though. We weren't in a relationship, and I had no say in who he was kissing. I would be lying if I said it didn't bother me, though.

Nick pulls back from me with my face still in his hands. "Now that that's settled, I have to go handle Paris. Can you give me two minutes? Don't leave."

I nod my head in agreement.

Watching him walk back to Paris, something swirls in my stomach. I don't know what she would tell him. How would she react? I haven't even spoken to Paris since the last time she was here. In a way, she was right. Nick and I would eventually end up with each other, but it's different. I don't feel like some random hookup to Nick. I feel it is more important than that. I feel like I matter more to him.

Which I know won't settle over well with Paris.

I look down at my feet. Not being able to look as Nick sends her off. But I also can't help but wonder if he would actually do it. I slowly drag my eyes from the ground to see Paris walking in my direction with Nick on her tail.

"You fucking slut!" she howls.

"Paris, I-" She cuts me off.

"I don't want to hear it. I told you I was into him. I was *really* into him. God, I can't believe you!" Her words cut deep into my soul.

I never thought about Paris's feelings for Nick. "Paris, we're not together." Is the only thing that I can think of to say. I'm not lying. Nick and I aren't together, but we *are* something.

When I look at Nick's face, I see the hurt shadowing his face. I know he wants more from me, but what I'm giving him is the best I can do.

"Don't fucking lie to me. I just fucking saw you kissing him. Then, not even two seconds later, he tells me it's not going to work between us!" She steps closer between us until she is right in my face. "You want to know why you have no one in your corner? It's because you're a traitorous bitch. Does Dean know you're fucking his captain?" She scoffs. "Yeah, I didn't think so. You don't care about anyone but yourself. You say you're dancing for Cassandra, but let's be honest. The only reason you're dancing is to prove to her that you're better than her. You only care if your light shines brighter than everyone else's."

Everything in me feels like I'm crashing. My heart sinks to the bottom of my stomach. "You don't mean that," I whisper.

"Yes, the fuck I do. God, I can't believe you. You're dead to me!" She knocks into my shoulder as she walks past me.

"Paris!" Nick calls after her while I'm glued to the ground. Of course, he cares about her. "Don't bring your ass back here anymore."

Nick grabs me by my shoulders and pulls me into a hug. "Please don't listen to her."

Isn't she right, though? I only care about myself. I mean, I'm literally sleeping with my brother's captain. If I care about Dean, I wouldn't be doing it. Over and over again, I've told myself that nothing can happen between us because of Dean, but I was so quick to say yes to him today. Without a second thought to Dean. He never crossed my mind as Nick kissed me.

I was so angry with Dean for sleeping with Gia. How am I any better for starting something with Nick?

I push out of Nick's arms. "Let go." I turn to my car and pull my keys out of my pocket. Before opening my door, I look back at Nick. He's looking at me like I'm this fragile, fine China plate.

"This isn't going to work, Nick. I'm sorry."

"What? Why? Because Paris thinks she has some claim over me? She doesn't." He walks over to me. "I already told you, I'm yours."

"No, you're not." I look into his eyes. "You're Dean's and Paris', but *you're not* mine."

"Fuck Dean. After everything he's put you through, you don't owe him anything. As far as Paris, I was never hers. Yeah, we had sex for the last year, but that's all it was between us. You and I are different." He cups my face. "This... between us, it's different. Please don't listen to her. Do not let her words affect what we have."

I slowly pull his hands away from my face. "They already did." Then I get in my car before driving away.

More than anything, I wish I had met Nick first. I wish he wasn't on my brother's team. But I didn't meet him first, and he is part of my brother's team. This was a mistake. I knew it, and so did he. We were fooling ourselves into thinking we could ever be anything more. Not with all of these roadblocks in the way.

We might as well give up while we're ahead.

✦

"Luna, what are you doing?" Madam Christine yells. "That was just sloppy. Again. This time, try to focus on your partner and not whatever is going on in that mind of yours."

It's been days since I've heard from Nick.

Why should it matter? This is what I want, right? I don't want to ruin what's left of Dean's and my relationship. If he were to find out that something was happening between Nick and I, he would lose his shit. I just don't have the energy or time to deal with more betrayal right now, especially if it's coming from my end.

"Luna!" I snap out of my head and return to dancing. "From the top," Madame Christine commands.

I try to shake away everything that doesn't revolve around dancing and focus on the choreography.

I watch as Giselle takes her place on the ground, her arm sprawled out in front of her. Her head rests on her bicep, and her other arm is underneath her.

Wrapping my right hand over Connor's eyes and my other over his chest, I give a nod, signaling to Madam Christine to start.

Then we start.

Connor takes a step on his right foot as mine shadows his. We glide toward Giselle, lunging on our seventh step. As we pause, Connor takes this time to lift his right arm as if he's reaching out for someone.

Then we continue walking, stepping off on our left leg, and we continue to glide to Giselle. Our movements are slow and fluid. On our eighth step, we take another small lunge before putting our weight on our right leg and leaning into it.

There's a moment of stillness, then I extend my arms like wings. Spreading his arms, he leans over, and Giselle sits on her thighs. Brushing her legs behind her, she meets him midway. Their eyes connect, and they have this moment of acknowledgment for each other. I walk around them as Giselle lays down on her forearm. I rise on my toes, and Connor's hands find my thigh and turn me slowly. My leg extended in the air as I circled around them for the remainder of the phrase.

I wave my arm gently and fall back on my feet. I melt onto my right leg, leaning forward into my left leg in a small bow. Then Giselle and I run toward Connor, pinning my chest to his back while Giselle pinned her back to his front. His arms wrap around both of us before we take elongated strides together.

Once we reach the middle of the room, Connor steps behind us. I use my left hand to grab his right hand, then reach up and relieve our hands from his. We lunge forward before sitting on our hips.

There is a slow clap, and the music cuts off. "That was beautiful. All three of you. Just beautiful."

Connor gives both of us a hand and helps us off the floor. "Thank you," I whisper.

We all stand side-by-side as we wait to hear Madam Christine's feedback.

"Luna, I'm glad to see you can leave your personal life at the door." I silently take a breath, trying not to let the sarcasm stab too deep. "You still need to work on your balance. Your feet are too wobbly. I said it before, and I'll say it again. If you cannot leave your personal life outside of here, where it belongs, don't bother coming into my studio and wasting my time. Do I make myself clear, Luna?"

"Yes ma'am." I nod.

Dance normally distracts me from my personal life. Today, it didn't. I can't be mad at Madame Christine for snapping at me. She's right. *I* broke it off with Nick. I need to accept that and move the hell on.

She continues on with her feedback with Connor and Giselle. After she finishes, she leaves us in the room. Before she walks out, she turns to me. "Luna."

"Yes?" I respond.

"Be in the studio tomorrow. Maybe you can make up for whatever that was today."

"Yes ma'am," I answer, while my pride takes another massive hit.

I want to continue in the studio today, but I don't think I can. I just want to go home, shower, and go to sleep. I start to gather my stuff up in my duffle bag.

"Hey." Connor taps my shoulder. "Just ignore her, yeah? She can be a little melodramatic sometimes."

"Maybe, but she was right. I should have been focused, but I have too much shit on my mind."

"It's life. Look, Giselle and I were heading out to get something to eat. Want to join?"

I look at Giselle and back at him. "I'm kind of beat. I just want to go home and sleep. Maybe some other time?"

A sympathetic smile grows on his face. "Yeah, sure." He grabs his bag off the ground and walks to the door. "I'll hold you to it."

I return his smile as he leaves.

After packing my stuff up, I grab my bag off the floor and head out. These last couple of days, I have felt like absolute crap. Paris' words keep ringing in my head.

You want to know why you have no one in your corner? It's because you're a traitorous bitch.

How could I be mad at Dean for sleeping with Gia when I'm doing the same thing? I keep telling myself it's not the same thing, but it is. Nick and Dean might not be best friends, but they *are* friends. Or at least they were. Nick is training Dean to be the new captain when he leaves. So, honestly, what's the difference? I'm being hypocritical.

When I walk outside, I run into a wall. Well, it felt like a wall. I look up to apologize but stop when I see Nick. "What the hell are you doing here?"

"You haven't talked to me in days. Why?" he asks, stuffing his hands into his jean pockets.

"I told you this wasn't going to work." I swerve around him and walk to my car. I try to open it, but Nick slams his hands into the door, closing it. "What the hell is your problem?"

"That's what I'm wondering too. *What the hell is your problem, Jay?* What, because Paris said some shitty things, you just call it quits?"

"No, it's because she wasn't lying. I can't be pissed at Dean for sleeping with my best friend while I'm out sleeping with you!"

"First off, Dean and I aren't best friends. Second, it's different."

I scoff. "How? Because I knew Gia longer? It doesn't matter. You're also his captain. Everything about this screams red flag."

I try to open the door again, but he pushes his hand against the top of it. "No, you're just looking for an excuse to give up. I've got to be honest, Luna. I didn't peg you as a quitter."

"I'm not a quitter! I just know what's worth fighting for." Waving my hands between us, I said, "This is not worth fighting for."

"How do you know if you won't even give it a try? Luna, you keep making these decisions about us without even trying to consider what I feel or want."

"Because I'm the only one using my head!" I yell. "Nick, you don't even see how much this is affecting me! Paris was the closest thing I had to a sister. She just told me I was dead to her! My brother, my twin at that, isn't talking to me. I lost my best friend as well. I'm losing everyone close to me." I sigh. "Nick I can't do this with you. I might not be ready to forgive Dean, but I don't want there to be something else that comes between us."

He inhales sharply, taking a moment before speaking again. "Your brother and Gia weren't thinking about you when they slept together. They didn't think about you when they were fucking in that room on your birthday either." He takes a step toward me, pinning me to the door. "They didn't consider you when they were keeping it a secret; they were fucking for months. They didn't think about you when Dean invited Gia to the game. In fact, he wanted you to leave."

"What?" I didn't know Dean saw me at the game. I knew he might have, but I wasn't there for Dean. I was there for Nick. "He wanted me to leave?" But he wanted Gia to stay. He really chose Gia over me?

"Don't you dare waste another fucking tear on them. My point is that they didn't think about you, so why are you thinking about them? If they loved you even a *fraction* of how much you love them, they wouldn't put you through this bullshit."

It didn't matter, though. I loved them. I couldn't lose anyone else. The pain I went through after losing Cassandra was the worst pain imaginable. To lose someone else, especially over something so dumb. I can't.

I don't forgive them for holding this secret from me, but they are my family. Somewhere down the line, I know that I'll want them back in my life. If I start anything up with Nick, I'll never get that opportunity.

"They're my family, Nick. You don't get it."

"No, I don't. I would never put my *family* through this. Stop making excuses for them, Luna. You deserve better than that. I want you, Luna. I don't care about the damn consequences. You deserve to be appreciated. I know how important your family is to you, but think about yourself for once. Think about what makes you happy."

Grabbing my face in between his hands, he says, "What about your happiness? What about what you want?"

Tears start to stream down my face. I've never had someone care so much about me. I want to trust that this is worth it because I want it to be worth it. I want Nick. But there was something in me that was telling me how badly this was going to end.

"Nick—" My words are cut off when Nick slams his lips into mine.

This kiss is different from any other kiss we've shared. It feels like a promise. Like he's promising to stay and stick by me. My body melts into his arms, finally giving up the fight. I don't want to fight anymore, not with Nick. He's been the only person to stick by me. Even when I'm being an ass, he stays.

My lips mold to his as he presses his body into mine. His kiss feels like a cold breeze on a hot summer's day. Something I've grown to want more and more every time he kisses me.

His rough, calloused hand finds my jaw, grabs hold of it, then tilts it upward. He breaks the kiss while still holding my jaw. "You're mine, Luna James Beitar. I don't want to hear any more of that bullshit about doing what's right. Because *this* is right, and I don't care what anyone else says. You understand me?"

I nod silently. "Good." He gives me one more peck on the lips before letting go of my jaw. "I'll drive. Give me your keys."

I place the keys in his hands and walk to the passenger side of the car, with Nick on my heels. He opens the door, letting me in.

Nick crouches next to me as I buckle myself in. "Get out of your head, Luna." Then he kisses my forehead before closing the door.

God, please don't let this be a mistake.

Chapter 24

Luna

I unlock the door to let Nick in first as I walk in after him. Having him here feels surreal. Even though he's been over a couple of times, he's here now as more than a friend, and it just doesn't feel real. But it's something I want. I don't want to be just friends with him anymore. I want more. No, scratch that. I *need* more.

I'm trying not to think about how badly this could end. I want this to work. But my mind keeps going back to the fact that he's Dean's captain. I don't want him to be, but he is. This situation is just so fucked.

I lock the door as I slowly walk to my room. Why am I walking to my room, you ask? Probably because a part of me just really wants to curl up in bed and cry. I'm so exhausted. Mentally and physically.

Everything that happened these last few months must have taken at least five years off my life.

"Hey, I found this envelope on the floor." Nick walks into my room with a bulky yellow envelope. "What is it?"

I shake my head. "I don't know. I remember bringing it in a couple months ago, but I never opened it."

"Do you want to open it now?" He holds up the folder for me, but I push it back.

"No. I just want to go to sleep. You can throw it on the desk."

He throws the envelope on the desk before crawling into bed behind me. Wrapping his muscular arms around my waist, he snuggles his head into my neck. I can't remember the last time I had a man in bed with me. Something about having Nick here just calms me. It feels like I'm safe and sound as long as I lie between his arms.

"What's wrong?" Nick asks, lifting my haze.

"Nothing."

"Luna."

"Everything." I twist in his arms until I'm facing him. "I just don't know what I'm supposed to feel right now. Should I be concerned with the fact that Gia and Dean haven't reached out? Or the fact that I just lost one of my biggest connections to my sister? Don't even get me started on you."

"Me? What did I do?" he asks, furrowing his eyebrows.

I look into his green eyes—something I could get lost in and be okay with never finding my way out of. I reach up to run my palm against his defined jaw. "Nothing. Absolutely nothing." I answer softly as a soft grin grows on his face.

"Good." He pulls me closer to his body until we're flush against each other. I close my eyes as I lay against his warm chest and listen to the beat of his heart.

After a beat of silence, I finally muster up the courage to ask the questions that has been bouncing around in my head. "So, what are we?"

"What do you mean?" Yeah, because that's a good sign.

I tilt my head back until I can see his face. "What are we, Nick? Please don't act dumb on me now."

He laughs. He pulls my head back to his chest. "I already told you, you're mine. Enough said."

My heart swells and butterflies take flight in my stomach at those six plain words.

I already told you, you're mine.

"Okay," I say simply. I'm happy to be his. As long as he was mine, I didn't care about anything else. Okay, that's a lie. I still care about the whole Gia, Dean, and Paris thing. But for right now, I wanted to get lost in Nick.

Although everything is basically mushy and muddled in my head right now, I know I can always count on Nick. I know I'm safe here in his arms. I don't have to worry about his intentions. I can just ...be.

Even though I'm in his arms, I want to feel more of him, and I want to be as close to him as I can get.

Pushing out of his arms, I reach up and grab his face, pulling his lips down to mine. This kiss was hungrier.

His hands explore my body. They edge their way down my back until they reach my hips. Leaving goose-bumps in their trail. I felt like I was on fire. My body is craving his touch.

I break the kiss before pushing him on his back. Then I crawl on top until I'm straddling him. "Nick, I want you." I mean that in more ways than one. Yes, I want him physically, but I want him emotionally too. I self-ishly want Nick all to myself. I wish he had met me before Dean; then I wouldn't be so pulled in so many different directions.

"I'm all yours. Have your way with me, Luna." He moans.

Then I reach down to grab the hem of his shirt. He sits up to pull it off, wrapping his arm around my waist to hold me against him. His lips find mine again. My hand curls in his thick, voluminous hair as warmth pools between my legs. He nips and sucks on my bottom lip, and I welcome a nice sting.

His lips starts to trail down my neck. I tilt my head backward to give him better access while his hand glides up my shirt. His hand pauses on my stomach, and he pulls back.

"What the hell is this?" He groans.

I look down to see what he's talking about.

A laugh bubbles in my chest. "It's a leotard." I forgot I even had it on. "I was going to shower, but someone distracted me."

He grins slyly. "I hope you don't mind if I just..." Then he rips it down the middle.

I jump. "Nick! These aren't cheap." No matter how hot that was, these are expensive as hell.

His hand dips in between my legs. "I'll buy you more."

I moan as his hands find my center. He starts to rub against my clit and my body vibrates with the motion. I'm trying to not lose myself, but his calloused hand is causing me to lose all common sense.

I start to rock on his hands.

"Fuck. You're so fucking beautiful riding my hand." His lips find the crook of my neck again as he starts to suck down and trail kisses along my collarbone.

I groan when his fingers slip into me. Pressure builds between my legs as I ride his fingers. My head falls back as I hold onto his shoulders for stability. "Fuck, Nick." I moan.

His free hand grips my ass. He slips in another finger while his thumb starts to caress my clit. My stomach starts to tighten as I grow closer to the edge. "Faster. *Please*," I plead. Then his fingers start to pound into me faster and harder.

I can't take it. My hips rise slightly, but he pulls me back down. My fingernails dig into his shoulders as the pressure bursts. "Oh, Nick! Fuck!"

I don't even have time to come down from the orgasmic high as Nick lifts me from his lap and flips me onto my back. He pulls his fingers in between his lips one-by-one, licking them dry. "Fuck, your pussy tastes good."

I can feel the heat rise in my face.

Nick grabs my shirt by the hem and lifts it over my head. Yeah, the leotard he rips, but he can safely take off a fucking t-shirt I give zero fucks about.

"Fuck, I'll never get tired of looking at you." He grumbles

A small giggle leaves my mouth before I can stop it. I lift my hips to help him pull it down with my sweats and toss them to the side. He sinks back down to my legs as he starts to trail kisses up my thighs.

His lips linger on my inner thigh, making me shake beneath his kiss. I could feel his lips quirk in a smile. He moves to my center as he makes eye contact with me. "When I'm done, there will be no question about what we are."

Then he feasts. My back arches into his mouth as I grab a hold of his hair. I grip on for dear life. I can't take it, but I'll be damned if I tap out. He pulls back just an inch before trailing his tongue from my center to my clit. I moan out in pleasure as he continues to suck on my bud.

My body twists to the side as I try to catch my breath, or a gasp of air. Whichever came first. Nick grips my hip and pins it to his face, holding me in place. My hips buck up from the invigorating feel of his tongue sliding up and down my clit.

I could feel another orgasm coming, but I push it back. I want to enjoy this a little longer. Nick spreads my legs a little wider, giving him better access. His tongue starts to pick up speed. I try to push away his face, but he doesn't budge. It's too much, but Nick pulls me back to him, gripping my hips and holding me in place.

"Oh, Nick. I can't." I moan. "It's too much."

He pulls just a little. "You can." He's back to lapping at my clit and pushing me down into the bed by my hips. Leaving me no room to squirm, no matter how hard I try.

He releases my hip before inserting three fingers into my cunt.

I want to tell him to pull back, but he starts pumping them into me as he continues to suck on my clit. I can't hold back anymore as I release into his mouth. My body trembles beneath him, but he doesn't stop.

"Nick. Fuck. Please," I beg, praying he stops but also hoping he doesn't.

He looks into my eyes. "Oh, come on," he grins. "You can give me one more." He continues to pump his fingers inside of me, sucking on my clit. His tongue enters into my pussy as my legs shake around his head. I'm a sweaty, hot mess, and I can barely breathe, but that doesn't deter Nick.

The room fills with the sound of my screams and moans. He finds my g-spot and starts pounding harder into me. Then I come undone again. Stars start to cloud my eyes as I come down from euphoria.

He licks up every drop of me before he leaves one last kiss. "I knew you could do it." I'm too exhausted to even have a comeback for that.

Nick pulls me down to the edge of the bed by my ankles before lifting one leg in the air. Resting it on his shoulder. He starts to insert himself but stops. "Fuck!"

My eyebrows scrunch together. "What?"

"I don't have a condom." Really? That's his problem?

"Nick, just stick it in. I'm clean and on birth control. Unless you're not-" My words are cut short as he shoves himself inside of me. A loud moan is hurled out before I can stop it. My vagina feels like it's been ripped into two. He's so big, and the way he forced himself in has me thinking I never lost my virginity.

He leans forward, resting both hands on either side of my waist and pushing my leg into my shoulder. "I'm clean."

I wrap my arms around his neck and pull him down to kiss me. It's soft and languid as he starts to move slowly. I moan softly into his mouth. It still kind of stings, but it also feels so good.

His hips start to rock into me as he inches further in. I pull from his lips to look between us. "Nick, you're not even halfway in?"

"I was trying to give you time to adjust." He laughs.

I knew he was big, but it still didn't prepare me. I shake my head and say, "Just do it. I can take it." I lie.

His hand embraces my face, and he leans in to kiss me again. Then he shoves himself deeper into me. I throw my head back, breaking our kiss. I can't take it! I *can't* take it!

My hands grip his biceps as I try to catch my breath. It's so fucking painful. My pussy is literally crying and begging me to take him out. I can feel my walls actively spreading farther apart, making room for him. Nick starts to kiss my neck, distracting me from the throbbing pain between my legs. Another moan bubbles in my throat.

"Are you okay?" he asks tenderly.

I nod my head. "Just give me a second." His thumb finds my clit, and he starts to massage. It slowly relieves the pain, and it earns him another moan. After a few more seconds, the pain is gone.

I rake my hands through his hair and nod my head. "Okay. You can move now," I say softly.

He gradually thrusts himself into me. I can't help but moan with every thrust. He fills me up like no one ever has before. You know when people say that a guy is so deep, they can feel it in your stomach? Well, Nick was so deep, I swear I could feel him in my *chest*. It might sound dramatic, but that's what it feels like. Like he's thrusting into my chest.

"Nick, move faster," I beg.

His eyebrow quirks. "Are you sure?" I nod.

Then he loops his hand behind my neck and sits on his knees, bringing me with him. Still holding my leg against his chest, he starts to thrust faster and harder. I grab hold of his arm that's linked behind my head for stability. My breaths were erratic as he pumps himself inside of me.

"Aghh, Nick." I moan.

I could feel how deep he was, and I could see it in his eyes. He didn't care. In fact, I think he likes that he's so deep in me. I love being this close to him. I want him closer. I want to touch every inch of him and mark him as mine in hopes that, in return, he will do the same to me.

I don't know where this primal beast came from. Or maybe it was always there, and Nick just brought it out of me.

Nick was right. I've wanted him for a while now. To actually have him now means I can never let him go. I didn't want him to look at another woman the way he's looking at me right now. Like I'm the last piece of pumpkin pie on Thanksgiving.

Nick is the only person who can make me feel this way. I'd be stupid to let him go now.

I can't, even if I want to. I'm hooked on him. He is the drug, and I am the addict.

"Fuck." Nick moans, lowering himself until his nose touches mine. "Luna, what have you done to me?" His voice is raspier now as he continues to thrust into me. The slaps of our bodies fills the space.

I grab hold of his sweaty face. "The same thing you did to me. I just wanted to even the score." Then his lips crash into mine. His kiss feels feral now, like a lion let out of his cage on a hunt for his prey.

Nick lifts his hips slightly before he starts to pound into me like a bat out of hell. "Oh, God!" I moan. I couldn't take it anymore. I try to push at his chest, but he just grabs my arm with his free hand and pins it above my head.

My stomach tightens, and I can feel myself on the precipice of another orgasm. "Fuck! Nick!" I moan louder, and all it does is boost his ego.

I tighten around him as the orgasm washes over me with vengeance. The room is filled with my screams. I shudder beneath him as he rides out my orgasm and finishes inside me. His body shakes before crashing his forehead into my neck.

"Yeah, that has got to be the best I've *ever* had." He mumbles into my neck.

I rake my hands through his hair as I come down from my high. "Yeah. I know."

He lifts me up from my neck just enough to find my lips. I'll never get tired of kissing this man. "Want to take a shower?" he asks, breaking the kiss.

I nod.

He pulls out, and my body shivers from the cold breeze. Then he walks into the bathroom and turns the shower on. My eyes gazes over his body. Nick really was beautiful, from his broad shoulders to his evenly tan skin. God clearly has favorites.

"What are you looking at?" he asks as he saunters back to me.

"You. You're kind of hot. Did you know that?"

He shakes his head. "Nope, not at all."

I throw the pillow at his head. I try to stand up, but my legs quickly give out. "Fuck, Nick." He just laughs. "I have to be in the studio tomorrow."

"You'll be fine. I think. Just take a hot shower with me, and then I'll give you a massage. Hopefully that helps." He wraps one arm around my waist, uses the other under my knees, and lifts me off the bed.

Then he carries me into the bathroom before setting me down in the tub. "I thought you said we were taking a shower?"

"Yeah, we were, but I figured a bath would be better." He turns the dial to turn off the water. My bathtub isn't as big as Nick's, so I hope he didn't plan on getting in here.

"Scoot forward." Nick demands.

"Nick, you're not going to fit."

"You said that about something else and look how that turned out." I open my mouth to retort but decide against it. I mean, he was right. I quietly scoot forward. "What? No comeback?"

"Shut up." He laughs, and slowly steps into the tub.

When he's fully in, he lifts me onto his lap, pulling me flush against his chest. Surprisingly, he fits. Well, technically he doesn't because I'm in his lap, but semantics.

His hands start to massage my thighs. I lean my head against his chest and let my eyes close. After tonight's festivities and dance class, I'm exhausted.

My eyes snap open when Nick starts to tug on my bun. "What are you doing?"

"I love seeing your hair down, but you never wear it down."

I laugh as I sit up and pull it out of the bun. "That's because these curls are hard to manage." I say and turn to look at him.

"I get that, but you look so hot with them down."

Heat rises in my cheeks. "Shut up." I rotate back around, throwing my back against his chest.

"Can I wash it?" he asks hesitantly.

"You want to wash my hair? Why?"

He shrugs. "I love your hair. I think it might be my new kink."

I laugh. "Please be careful. My hair can break off easily. It's black people hair."

"I'll be delicate." He promises before he starts to cup water in his hands and brings it to my head. He uses the water to rake my hair backward. There's something so therapeutic about him doing it, too. His fingers begin to massage my scalp as my eyelids fall close.

I don't deserve Nick Beckett, but I'll be damned if I lose him now that I have him.

Chapter 25

Nick

I watch as Luna scrambles around the room, getting dressed for her dance class. Last night was unlike anything I've ever experienced. A big part of me just wants to grab her and hold her hostage in this bed. But I know how important dance is for her, so I don't. Instead, I gawk at her as she pulls on her leotard.

She pulls her arms through the straps, then pulls on a pair of pink sweats. "How long is your class?"

"I don't know. I really fucked up yesterday, so she's making me come in today as a punishment. Which I don't mind. I should've been focused yesterday."

"What was on your mind?"

She has a look in her eye, like I should already know. "Honestly? You." She walks back to the bed and sits down next to me. "I hated how I ended things the night before. I thought I was doing what was right, though."

I cup her face. "Why does doing what's right always come at the expense of your happiness?" She just shrugs. "Not with me, okay? As long as you'll let me, I'll make sure your happiness always comes first."

A small smile grows on her face before she leans in and lands a kiss on my lips. I pull her down on the bed before she can get up again and deepen the kiss. I want to stay like this all day. I just got her. It feels like if I let her go, she'll tell herself how bad of an idea this is and then break it off again.

But I pull back and stare into her eyes. They sparkle with happiness. Something I haven't seen in her eyes in a while. "You should get going."

She runs her hand through my hair. "What are *you* going to do?"

I look around the room and then back at her. "Stay here. Waiting for you to come home. I'll be your house-wife today." I smile.

"I could be into that. Does that mean you'll cook dinner and clean my house?"

I laugh boisterously. "Hell no. I like you, but I don't like you enough to clean your place. I'll make you dinner, though. Deal?"

She rolls her eyes. "Deal." Then she pushes me off her as she continues getting ready.

She picks her duffle bag off the floor and walks to the door. "I'll text you when I'm heading back." She shouts over her shoulder.

I jump from the bed and follow her to the door, wearing nothing but my briefs. Before she walks out the door, I grab her hand and turn her back to me, giving her one more kiss.

She laughs into my mouth. "Nick, I'm going to be late."

"Okay. Go." Then she's gone.

Fuck, I miss her already.

It's been four hours since Luna left, and I'm bored out of my mind. I've been flipping through Netflix trying to find something to watch, but nothing looks appealing. I don't know when Luna's supposed to get home, but she's been gone forever.

I pull out my phone to shoot her a text.

Luna J <3

When do you think you'll be home?

I miss you.

There's no reply so I text her again. I know she's probably dancing, but it doesn't make me feel any better. So, the only logical thing to do is blow up her phone.

Luna J <3

I'm lonely

like really lonely

I ransacked your kitchen there's nothing here to eat

How do you survive with no food?

it's fine I ordered you groceries

you can thank me later ;)

no seriously, when are you coming home I need you in my arms like yesterday :(

omg! you're going to get me in trouble

Shut up already!

I'll be back in about 20 mins

she's just giving me my critiques now stop

being so clingy

Me, clingy? For her? Yeah, the fuck I am. I want all of her time and her attention. Clearly, I'm down bad for this girl. I don't care who knows either.

Luna J <3

well, I'll stop now that you answered

see you soon lunar moon <3

I don't like that one bit

see you soon

I throw my phone on the sofa beside me and walk to the kitchen. I told her I would have dinner ready for her when she got home, but I have no idea what I should cook. I'm not entirely sure what she likes. Especially with her being a dancer, I'm sure she only eats certain things. Not that it matters. That girl could eat all of McDonald's and still have a sexy ass body.

I open the newly stocked fridge, smiling to myself. I'm sure she had to have starved herself because there was literally no food in this fridge when I looked in here. So how did she eat? What did she eat?

I decide to make her my mom's famous chicken Parmesan.

Thirty minutes later, as I'm putting the chicken in the oven, the door opens. It's about damn time.

"Mm, something smells really good." Luna moans, walking into the kitchen, setting her bag down by the trash can.

"Yeah? It should be done soon." I lean in to kiss her as she wraps her hands around my neck. This girl was literally made for me. We fit together like two puzzle pieces. She's not that much shorter than me. She's probably five-foot-eight, while I'm six-foot-three. My perfect size.

She breaks the kiss but stays in my arms. "Now what's this I hear you buying groceries for me."

"Yeah, about that. We need to talk." I push her far enough for her to see my disappointment. "What the hell have you been eating? Your fridge is always empty. The first time I ever came over here, there was nothing in there. Today, there was nothing in there either. So, what do you eat?" Her arms fall to her side, and she takes another step back.

"To be completely honest, I rarely eat when I'm home. I'm either too tired or too busy studying. I rarely have time to eat."

"Unacceptable, Luna. From this day forward, you won't miss another meal. Understand?"

"You do realize you're not my boss, right? You're my boyfriend, not my father," she says, rolling her eyes in annoyance.

I should have a smart comeback, but all I hear is that I'm her boyfriend. So right now, I have this big, cheeky grin on my face.

"Why are you looking at me like that?" she asks, furrowing her eyebrows.

"I'm your boyfriend?"

She scoffs, but I see the smile she's trying to hide. "I thought you said there would be no question about what we were after last night."

"Yeah, I know that. I just thought you would put up more of a fight." I shrug.

Her eyes fall to the ground as regret clouds her face "Nick, I'm sorry. I've made this complicated, and I didn't mean to. I really do like you. I just-"

"Think of your family first." I finish her sentence for her. She nods her head in agreement, even though I know I'm right. "It's fine." I pull her into my chest. "I have you now. I don't really care how we got here, just as long as we stay."

That beautiful smile I love grows back on her face. A timer goes off on my phone, which makes both of us jump. I pull back and grab the oven mitt off the counter before pulling the chicken Parmesan out of the oven. I already cooked the spaghetti, so I just need to let the chicken cool down a little before serving it to her.

"Okay, give that a couple of minutes, and then we can eat."

"Nick, that smells amazing. I didn't know you could cook."

"You never asked." I shrug, and she pushes me in the chest.

She leans down to grab her bag off the ground. "I'm going to get washed up, and then we can eat." I nod, and she runs to her room.

It feels like we've done this a million times. You would think this was our normal routine because of the way we're acting. I wouldn't mind doing this forever with her.

Am I crazy? Thinking about the future already. I mean, we've been officially dating for less than twenty-four hours. I'd say it's too soon to plan a future with her, but honestly, I couldn't see myself with anyone else but her. She's the only person who makes me feel this way.

I shake my head at the thought and start to make our plates.

As I'm setting the plates on the island bar, my phone starts ringing.

I look to see who it is, and Overstead Nursing Home is flashing across the screen. I quickly hit answer and hit the speaker button.

"Hello?"

"Mr. Beckett?"

"Speaking. Is everything okay? Is my mom lucid?" I went to see her last weekend by myself, and she thought I was my dad. I didn't mind it, but I haven't spoken to her since. I planned on going back up there with Luna this weekend. I saw how much my mom really liked her.

I think she would probably like to know I'm finally dating. Something she doesn't have to worry about is me ending up single and alone. I have Luna now. My mom is going to be so happy.

"No, I-I really don't want to do this over the phone. Do you think you could come to the nursing home?" My heart leaps into my throat. The way she phrased that has me panicking.

Before I speak, Luna walks into the room with a confused look on her face. "What's wrong?" she whispers, pulling her shirt over her stomach.

"Mr. Beckett, are you still there?" the lady on the phone asks, snapping my attention back to the phone.

"Ca-Can you j-just..." I couldn't get the words out. You know those moments when you know exactly what's about to happen without actually knowing. That's what this feels like.

Luna steps beside me and wraps her hands around my bicep, trying to comfort me. I clear my throat, bracing myself. "Can you just tell me now?"

"Mr. Beckett, I'm sorry to inform you that last night your mother went into cardiac arrest. Someone contacted your father, and he was here with her the whole time. We really thought she was fine, but then she had a stroke today. The-They did everything they could. I'm so sorry for your loss."

My legs completely give out, but Luna catches me before I hit the ground.

"Babe!" She slowly lowers me to the ground, wrapping her arms around me. "I'm here. I'm right here," she says, stroking my back.

Despite the fact that Luna is holding me, none of this felt real. My mind couldn't make sense of what the nurse said. It's as though I hear it, but it was something I heard on TV rather than something I am experiencing. It can't be real. I had seen her just last weekend. She was perfectly healthy. She's now, what, gone?

The news hit like a tidal wave, and everything around me blurs into nothing. Numbness envelopes me as the words "your mother" and "stroke" echo in my head. Reality fractures, and I'm lost in a space where time loses its meaning. My emotions surge, but I'm trapped in a state of shock, grappling with the cruel truth.

My mom is dead.

Chapter 26

Luna

Nick has been staying at my apartment for the last couple of days. I called his coach yesterday to let him know what happened. He excused him from practice for the remainder of the week. He's been in bed the entire time. He won't eat. He won't shower. He won't even look at me.

I hate how helpless I am. I hate that there is nothing I can do to make him feel better or even just ease his pain. His phone has been ringing non-stop from his dad.

I kneel beside the bed and grab his phone. "Nick, babe. Your dad is calling." He doesn't say anything. He just stares at the wall behind me.

"I'm going to answer it." I expect him to tell me no or to stop me, but he doesn't even flinch.

"Hello?" I answer.

"Oh, um, is this Nick's phone?" A deep, husky voice answers.

"Yes, sorry. This is his girlfriend. He hasn't been answering his phone." Not that I blame him. The last time he answered, it was the worst phone call he ever received.

"I wanted to check in on him. I'm at his house, but there's no one here."

"Oh, right, yeah. He's, um, staying with me. I can text you the address," I offer.

"Perfect. Thank you..." He pauses.

"Oh, sorry, Luna. My name is Luna."

"Okay, Luna. I'll be there soon." Then he hangs up.

I put in Nick's password, 1022. My birthday. And my insides turn to mush. The day Nick told me his password, I just wanted to delete some dumb picture he had of me. We weren't even dating. I should have known then how serious he was about me. I wish we could go back to that day. I hate not seeing him with a smile on his face.

I quickly send my address to his dad. Then I lock his phone and put it back on the charger. I rub Nick's shoulder as I sit on the edge of the bed. "Your dad is on his way." Once again, he doesn't even flinch.

It breaks my heart to see him like this. Since he got that phone call, he hasn't even cried. Not once. I expect him to cry considering how close he was to his mom, but he hasn't. I'm not sure if it's shock or if he's just numb, but he has shown no emotion besides what he is right now. It's like his whole life came to a halt.

I plant a kiss on his forehead and rest mine against him. "Tell me what to do." My voice cracks. "I hate seeing you like this. Please j-just tell me what you need."

Then there's a knock on my door. I quickly wipe my eyes and run to open it. I open it to see a man who looks almost identical to Nick standing there. "How did you get in?"

"Oh, someone at the front desk let me up. I guess Nick is popular around here. I just told them I was here to see him." He laughs humorlessly.

He has bags under his eyes, as if he hasn't slept for weeks. His salt and pepper hair is disheveled, and he's wearing a suit that looks worn out, like he's been wearing this suit for days. He probably has. I remember the nursing home telling Nick his dad came to see his mom right before she died.

That will always feel weird to say aloud.

"Sorry, please come in." I open the door wider as he steps in.

"Where is he?"

I point toward my room and lead the way. I open the door to my room and see that Nick still hasn't moved. My heart tightens, and I push back the tears that threaten to break free. Seeing him this broken does nothing but rip me apart.

"Nick?" He sits on the bed next to him. "I'm sorry, son. You should've been there. Everything just happened so fast. I had no time to react or to even call you. That's on me, son. I know, and nothing I say will make up for you not being able to say goodbye, but you can't... You can't stay like this. I'm worried about you."

Nick doesn't move a muscle, and neither does his dad. His dad looks up at me and back at Nick before standing up.

Is that it? He's just going to give up that fast? He drove all the way out here, only to give up on him when Nick doesn't answer him on the first try. What was the point of driving up here, then?

"No!" I demand, kneeling in front of Nick. I grab his face and turn it toward mine, forcing him to look at me. "You do not get to quit on yourself. Do you hear me? This sucks. I know it does, but please get up, babe. Your mom would want you to keep living your life. She wouldn't want you holed up in this bedroom." I sigh softly. "I don't know when it will get better, but it will. I promise."

My voice cracks again as the tears start to spew down my face. "Please, baby. I need you to get up. I need you to move. For me, can…can you p-please just get up? I hate seeing you like this." I look at his dad as defeat covers his face, but I refuse to give up on Nick. "What if you just take a shower? That's it."

His eyes finally drag to mine. Then my tears break free. He hasn't looked at me in days. Staring into his eyes, I can see the fullness of hurt and depression swimming around.

He slowly pulls the blanket off. "A shower."

"That's it. That's all I want for you." I cry.

He reaches for my face as his thumb brushes my tears away. "Please stop crying," he begs softly.

I grab his hand and smile. I watch as his eyes trail to his father. "Hi, Dad."

"Hey, son. I'll be in the living room waiting on you, Nicholas."

"Dad!" Nick yells.

His dad leaves the room, shaking his head. My attention is back on Nick sitting in front of me. I still see how broken he is, but he's sitting up now, and that's something.

"Let's shower, yeah?" I rub my palms along his thighs.

He nods, "Okay." I stand up and hold out my hand. He grabs it, and we walk into the bathroom.

Slowly, I start to help him out of his clothes. "Luna," he says, stopping my hands when I reach for his waistband. "I'm not in the mood for anything more."

"I know. Trust me. I just want to shower with you. That's it. I promise." He nods his head, and I continue to help him out of his clothes.

I turn the knob to turn the water on as warm as I can get it. Then I watch as he steps in, letting the water cascade down his body. After undressing, I step in behind him. As I run my hand up his back, his shoulder starts to shake.

"Nick?" I twist his body around, and he's crying. "Babe?"

"Sh-she's re-really go-gone," he cries out.

I pull his head down to my shoulder. "I know. I'm so sorry. I know that does nothing for your pain, but I'm here for you. We'll get through it. I promise."

We fall down in the shower until we're on our knees. I hold him in my arms as he cries. He finally broke, and it was good. It's what needed to happen. I need him to feel his feelings. It's the only way he'll be able to move forward. Not move on because that will never happen. The pain of her death will always hold a place in his heart, but hopefully, with time, it'll be easier to bear.

When we finish our shower, we walk into the living room with his dad.

"Nick, how are you?" He holds his hands up before Nick can answer. "Don't answer that. I know how you are. I should have called you. I should have told you to come down with me. I'm sorry."

"It's not your fault, Dad," Nick responds.

"It is. I should have called. You needed to say goodbye to her. I'm sorry I took that from you."

"Don't. I promise, I don't blame you." Then Nick hugs his dad.

"Nick, I understand you're in pain, but think of it this way. She's not in pain anymore. She's not hurting, and she's happy again. She will always be with you. Always." Nick sniffs. "You can't stop living your life, son. That's not what she would want."

"I know." Nick mumbles.

"Why don't I order us food?" They both give me a nod, and I order a large pizza.

Nick's dad has been staying at a hotel down the street from my apartment for the past couple of days. I've told him he could stay here, but he says he doesn't want to intrude. Not that he was. I think having him here is good for Nick.

He's starting to eat again. It's not a full meal, but he's getting food in his stomach, and I call that another win. He's also been crying at night. Every tear he sheds feels like a shank in my heart. I know it's good for him, but it hurts to see him this sad.

There's a soft knock on the door. I open it to see Nick's dad standing there. "Mr. Beckett, please come in."

"Please, Luna. Call me Evan." He hands me a white bag. "This was on your doorstep."

"Oh yeah. I ordered food for us. If I had known you were-"

He shakes his head. "Don't worry. I ate before coming over." He looks around the living room before shifting his attention back to me. "Also, I want to say thank you."

My brows furrow. "For what?" I walk into the kitchen and start to lay out the food on the island.

"Being here for my son. You let me into your home this past week. I know it's a lot, and you didn't sign up for this. My son is really lucky to have you." He smiles sympathetically.

"I'm really lucky to have your son, Mr. Be-" He scowls. "Evan. Sorry." I grin. "He means the world to me. He's been there for me through a lot of crap, and we weren't even dating."

As if he heard us talking about him, Nick walks into the kitchen with us. "Hey, babe," I say softly. "I ordered us food if you're hungry."

"Sure. Hey, Dad."

"Hey, how are you feeling today?" he asks, rubbing Nick's shoulder.

"A little better, I guess." His eyes are puffy and red, as if he just finished crying.

"There's actually something I wanted to talk to you about." He pauses. "The funeral."

Nick's eyebrows shoot to his hairline. "Funeral?"

"Yeah, this weekend. I've already ordered a casket. It'll be beautiful. I wanted to know if you could give the eulogy."

"Dad I-I don't know. I can't."

"He'll do it." I interrupt. Nick gives me this look, holding me with his glare, like I'm overstepping. But I ignore it. "He'll be ready by Saturday. I'll make sure he's ready."

Evan blows out a breath. "Okay, well, it looks like you both need to talk. So, I'll be at my hotel when you're finished."

"Bye, Evan," I say sweetly as I walk him out.

When I close the door behind him, I turn around to see Nick standing right behind me with his arms crossed over his chest. "What the hell was that?" he yells.

"Nick, you need to do this."

"You don't know what the hell I need, Luna. So mind your own goddamn business." He turns away, but I grab onto his elbow, pulling him back to me.

"No. You're right. I don't know what you need because you won't tell me. But what I do know is that you'll regret not doing this, Nick." I grab his face, so he's looking me right in the eyes. "I'm going to be there the entire time. Okay? You didn't get to say goodbye. I know that's what hurts the most right now. You need to say goodbye. Please?"

His eyes water again, and I wrap my arms around his neck and pull him to my chest. He thought he had a while with his mom. Her death was so sudden that it made everything else around him fall into a muffled silence. He needs to push play on his life, and this funeral will do that for him.

"I don't know if I can keep going." He cries into my neck, and a part of me breaks.

"Don't speak like that, Nick. Please." I beg, "You'll get through this. This pain. It's not forever. You have to find something to hold on to. Everyday. Find something new that makes you want to get out of bed. That's what's going to get you through this."

I rub his back as he cries in my arms. There's no pain like seeing the person I care about the most hurt and not being able to do anything to ease it. I didn't want him to give up. I need him to keep pushing. Selfishly, I want him to use me as his anchor. Use me as the reason to get up every single day. Because he became mine. After losing Gia, Dean, and Paris, I felt like I had no one. Then he came into my life and gave me a love I'd never felt before.

If I lost Nick, I wouldn't make it. The only word I can use to describe it is love.

Fuck. I love Nick Beckett.

Chapter 27

Nick

I'm in the bathroom fixing the tie on my suit, or at least attempting to. My hands keep shaking, and I can't seem to make them stop. In two hours, I'll be saying goodbye to my mom for the last time. There isn't enough time in the world to prepare me for this. Mentally, I know she's gone, and I understand it, but every fiber in my body is telling me she's waiting for me at Overstead to come visit her. Which just makes this that much harder.

I hear a click on the door from the bedroom. When I look into the mirror, I see Luna. She has her hair down today, wearing a flowy black off-the-shoulder dress. She looks stunning; she always does.

Luna has truly been my rock this past week, and I'll forever be grateful for her, but I feel like I'm dragging her down. I've been depressed and stuck in bed for the better part of the week, and she never once complained. She's been home with me every day, so I know she's missed her dance classes.

One thing I've always promised her is that I would never make her choose me over dancing. Then I go and do exactly that. Her showcase is in a couple of weeks. Her entire focus should be on that, not me, but here she is again focusing on me.

It seems like every time we give each other a chance, there's something new that's keeping us apart. Maybe it's the universe's way of telling us we shouldn't be together. Maybe this time I should actually listen.

"Need help?" she asks as she turns me to her and starts to fix my tie. I drop my arms to my sides as I watch her brown eyes glisten from the bright lights in the bathroom. She doesn't have any makeup on today, not that she ever needs it. Luna has always been naturally beautiful.

"There. All done." She pats me one last time and looks me up and down.

"Luna." She gazes up at me and completely takes my breath away. She's so beautiful. I reach for her face and sink my lips into hers.

I haven't kissed her in what feels like forever. This one is different, though. Every time we kiss, it takes on a whole new meaning. This one was filled with longing. I've missed touching her. I've missed holding her in my arms. But she was a beautiful butterfly that needed to spread her wings, and I was the needle pinning her from doing so.

Losing my mother took a toll on me that I didn't see coming. I knew I would be crushed when I ultimately lost her, but so soon. It was unexpected, and I was nowhere near prepared. Every day, I struggle to find a reason to get out of bed. I miss my mom so much that it physically hurts. I'm doing my best to keep my head above the rising water because I know that's what my mom would want, but I can't do that with Luna.

I break the kiss, and she takes a deep breath. "I've missed-"

"I think we should break up." I pant, cutting her words off.

Tears spring into her eyes. "What the hell did you just say?"

"Luna, this isn't working. I'm sorry." Then I push past her as I walk downstairs. It feels like I left my heart in that bathroom, because I did. But I did what was right. She needs to focus on dance. I don't know what I'm doing or what tomorrow even holds, but I know I can't drag her into the unknown. Staying with her is too much work right now. I feel like I have to keep her happy, and I'm doing a shitty job at it right now. How can I make someone else happy when I don't even know how to be happy myself?

I want her more than anything, but I can't have her right now. It's not fair to her or me.

I walk outside to get in my car.

"Nicholas Beckett!" My head swivels around to see an angry Luna running down the steps.

"Luna-" She pushes me in the chest, hitting my back into the car.

"No! Shut up! I'm talking." I close my mouth. "*You* fought tooth and nail to date me. *You* told me to give us a try. *You* told me this was worth it. *You* did. I told you to leave *me* alone. I told you I didn't want a relationship, but you wouldn't listen. Now you want to break up?" She sobs. "No, fuck that! You are not breaking up with me! Do you hear me?" She takes a step toward me. "I fought so hard not to like you. Now I love you. I can't lose you, nor do I want to. This, us." Running her hands up my chest until she cups my face, she says, "That's all I want. *You're* all I want. I don't want to lose you, Nick. So please, don't leave me. Please don't give up on us. Please!" she pleads as her tears fall.

She *loves* me. It doesn't matter right now. I'm doing this *for* her. "Luna, I can't be with you right now. Everything in me hurts. How can I be with you like this? I'm just holding you back." I sigh. "Dammit Luna, you're supposed to be practicing for your winter showcase, but you're too busy worrying about me. I can't do that to you. I know how important that showcase is to you."

"You're not holding me back, babe. I promise. Madam Christine knows. She understands. I'll be back next week." She glides her hands across my cheeks, a warmth worms its way through my chest. "You're going through something unimaginable. If you thought I would just leave you to go through that by yourself, then you're absolutely insane. You mean the world to me. I can't lose you, Nick. Do you understand me? I *cannot* lose you." Her voice cracks.

I pull her into my chest and wrap my arms around her. What am I supposed to do when she looks at me like that? Her eyes are all puffy and filled with love. No one has ever looked at me the way Luna does. "I can't lose you either. I'm sorry." I'd be stupid to let her go, I know.

"Then don't pull this bullshit again. Or I *will* murder you." She cries into my chest.

My chest rumbles with laughter for the first time in a while. She pulls back and wipes her eyes. "Come on. We have to go say goodbye to your mom."

When we arrive at the cemetery, I see the entire hockey team here. Including Coach. I look down at Luna, and she smiles.

"I figured it takes a village. They all wanted to be here for you." She squeezes my hand twice before she pulls me toward the coffin. My dad decided to make it a close casket. Something I'm grateful for. I don't know if I could see her there and not completely lose it.

Coach pats me on the shoulder as I walk past him and stand in the front row. Luna is still holding my hand, and she's probably in pain from how tight my grip is. Holding her hand is the only thing keeping me standing.

"Thank you all for coming," my dad starts. "I, um, I never thought this day would come. I used to tell my wife she was immortal. I think I told her that because I wanted to believe it." He sniffles. "My wife made my world turn. She was everything I've ever wanted and needed. I will never love someone as much as I love her—besides my son, that is." He glances at me. "He is our greatest accomplishment." A soft smile touches his face.

"I could stand here and tell you how wonderful my wife was or how everyone she met loved her. But I'm sure you already know that. Instead, I'll tell you how she lived. She lived every day like it was her last. Even when she was sick, she never stopped smiling. She constantly told me about adventures she still wanted to take together. Or how she gambled the nurses for a month's supply of German chocolate cake." Everyone laughs lightly. "She was the most beautiful woman I have ever met, and I'll miss her for the rest of my life." He looks down at the coffin. "I love you, Jenna. I'll see you later."

He clears his throat. "Now, my son has prepared a few words. Nick."

Luna squeezes my hands one last time before letting them go.

I walk to where my dad was standing and pull the paper out of my jacket pocket. I clear my throat before speaking. "I, um, I don't even know where to begin. I was put in charge of writing my mom's eulogy, but I didn't know where to start." I look down at my mom's casket as my emotions start to overwhelm me. "I kn-knew she was si-sick and I, um, couldn't bring myself to wrap my head around it. No matter how many times I we-went to see her, she was fine in my eyes."

I swallow the thick lump growing in my throat. "Words can't describe how much my mother means to me. She's the reason I started playing hockey. She took me to my first game when I was a kid. I never knew I would love something as much as I love hockey, and it was because of her that I found it. I owe my mom the world." I take another breath. "I didn't get to say goodbye to her before she died. I had planned on going to see her this weekend. To tell her, I finally tricked Luna into dating me."

Everyone laughs again. "I wanted to tell her I finally found someone to put up with my bullshit. There was now someone I loved just as much as I loved her." My eyes connect with Luna's, and they tell me what her words don't.

"Luna was the first person I ever introduced to my mom. She's actually the only person I've ever introduced to her. I think my mom knew before I did that she was going to be the love of my life. My mom knew that Luna was in my life to stay. When she asked her to take care of me, I should've known right then and there what she was doing. Even sick, my mother always liked to play matchmaker."

My eyes find Luna again. "She wanted Luna to stay in my life forever. My mother always knew what was best for me. Something I will always be grateful for. My mom knew what I needed before I ever did. My mom knew that no one on Earth knew me as well as she did, except this girl here. My mom didn't introduce us, but I can almost guarantee she had a hand in us finding each other."

I clear my throat. "I didn't get to say goodbye to my mom. For a while, I thought that was the worst pain imaginable. But then I remembered what my mom would always say. *Don't say goodbye, because that means I'll never see you again. Instead, say, You'll see me later.*" I look at my mom's casket one more time. "So, Mom, I'll see you later. Save me a place in heaven. I love you." I walk to her casket before landing a kiss on the mahogany-glazed wood. Then I stand next to Luna.

She kisses me on the cheek and whispers, "That was beautiful. I love you."

I turn to kiss her forehead. "I love you too."

Was it too fast for me to tell her I loved her? Maybe, but I really don't care. It's the only way I can really express how much I care about this girl. I love her. Through all of this, she has stuck by me. She never pushed me or made me feel bad for feeling like crap Instead, she showed up every day, pushing me further and further into healing.

Luna

"Okay, so what are you thinking for dinner?" Nick asks, setting out a variety of takeout menus.

"Why do you have so many takeout menus?" I question, eyeing each one. I don't think I know anyone under the age of thirty who owns takeout menus.

"Because I like to eat in. You've got a problem with that, Beitar?"

I shake my head. "Not at all. It is weird, though."

It's been a few weeks since his mom's funeral, and every day his smile has grown. I know it'll be awhile before he can smile without thinking about it, but every day is a step in the right direction. Some days are better than others.

He did start going back to practice a week after the funeral. So, that's good. I also went back to dance classes. Madam Christine was understanding of the situation, but I had to be in the studio every single day to make up for lost time. Four hours, seven days a week. It was hell, but now I'm all caught up, and we're back to normal scheduling. This is perfect timing because finals are coming up and I need to study. The weekend after the finals is our showcase.

Nope, I'm not stressed at all.

"Can we just get burgers?" I ask while pouting.

"Sure. Do you want fries with that?" He pulls out his phone and starts typing in our order on an app. Why did he pull out these takeout menus if he wasn't going to use them?

"No. I can't put on weight before the showcase." I rub my stomach, thinking about how I'm going to regret eating this burger. He looks at my stomach and then at my face with a look of annoyance. "What?"

"There's no way you'll gain weight, Luna. Even if you did, you'll still look hot as fuck."

"It's not about looking hot, Nick. It's about not weighing the same amount as an elephant. My partner needs to be able to lift me in the air," I explain.

"Okay, first off, eating one hamburger will not cause you to gain three hundred pounds. Second, if your partner can't lift your light ass, you need a new partner."

I laugh.

"I'm ordering you fries. End of discussion." He says it with finality.

I don't say anything else as he orders the food.

"How long till it gets here?" I ask.

He looks down at his phone before tossing it back on the counter. "Forty-five minutes. Which is enough time."

"Enough time for wh-" His lips are on mine before I can finish the question.

"God, I've missed kissing you," he says against my lips.

I've missed it too. A wave of emotions surge within me. As we kissed, the air cackles with the electricity of anticipation. His touch was so familiar and yet so foreign. This wasn't just a kiss; it's like something inside of him has finally reignited. I cling to his shirt and mold my body against his. His body heat sends a shiver up my spine.

His grip on my face tightens, and I moan into his mouth. He lifts me by the waist and sets me onto the island, stepping in between my legs. My hands roam over his body as if it's the first time I've ever touched him. I try to memorize every muscle and every vein. I feel his hands journey up my thighs and around my waist, leaving a fiery pulse in their wake.

I start to rock into his touch as my body feels this sudden urgency and need to have him. He steps back, breaking the kiss, and he unbuttons my pants and slowly pulls the zipper down while keeping his dark green eyes trained on mine. Before, you would have been able to see the golden hue in his eyes. But right now, all I see is the dark green.

I want him to move faster, but he won't. My need for him was only getting stronger. Grabbing him by his shirt, I pull his lips back to mine. As my tongue invades his mouth, we're both fighting for dominance.

His hand finds my neck as he pushes me away. "Tsk. Tsk. Tsk. Someone's needy."

A moan escapes my lips as I try to bring my face back to his, but his hand is firm. "I want to take my time. Enjoy every last minute of this," he says as his hand dips into my jeans and finds my swollen clit.

"Fuck." I whimper. His hand tightens, just a fraction, around my throat. I feel my eyes roll to the back of my head as the air supply slowly drains from my body.

His fingers start to move up and down as I start to create a rhythm with his body. Then he sinks two fingers inside my entrance as his groan fills the space. "You're always so ready for me, aren't you?"

It's been so long since I've had him touch me that my body is on fire. My hand wraps around his wrist as I ride his fingers. Our eyes locked on one another neither one of us looking away.

"Nick, don't stop." I cry out.

"I love it when you call out my name," he whispers into my ears as his beard scratches against my cheeks. He kisses my neck and starts to pick up his pace, and I try to stifle my screams, but I can't. His neighbors are going to hate me, but I really don't care.

I drag my hands into his hair and grip onto him for dear life. His thumb starts to draw circles on my pulsing clit, and it takes everything in me not to lose it.

His thrust grows faster and harder until I completely combust under him. Before I have time to come down from my high, Nick rips off my pants and tosses them to the side.

"You seriously have *got* to stop destroying my clothes," I complain.

"Stop wearing clothes, then."

The reply gets caught in my throat as he pulls his pants down and his dick bobs free.

Pushing my chest down until I'm lying flat across the kitchen island, Nick grabs my leg and wraps it around his waist. I gasp loudly as he inserts himself into my wanting pussy. His thick length inside me causes me to jerk in pain. It hurts, but it feels too good to make him pull out. He doesn't move while he gives me time to adjust to him.

I slowly start to rock back and forth against him, signaling for him to move. My hands tighten around the edge of the counter as he starts to thrust in and out of me.

I feel so filled with him inside of me. My skin is crawling with pleasure as I moan out his name over and over again. I lean up on my arms as I meet him with each thrust. He wraps his hands around my breasts and pulls them into his mouth, sucking on them like they're his last meal. The pleasure is too much. The kitchen fills with the sounds of our bodies slapping together.

My stomach tightens, but I push back the release until I know he's ready. I don't want to finish unless I finish with him.

He pulls completely out before pulling me off the counter and turning me around until I'm face down on the surface. He kicks my legs apart and thrusts himself roughly inside of me. "Fuck!" I cry. The pressure builds in between my legs as he continues to work himself in and out of me.

He leans down and picks up my leg before resting on the island, repeating the same movement with my other leg until I'm spread eagle. I was resting on my stomach, holding myself up with my forearms. It wasn't very comfortable, but the way Nick is fucking me right now, I didn't mind it.

With this position, he's able to go so much deeper. My toes curl with each thrust. "Nick, I-I can't hold it in. Please." I beg.

I start to bounce backward as he continues to pound into me. His thrust becomes faster, and I release myself as euphoria blinds me. Nick is right behind me as his deep groan fills the air. We're a hot, sweaty mess as he slumps over and rests his head on my spine.

There's a knock on the door, and we both snap our heads to it.

We both look at each other and back at the door. "So, who's getting that?" We both laugh.

Chapter 29

Luna

I've been in the library every day this week. If I'm not at the dance studio or class, I'm here. I rented out a study room for the next two hours. I'm not really worried about my finals, considering I have a 4.0 GPA, but I still wanted to study to make sure I keep that 4.0.

My phone buzzes in my pocket. I pull it out to see if it's a missed text from Nick. Is it weird? I was kind of hoping it was Gia or Dean. I still haven't spoken to them in over a month. I want to move past everything, but they haven't reached out. I could easily text them first, but it's not my responsibility to fix everything. I didn't fuck up; they did. At least that's what Nick reminds me of every time I think about calling or texting one of them.

I've become so dependent on Nick lately. I turn to him when I'm stressed or when I'm feeling anxious about something. He always knows exactly what to say. I had to talk to Katherine and ask if this was healthy behavior. She did tell me I could lean on Nick if I needed to, but I also need to learn how to do it on my own. She doesn't want me to become too dependent on him, so I look to him for all of my answers. But isn't that what she does for me?

Anyway, I know she's right, though. I can't look to Nick to solve all of my problems. No matter how badly I wanted him to.

I unlock my phone to respond to Nick.

My Headache <3

Where are you?

library

why?

what room number?

317?

He doesn't text back, so I shove the phone back into my pocket. I continue to write notes for my Gender

Studies course. This is probably one of the easiest A's I've ever gotten. The professor doesn't really give exams throughout the term. She mainly gave us writing assignments and then one overall exam at the end of the term. This exam is worth thirty percent of my grade, but I wasn't worried. Everything we learn in this course is pretty simple. I'm just using this study time as a refresher.

As I turn the page in my book, the door to the study room opens. Without taking my eyes off the book, I ask, "Can you not read? The sign clearly says in use. Please get out."

"What if I don't want to?" That raspy voice is all too familiar. I look up to see Nick standing in the doorway with his arms crossed over his chest.

A smile grows on my face. "Sorry, I didn't know it was you."

"How would you, if you keep your nose in your book?" he asks rhetorically. "How long do you have the room for?"

"Two more hours." I answer, and he checks his watch before sitting right next to me, throwing his bag on the ground.

"Cool, I don't have practice till later, so I *guess* I can spend some time with you." He shrugs nonchalantly.

"You *guess*? You don't have to. You can walk your ass right back out the same way you came in." I point my pen at the door.

He leans in and kisses my cheek, causing me to blush. "I'm just kidding, babe. I've been looking for you everywhere. I even went by your apartment."

I scrunch my eyebrows. "How did you get in without a fob?"

He pulls out a fob card from his back pocket. "I had the front desk make one. I told them you were my girlfriend, and you requested it."

I raise a brow. "And they just believed you?"

"I'm Nick Beckett. All I have to do is show this pretty smile, and they'll be putty in my hands."

I roll my eyes and return to writing my notes.

The last thing I need to do is boost this man's ego. It's big enough for the both of us.

He spreads his arms out in front of him and rests his head on his biceps as he stares at me. Even though his gaze was quite literally causing me to overheat, I continue to focus on my notes.

"You know you're truly stunning," he says randomly. "From your golden-brown eyes to your beautiful curly hair, which I wish you would wear down more often, by the way. To how beautiful your skin glows under this ugly ass fluorescent lighting."

I snort. Oh god, I just fucking snorted.

"Even your snorts are cute," he adds.

"Nick, shut up or get out. I'm trying to study." I try to say it as seriously as possible, but I can't seem to wipe the grin from my face.

"I'm sorry. I just wanted you to know how lucky I am to be dating you." When I turn my gaze to him, his eyes soften, filled with love and awe. Not with lust, but with genuine love. No one has ever looked at me the way Nick is looking at me right now.

I throw my pen down, grab him by the strings on his hoodie, and pull him in for a kiss. He instantly kisses me back with languid fervor and want. I break the kiss before it goes any further. "I love you too." He smiles and returns to laying on his arm and staring at me.

I'm down to my last hour in the study room, and I've retreated to lying on the floor. I got too uncomfortable in the chairs and needed to spread my legs. So, I'm currently lying underneath a table, writing notes on gender mainstreaming.

Nick went to get food for us because I hadn't eaten all day. According to him, that's a crime worthy of prison time. His words, not mine.

The door opens and closes. "Luna?" he calls out as if this room wasn't a square box.

"I'm down here."

He kneels down and laughs.

"Why the hell are you on the floor?" he asks.

"I got uncomfortable. Did you bring food?" He hands me a bag of Panda Express. "God, I love you so much!"

"I love you, too!" he replies.

I look up at him. "Oh, I was talking to Panda, not you." Then a frown clouds his face. "But I do love you." He shakes his head and laughs.

Nick lays down next to me and opens his mouth. I chuck a piece of orange chicken in, and a smile grows wider on his face.

"What are you studying?" he asks while chewing.

I run my hand through my hair, which I took down thirty minutes into Nick arriving. *The things I do to make him happy.* "Gender studies. I'm not gonna lie; this section is hurting my brain."

I've been studying the same course for the past two hours, and it's starting to actually hurt. I know I said it was easy, but I swear I don't remember her teaching some of this.

"So, take a break." He closes the book in front of me and pulls it toward his body.

"Okay." I return to eating the orange chicken.

It's weird. I've never felt so comfortable with someone as I do with Nick. The way he takes care of me and puts me first will never get old. I want to stay like this for as long as I can. Just Nick and me and no one else.

"What are you thinking about?" Nick asks, bringing me out of my thoughts.

I shake my head. "Nothing."

He pulls the carton of chicken out of my hands and sets it a safe distance away from me. Before I can complain, he crawls over to me and pushes me onto my back. He towers over me, resting his palms on either side of my head. It feels like we're recreating that one *Spider-Man* scene where he kisses Mary Jane upside down.

"What are you doing?" I gulp.

He doesn't answer. He just stares at me. The golden hue in his eyes sparkles a little brighter today. It looks like sunflowers bloomed in the tall field of grass. It just makes him that much hotter. I've always found his dark green eyes sexy, but when the golden flecks shine, ugh. I'm ruined.

"What?" My voice is barely above a whisper. He's looking at me like I'm the most beautiful thing on Earth. It's making me anxious; he's just staring at me.

Before I could ask again, he leans down and kisses me. I run my hands up his face and wrap them around his neck before pulling him lower. His palm reaches under my chin as he deepens the kiss, gliding his tongue into my mouth.

I don't have time to pull him closer as he breaks the kiss. "Sorry, I just needed a reminder that you were really mine," he finally says.

I shake my head as my chest quakes with laughter." You know, you've kind of ruined other men for me."

His brows furrow. "What makes you think there are other guys for you, Luna James?"

"Are you it for me then, Beckett?"

"Yeah, I am." He kisses my nose softly before my phone starts ringing.

Nick looks at it and then hands it to me. "It's your mom," he murmurs.

Even though he's been getting through his mom's death, it's still hard for him to think about. I never really talk about my parents in general, but I make sure to not bring up my mom around him. At least not yet. I want to give him time to really mourn his mother.

I quickly hit answer. "Hello?"

"Luna, honey, I haven't heard from you in forever." I haven't heard from them either. The phone works both ways. Although I haven't put in any effort to reach out to them, especially since neither one of them even wished me a happy birthday,. Even though there was nothing happy about it.

"I've been busy with dance and school." I lie, which isn't really that big of a lie because I have been busy with dance and school.

"I understand. I know the showcase is soon, and I know how busy it gets around this time of the year. I just wish you could make more of an effort to call home often." I roll my eyes. "I also wanted you to come home for dinner tomorrow. Can you make it?"

"Will Dean be there?" It was a stupid question to ask, but of course Dean would be there.

"Yes. He said he was bringing someone home. Do you know who?"

My heart leaps out of my chest. He wouldn't bring Gia, right? He's not that dense. Neither of them has made the effort to try and fix things with me, but they can flaunt their relationship in front of our parents.

I look at Nick, and I know I'm going to regret this. But fuck it. "I'm bringing someone too."

"Oh really? You're finally dating someone?" I try to ignore the stab. I can hear her running to tell my dad. "Honey, your daughter's finally got a boyfriend, and she's bringing him home! So, prepare an extra seat for him."

Nick gives me this weird look. He mouths, "*What happened*?"

I just shake my head. "Mom, I have to go. I'm kind of studying for finals."

"Oh, yes, right. Okay, well, I'll see you tomorrow, Luna," she says sweetly. "I love you."

"I love you too, Mom." Then I hang up with a groan.

"What happened, and why am I going to your parents' house?" Nick asks with cinched brows.

"I'm sorry to drag you into this, but you're the only person who can get me through this dinner."

He gently kisses my forehead. "I'm honored. When is it?"

I grin. "Tomorrow night."

He shakes his head and smiles. "Okay, I'll be ready."

"Nick, thank you so much. I owe you big time."

"Yeah, you do." Then he grips my chin and kisses me hard. "I have a few ideas, too."

I'm going to regret this dinner, I can already tell.

Chapter 30

Nick

I hold Luna's hand as we pull into her parents driveway. She's been a nervous wreck all night while preparing for this dinner. She told me today that Dean's going to be there with Gia, and that's why she invited me. I don't know if I should be offended or not, but she's been there for me since my mom's death, so it's the least I could do for her.

I put the car in park and shut the engine off. "You ready for this?" I ask, turning to look at Luna.

"No. Dean doesn't know about us, and I'm not sure how he'll react," she answers, picking at the hem of her dress.

"Why do you care?" It shouldn't matter what Dean thinks about us. He literally doesn't care how she feels about him dating Gia. So, why should she care what he thinks about us dating?

"Because he's my brother, Nick. I might not like his ass right now, but he's still my brother. Ugh." She grunts. "I just want to move forward and put all of this shit behind us. Please, Nick, can you play nice? Just for tonight."

I roll my eyes. "Fine." I will only play nice if he keeps his mouth shut. He always seems to put Luna down, and she never stands up for herself. So, if she won't, then I will. I lean over and kiss her.

"Best behavior, promise." I hold out my pinky, and she stares at it like it's a fish out of water.

"What am I supposed to do with that?" She huffs.

"This." I grab her hand and wrap her pinky tightly around mine, linking our thumbs together, before dropping my lips on it. "I pinky promise to be on my best behavior."

A smile quickly grows on her face before she returns the same action. She kisses her thumb and says, "There, it's sealed. Meaning you have to keep it."

I kiss her on the lips one more time. "I'll keep my promise." I smile. As I take the keys out of the ignition, I see Dean standing in front of the car with Gia's hands in his.

"What?" Luna asks before turning her attention to Dean. She quickly jumps out of the car. "Dean!"

"Are you fucking kidding me, Luna? You're fucking my captain?" Dean yells.

"Dean wait." Luna whimpers.

"You're such a hypocrite, Luna. You were so pissed at me for sleeping with Gia, but you're literally dating the captain of my hockey team. Are you serious? Come off your damn high horse. You're no better than the rest of us, and I'm tired of you acting like you are." I watch as Luna shrinks in on herself. This is exactly what I mean.

I think I've heard enough. "You need to back the fuck off, Dean."

He takes a step in my direction. "You really want to do this right now?"

"Yeah, I really do," I respond, stepping in front of him until we're nose to nose. "I'm so fucking sick and tired of you treating your sister like shit. She gives up a lot of herself to make sure you're happy. You didn't give a shit about her and started dating her best friend behind her back. You brought her to the hockey game and told me *Luna* needed to leave, not Gia. Then you bring her to your house, holding her hand. Yet *you* feel the need to tell Luna *she's* selfish and in the wrong? You come off *your* damn high horse."

I hear the front door open, and Luna's parents walk out. "What is going on out here?" her mom shouts.

Luna takes a step next to me and presses her palm into my chest. "Nick, just let it go. It's not worth it. Please?"

I grab her hand off my chest and intertwine our fingers. Then I walk to her mom. "Hello, Mrs. Beitar. I'm Nick Beckett. I'm Luna's boyfriend."

She looks just like Luna. Except her eyes are hazel to Luna's light brown. Her brown skin is a little darker than Luna's, too. Her hair is just as curly as Luna's, but it's shorter, reaching her shoulders. They both have that button nose. Something I adore about Luna. "Oh, well, it's very nice to meet you! Please come inside. It's cold out here. Dean. Gia. You both come in too."

I press my palm into Luna's back and let her lead the way in.

When we walk inside, Luna quickly grabs my hand on her back and ushers me into the living room.

"Nick, I love you. You know I do, but we can't do this tonight. Okay, not in front of my parents. So, please, for the life of me, let all of the bullshit go. At least for tonight."

I grab her face and land a quick kiss on her lips. "Just for tonight," I promise, leaning my forehead against hers. She holds onto my wrists, closes her eyes, and takes a deep breath.

"It's going to be a long one." She sighs.

I'm sitting at the dining room table next to Luna, with Dean sitting right in front of me and Gia in front of Luna. I've never felt more uncomfortable. The uncomfortableness was from wanting to really punch the dog shit out of Dean, but I couldn't since I promised Luna I'd be on my best behavior.

I still hadn't met her dad yet. He's been in the kitchen all night, cooking. It's like he's purposefully avoiding everyone. Not that I would blame him. It's a damn shit show out here.

Luna's leg starts to shake anxiously. I rest my palm against her thigh. "Are you okay?"

She shakes her head. "No. I shouldn't have come tonight. I should have made some lame ass excuse for why I couldn't be here."

"No, you shouldn't have. This is your family, too. Not just his," I whisper, then land a kiss on her cheek. I hear Dean scoff under his breath. "Problem?"

Luna squeezes my hand, reminding me of my promise to her. "Nick."

"Luna, can we please talk?" Gia finally speaks up.

"What's there to talk about, Gia?" Luna snips. Now who's not keeping their promise?

"Please? We've been best friends our entire lives. I don't want to throw it away for this. Please?" Gia pleads, resting her arms on the table.

"Don't beg her for her forgiveness, Gia," Dean interjects. "You don't owe her anything."

"Dean, stop it!" Gia slaps Dean in the arm. "Luna, I do owe you an apology. I know I messed up royally. I didn't mean for it to happen; it just did."

"Yet, you felt no need to reach out to me before tonight. You don't want our friendship back. You want to be let off the hook for fucking my brother. I've told you countless times about how I feel about your feelings for Dean. You didn't care, then. Why should you care now, right?"

I've never been so proud of my girl. Fuck, she looks hot standing up for herself.

"So, what's your excuse for fucking Nick?" Dean interjects *again.* "He's my captain, and yet you don't see a problem with that."

"Oh, she did. Actually, that's all she fucking talks about." I defend. "Even after you betrayed her. All she cares about is your fucking feelings!" I promised I wouldn't get in the middle, but he's not going to keep trying to make her feel guilty for something she shouldn't feel guilty about.

"Nick, please," Luna pleads. "Just, don't. It's not worth it, okay?"

I turn my head toward Luna. "What?"

"I can't keep doing this." She looks at Dean and Gia. "You clearly both don't care. I'm tired of fighting. Dean, you're supposed to be my best friend. My *twin*. If you don't understand why this hurts so badly, then I don't know what else there is to say." She looks at Gia. "Gia, you say you're sorry, but you're not. You're only sorry you got caught."

Luna sighs, "Maybe if you had told me this when it first started, I would have had a better reaction, but you didn't give me that option. You hid it from me. You didn't think you could come and tell me. I'm supposed to be your best friend, and you *didn't* tell me. So, yeah. I'm over it and done."

Then she pushes back her chair and stands up. "I can't do this. I can't sit here and pretend nothing happened in front of mom and dad. You might not care, but I do."

Dean exhales. "Luna, I'm sorry."

"It's a little too late for that." She grabs her purse off the back of the chair and walks out of the dining room.

I quickly follow suit. We walk into the kitchen, where I see an older white man cooking. I don't know what I was expecting her father to look like, but white was not it.

"Mom, Dad, I'm going to head out."

Her parents both look at her with hurt in their eyes. "But you haven't even eaten yet."

"Yeah, I'm not really in the mood anymore."

"Why?" her dad pushes.

"Ask Dean." She walks up to her parents and wraps her arms around both of them. "I love you. Also, next time you forget my birthday, you will not be receiving a Christmas present," she adds.

They look at each other in confusion. "Luna, we didn't forget your birthday." Her mom finally says.

"Neither of you called and wished me a happy birthday. So, by definition, that's forgetting my birthday."

"Then, by definition, we didn't forget. We called Dean, and he said he was planning a party for you. You know we can't keep a secret, so we told Dean to tell you Happy Birthday for us." I watch as Luna tenses at the mention of her birthday party. "Also, we sent you a birthday present. Dean said he would give it to you."

"I didn't get anything from Dean." She quickly turns on her heels and walks back into the dining room. "Where is it?" she yells.

"Where's what?" Dean asks, confused.

"My present. Mom said she gave it to you, but you never gave it to *me*. You made me think mom and dad forgot about my birthday. God, who are you? I don't even recognize you anymore. You would never do this to me before..."

"Before what? Go ahead and finish that sentence. Luna, I don't know who *you* are anymore. You used to be my best friend. It was always us against everyone else. You traded me up. Let's be honest, we haven't been close since Cassie died. I'm tired of walking on eggshells around you." Dean pushes his chair back, standing up. "I get it. Cassie was a big part of your life, but you act like she was your only sibling. I was hurting too, but everyone was too busy making sure you were okay to even notice. I had to push all of my feelings down just to make sure you were good.

"Luna, I'm fucking tired of it. I'm tired of pushing my feelings down just to benefit you." He inhales slowly. "You want to know why I didn't tell you about Gia? It's because I wanted her just as badly as she wanted me. But I couldn't tell you that because you would have made it about you. This whole bullshit about she's your best friend and I can't be with her is crap, and you know it."

Dean takes a step towards Luna. "If you took a fraction of the time you put into dancing into actually being my sister, you would have known I've had a thing for Gia since high school."

Luna silently gasps, "What?"

"But of course, I couldn't do shit about it because you always had to make it a point that she's *your* best friend. God, Luna, she's your only friend. You don't make any other friends because you let dancing consume your life. I get that dancing is important to you because of Cassie, but Cassie's gone. We've all moved on. Why can't you?"

Chapter 31

Luna

My heart drops to the floor. I never knew Dean felt this way. I always thought he was just the tougher sibling when it came to dealing with Cassie's death. The only time he cried was when we found out. Instead, he just stood by my side, helping me through it. He never complained, either. He never uttered a single word about how he felt. How was I supposed to know he was hurting?

To add to it, he's had feelings for Gia too. Something he's never mentioned. I've never seen Dean act differently with Gia since we started high school. He never had those long stares. Never talked about her. Nothing.

How would I know about Dean's feelings if he never talked about them? I wouldn't. I can't force him to talk about them either. I'm not that narcissistic that I can't realize when other people are hurting. Dean is just really good at bottling that stuff up.

"Dean, why didn't you say something?" I sob.

"How could I? Anytime someone even mentioned Cassie's name, it brought you to tears. We were constantly coddling your emotions. Ask Mom and Dad, and I bet they'll agree with me. Or maybe they won't because, once again, we have to coddle you." Dean slaps his hands against his thigh in frustration.

"What about Gia? You never said anything about that either."

"Look how you're acting right now! Why the hell would I?"

I scoff. "You still don't get it, do you?"

"Get what?"

"Yes, I'm upset you're dating Gia. But I'm more upset that you kept it from me. That hid something so big from me. You're trying to make me feel guilty about this, but I don't." I glance at Nick and back at Dean. "You want to compare situations, but they are not the same. Nick is your captain. Maybe I should have told you, but we *just* started dating. You've been dating Gia for *months*. Months, Dean." I wipe my tears with the back of my hand. "It killed me to fight against dating

Nick. I kept telling him no because of *you*. Did you once *ever* consider me when you and Gia started dating?"

There's a beat of silence, and no one says anything. "I didn't think so. So, no, Dean. We are not the same. I'm sorry you had feelings for Gia for so long, but *you* decided to keep that to yourself; I didn't. I would have gotten over it. But you didn't think; you just did."

Our parents walk into the dining room, looking more confused than ever. "What's going on?" my mom asks.

No one answers. Dean and I just look at each other in an uncomfortable silence.

I finally say, "I never asked to be coddled."

"What?" Dad glances around the room. "Bean, what are you talking about?"

"I didn't ask to be coddled after Cassie's death. She was my best friend, and yeah, I got depressed, but I didn't ask to be coddled. I also didn't want you all to treat me like breakable glass."

Dean sighs. "You didn't need to. You were so sensitive; it was a natural setting for everyone."

My stomach tightens as I register Dean's words. "How is that my fault? I didn't ask for you to treat me like some sensitive ass child either. You all did that by yourselves."

"Bean, we did it because we love you. You were going to therapy, and we weren't sure what you were capable of," my dad says as he rubs my mom's arms.

"What, like killing myself?" Everyone in the room is silent, including Nick. "I never once thought about that. Maybe if you had just talked to me like a normal fucking human being, you would all know that. I feel like none of you know me. Not really. You all have this image of me inside your heads that I break easily, but I don't. My anxiety does not cripple me. I wish you would all stop acting like it does."

I wipe my face harshly and sniffle. "I'm leaving. When you all are ready to start treating me like the adult I am, let me know."

I brush past Nick and walk out of the house. I hate the way my family sees me. I'll admit, Cassie's death was extremely hard on me, but I *did* move on. Ballet was something we both loved and cherished. I'm keeping her dream alive because it does help me feel connected to her. It's not because I can't let go. I love dancing because it has become my sense of therapy.

Dean has had these feelings for years and has told no one. That's not my fault. I refuse to feel bad about it, either. I love my family, but they can't keep treating me like a kid and expect me to go along with it.

I hear Nick's footsteps finally start to trail behind me. I quickly turn around, grab him by the neck, and slam his lips into mine. He instantly kisses me back with just as much fervor.

Pulling back, I stare into his eyes, catching my breath. "Thank you."

He flashes a smile. "For what?"

"You see me as me. You're honest about everything with me. I know I can always trust you. No scratch that; I know I can trust you with my life. I think that's what attracted me to you. That's a lie; I hated you at first. I *really* hated you." He chuckles. "But you never gave up on me. You kept coming back for more. You've been my best friend and lover. Something I will forever be grateful for."

He wraps his arms around my waist. "You don't need to thank me, Luna Moon."

I roll my eyes. I hate that nickname so much. It's stupid and corny. "Nick, promise this is forever? You and me. Because this is it for me. I don't want to see other men who aren't Nicholas *whateveryourmiddlenameis* Beckett."

He laughs. "I'm not going anywhere. I'm here as long as you'll have me." He quickly pecks my lips. "I love you, Luna James Beitar."

I beam. "So, you're just not gonna tell me your middle name, then?"

"No, I'm not." Then he kisses me again.

I didn't care if I ever spoke to Dean again. Nick is my family now. The one person who has stayed consistent in being there for me. He's never wavered. Nick makes me feel more like myself than any other person ever has. I feel safe when I'm with him. I can always count on him to tell me exactly how he feels. Even when I don't want to hear it.

"Let's get you home," he whispers, breaking the kiss. I nod as he leads us to his car.

The next morning, I wake up in Nick's arms. My face is resting against his solid, warm chest. I've never felt more at peace than I do when I'm in his arms. I lift my head to rest my chin on his pecs.

I rarely get to just stare at Nick. He's always on the move, and I'm always busy. The only time I get to admire him is when I wake up first. His beard is scruffier and desperately in need of a trim. My whole body pulsates at how sexy this man is. How muscular his arms are—I can see his veins if he flexes just the slightest. How dark his brown hair is—it's almost black.

I drag my hands along his sharp jawline, soaking in his beauty.

Nick's eyelashes flutter open and immediately dart to mine. "Why are you staring at me while I'm sleeping, you weirdo?"

"I just wanted to admire the view." I grin.

He shakes his head, laughing. "I'm going to go take a shower." He beams, wiggling his eyebrows. "Wanna join?"

"Uh, no. If I join, I'll be late to meet with Madam Christine. We're going over the final touches for the showcase." I stand up from the bed and walk to the closet to pick out my clothes.

We're entering finals week, and I'm spread almost completely thin. Madam Christine decided it would be a good idea to run through the entire choreography a couple of times with the other dancers just to make sure we had it memorized. At that time, we would be able to tweak any mistakes. Also, we would be rehearsing in our skirts.

It's the skirt we're wearing for the performance, which is long and loose. So, we have to get use to performing in them. I'm meeting with her today so we can select times to gather the entire company to practice. It has to work well with everyone's final schedule, too.

One of the dancers, Clarissa, for instance, has Wednesday and Thursday fully booked with finals. Therefore, we can't schedule any rehearsals for that day. So that leaves us with Monday, Tuesday, or Friday. We might have to do all three, but they would have to do late rehearsals because most of their finals don't finish until six.

It was all confusing, and it was also stressing Madam Christine out, so I told her I would help her figure it out.

I walk back into the bedroom wearing my black tights and Nick's BSU hockey hoodie. I stole it out of his closet the last time I was there. It has his last name spread across the shoulder blades and Captain on the front left-hand corner. It smells just like him—bergamot and something manly—and I inhale it every chance I get.

I sit down on the edge of the bed, pulling my legs under myself, waiting for him to finish his shower. A couple of weeks ago, Nick brought over some of his body wash and took some of mine to his house. Every now and then, I like to shower in it before going to bed. It tricks my mind into believing he's there with me.

I've grown to always want to be around Nick. He's everything I never knew I needed or wanted. I've realized that being in his presence has done things for me mentally. My anxiety has been at an all-time low since I started hanging out with Nick. This is before we started dating. Before anything physical happened between us.

Nick has just been my rock. He constantly uplifts me and makes me feel seen. He doesn't make me feel like I'm a burden. He genuinely cares about me. He cares about my feelings, my goals, and my aspirations. I don't know where I would be if he wasn't by my side right now.

I hear the door open to the bathroom, snapping me from my thoughts. Out walks Nick with a towel wrapped around his hips and water dripping down his chiseled torso.

Fuck, I should've taken a shower with him.

"What are you looking at, Beitar?" Nick asks mischievously.

"You have a body that would make the gods jealous," I say, biting my lip, trying to restrain myself from jumping on him.

"Are you objectifying me, Jay?"

"Maybe I am?" I shrug as I stand from the bed and slowly walk toward him.

A shocked gasp slips from his lips. "How dare you? I am more than just my body, Ms. Beitar. I shall not be objectified by your gaze." He wraps his arms around his body and turns in the opposite direction, shielding me.

I laugh. "You're kidding, right?"

"No, I am more than just my body, Luna."

My boisterous laugh fills the room. Nick stares at me, confused. "I'm sorry," I say breathlessly. "It's just that you're such a hypocrite. All you do is objectify me."

"Yeah, but you're hot. Like out of my league hot," he says, turning around to continue picking out his clothes.

"Whatever. Anyway, what's your plan for the day?" I wrap my arms around his waist, resting my chest against his back as he sifts through his one drawer for something to wear.

"I have practice. After that, I have a meeting with Coach. He said there was someone who wanted to see me. I'm not entirely sure who, though."

"Entirely? So that means you kind of know?" I pause. "Do you think it's a scout?"

Nick told me that scouts from all over have been taking notice. None of them have made any actual offers, but it's a possibility. We just started this relationship, and I don't want it to end because he gets an offer from a team halfway across the country. What if he gets an offer in a *different* country?

I still have to graduate college. Not to mention, I want to join a dance company as well. The only way I can do that is if I continue to dance at my current dance studio. They'll help get my foot in the door. As much as I want to follow Nick, I can't. I have to think about myself and my career. I refuse to be the girl who follows a man across the world just because *his* career is taking off.

"I think so." He must feel me stiffen because he turns around and grabs my shoulders. "Hey, what's wrong?"

I shake my head. "Nothing."

"Don't start that again, Luna. You said you would start being more open about what you're feeling. So, tell me, what's wrong?"

I huff, burying my head into his chest. "I'm just scared. I don't want you to get signed to some team and move halfway across the country without me because I'm still stuck in college."

"Luna, where I go, you go. Simple."

I push myself out of his arms. "That's the problem, Nick! I don't want to sign up to be your groupie. I love you, but I also love what I do. I love dancing, and I want to continue to do it for as long as I can. I can't do that if I'm following you everywhere."

"Luna, I don't expect you to follow me everywhere. I know you have school, and I know you have ballet.

I know how important that is to you. I'm saying that wherever we go, we'll choose together. It's a decision for the both of us."

Tears gather in my eyes, but I push them back. Nick wraps his arms around my shoulders and pulls me back into his chest, leaving a kiss on the crown of my head. "I love you, Luna James. Like you said, we're forever. This isn't a fling, and it's not some situationship. This is a permanent relationship. One day, I'm going to marry you. We're going to buy a house together to raise our six kids. You're going to want to murder me every day for the rest of our lives, but you'll love me nonetheless. The same way, I'll love you. You're my whole world, Lunar Moon. There's no way I'll decide our future without you deciding right along with me."

Butterflies take flight in my stomach. Pulling back from his hold, I rise on my tiptoes and kiss his lips. He planned our whole future. Not only did he plan it, but he imagined that we would do it together. Every step along the way, we do it together.

I pull back to look into his eyes. "Okay."

His brows creased. "Okay? No fight? Just, okay?"

"I mean, we need to revisit that six-kid thing of yours, but yeah. No fight. *Just,* okay." I shrug.

He kisses me one more time. "Okay, well, I'll let you get to your meeting while I go to mine."

"Will you be here when I get back?"

"Yes. I might even have dinner." He wiggles his brows.

"Nice!" I release his neck and turn to grab my bag. "I'll see you later, then. I love you."

"I love you, too," Nick replies.

Before I leave, Nick grabs my wrist, causing me to drop my bag, and pulls me back to his chest, kissing me one last time. A giggle rumbles in my throat as I wrap my arms around him.

"Sorry, I just needed one more," Nick murmurs.

Nick

"Nick!" I turn around to see Dean running toward me.

I've been trying to limit the number of encounters I have with him. So, if it doesn't pertain to the team, there's no need for us to talk. I don't want him to be captain anymore, so there's also no need for us to talk about that either. I haven't told Coach this, but I will soon. Dean is not captain material. If he doesn't have the ability to put others before himself, he wouldn't make it as captain.

"What?" I turn on my heels and continue walking.

"Look, I need you to give this to Jay." I whip back around to see him holding out a wrapped package. "I already saw what it is. I had to re-wrap it. She'll love it. Look, I've been a dick to Jay. But she's my sister; I shouldn't have kept it from her."

His eyes soften, with a hint of remorse behind them. "Why can't you give it to her yourself?"

"Because she's pissed at me. Not that I blame her." He sighs. "I haven't been the best brother to her. I've been treating her like shit. Fuck. Where did it all go wrong?"

"When you slept with her best friend, for starters," I answer matter-of-factly. I know it was a rhetorical question, but it was the truth, wasn't it?

"Yeah, well, we broke up." My eyes practically shoot out of their sockets.

"When? Why?" I mean, I knew why, but I wanted to hear him say it out loud.

"I don't know. Gia broke up with me. If I'm being honest, I didn't want to end it. She's the one who ended it." Okay, I guess I don't know why.

For someone who says they feel bad, he's not really acting like it. "Fine. Give it here." I grab the package out of his hand and pack it into my duffle bag.

I continue to walk to the locker room. "Nick. Wait, dude."

"What?"

"I want to apologize." That causes me to stop. "Look, I understand you were just trying to be there for Luna.

Gia and I should have handled that situation better. But I shouldn't have bitched at you."

"Dean, I take everything you say with a grain of salt. Until you start treating your sister right, I couldn't really care less about what you say. Your words mean jack shit to me. If you want the God's honest truth, I don't think you should be captain anymore." His jaw gapes into a giant O. "You like to say you think of other people first, but then you turn around and make them feel guilty for doing it. As captain, you're supposed to put yourself last. You don't get to keep score either. You do it for the betterment of the team. If you can't even do that in your personal life, what makes you think you can do it for the team?"

With that, I turn on my heels and walk away. I've said my piece, and there's nothing else I need to say to him. I still have a couple of months on the team. Until I graduate, I'm still captain. Therefore, I will do whatever it takes to make sure this team has the best leader I can find.

As soon as we finish practice, Coach calls me into his office. "Yes, Coach?" I wasn't a hundred percent sure why I needed to meet with him, but I had a feeling for what its about.

Different scouts from different teams have shown interest in me, but I haven't heard about any final offers. I know Luna is nervous about it all, but I'm not. No matter where I choose to go, I know that I want her there for it all. I have to keep in mind that she wants to sign with a dance company. So, whatever company she signs with, I would go there in hopes that a team would want me in that state. Either way, I would follow that girl to the ends of the world.

"Yes, come in, Beckett. Take a seat." He ushers me to the chair in front of his desk.

I close the door before sitting down. "What's going on, Coach? You're making me nervous."

"Look, Beckett. I'm only going to say this once, so listen closely." He clears his throat as if he's choked up on tears. "I see you like a son. I want nothing but the best for you. You're one of the best captain's this team has ever seen. I'm proud of everything we've accomplished together. I'm going to be sad to see you go, but I'll be proud to see what more you can accomplish in the real world."

"Aww, Coach. And here I thought you hated me," I say, pressing my hand into my chest. "You love me?"

"No, I do not. Don't go spreading that nonsense either."

I laugh.

"Anyways, the reason I brought you in here is that we need to discuss this new captain business."

The smile fades from my face. "No one. I haven't found anyone deserving of the spot. Plus, I still have a couple of months left on the team. Are you trying to get rid of me already?"

"Beckett, don't be like that. We need to train the captain soon. So, yeah, you need to choose one already. What happened to Beitar?"

I shake my head. "I was wrong about him."

"You're wrong about a lot of things. Beitar being captain is not one of them."

"Coach-"

He cuts me off. "Don't *Coach* me. I've seen him play, and I've seen him interact with the team. He's the perfect choice. So, unless you have a legitimate reason why he shouldn't be captain, he's who I'm choosing."

He pauses, giving me a chance to rebut, but what could I say? *Oh yeah, he's been treating my girlfriend, who's also his sister, like shit.* I'd sound like an immature high schooler. I had no other reason. I could tell him the whole selfless thing, but that wouldn't work with Coach.

So, I'm stuck with making Dean the fucking captain.

Fucking hell.

"Is that all, Coach?" I ask, ready to leave and go home to my girl.

"No, actually." The door opens behind me. "Right on time. Beckett, this is one of the coaches for the Seattle Rays hockey team, Jeremy Longings."

I hold my hand out to shake his. "Nice to meet you, sir."

"Oh, please call me Jeremy. Nick, I've heard a lot about you. I've seen your film as well. You're really good. I hear you're also the captain."

"Yes, I am."

"Well, then, you're the full package. Unfortunately, we already have a captain for our team, but we want you. Like I said, we have the captain position filled, but we want you to be part of our team. So, what do you say?"

My heart climbs up into my throat. I thought there was going to be a scout coming to tell me how much they liked me. But this guy is offering me a spot on the team. Wait, is this an official offer? I turn my head to Coach and then back to Jeremy. "Is this like an official offer?" I ask.

He grins. "Yes, it is. By tomorrow afternoon, we can have the paperwork prepared for you to sign. We would like you to come join the team in the spring."

"Oh, shit," is all I can say. I couldn't believe what I was hearing. This is everything I've worked for.

He laughs. "Yeah. It's the big leagues, kid. It's all real. So, the question is, Do *you* see yourself as a Seattle Ray?"

Of course I did, but I couldn't make this decision without talking to Luna. "Can I have some time to think about it? I have a girlfriend, and I can't make this decision without her," I say hesitantly. I wonder how they would feel to know that I needed to talk to my girlfriend before actually making any decisions. I don't want to make any decisions without her because this is our life. Not just mine. I want to make sure we do things that would benefit both of us.

"I totally understand. I respect you for thinking of your partner. It says a lot about you." He looks at Coach before pulling out a business card from his blazer's pocket. "Here's what we'll do. I'll give you the week to mull this over with her. Next Monday, I'll need to hear your answer. Sounds good?" He holds out his business card.

"Sounds great. Thank you," I answer, grabbing the card from his hand.

"Alright, well, now that you have my number, feel free to call or text me with any questions that you have. I'll be seeing you, Nick. Lasiter." Then he leaves.

I turn to Coach as my brow peeks up. "Lasiter?"

"Shut up and get the hell out of my office, Beckett."

I laugh haughtily and leave.

I can't wait to get home and tell Luna.

Chapter 33

"**M**om, I don't want to talk about it anymore." I've been on the phone with my mom since I arrived home. I'm guessing Dean filled her in on every-thing that happened, but I'm sure he only told her his fucked-up side of it.

I know I should care about telling my side of the story, but I don't anymore. I'm moving on. He chose Gia over me, and that's that. I know where I stand now, and I refuse to beg for either one of them to stay in my life. We were supposed to be the indestructible trifecta, but clearly, that's not true.

"Luna, sweetie, please. He's your brother. Just forgive him and move on. It's really not that serious." I push back the anger boiling in the pit of my stomach.

It always annoyed me how she could so easily take Dean's side in everything. Which is why I was so close to Cassie. She always listened to me. She wasn't biased, either. She would tell me when I messed up, but she would also tell me when I'm right and that I'm able to feel whatever it is that I need to feel. With my mom, it's always been the complete opposite.

"Mom, can you take my side for once?" I beg. "He slept with my best friend, for God's sake! Then she hid it from me. How do you not understand how fucked up that is?"

"Watch your mouth, Luna James!" she demands. "I don't care how old you get; I am still your mother, and you will respect me," she snaps. "Look, I get you're upset, but you get pissed at your brother for the dumbest things. This is one of them." She clears her throat, and her voice softens. "I'm sorry, but no, I don't agree with you. He's your brother! How do you not see what's more important here, Luna?"

Tears well up in my eyes as my mother's words wash over me. Once again, I'm not being chosen. Once again, it's Dean over me. Why am I never good enough for anyone? "I'm going to go. I can't deal with this right now."

I hang up the phone before she has a chance to respond. It immediately starts to ring again. I throw my phone on the couch and walk into my bedroom.

Tossing myself on the bed, I pull my legs into my chest and let the tears start to fall. I feel my heartbeat start to rise. This can't be happening right now. I've been fine these past couple of months. I haven't had a panic attack since the woods, where Nick kissed me.

Nick. Where's Nick?

As I try to gasp for breath, the air seems to thin. Each breath becomes a conscious struggle, as if the air itself were resisting entry into my lungs. My heartbeat, once a reliable metronome, quickens into a frantic percussion that reverberates in my ears. The room fills with eerily silence, punctuated only by the erratic rhythm of my own pulse. An overwhelming sense of my own self-worth grips me and races through my mind like a runaway train, derailing the semblance of rationality.

Reality itself seems to be uncertain, slipping through my grasp. I find myself suspended in a surreal limbo, surrounded by a thickening fog of fear of never being loved for who I am. Of never being enough for anyone, no matter how hard I try. The dreams of Nick and I's future from this morning now loomed as insurmountable obstacles that I could never achieve.

Desperation claws at me, urging me to escape from the confines of my own mind. Yet, my limbs feel too heavy and unresponsive, as if shackled by the weight of my anxieties. My bedroom, once a sanctuary from all of the fear and anxiety from the outside world, now becomes a disorienting battleground where the struggle for composure unfolds within the confines of my own mind.

"Luna! Babe, I want to talk to you about…" I hear Nick walk into the room, but I can't get my body to move. "Luna!"

He runs to the bed, resting on the side of me. "Hey," he says softly. "I'm right here. I'm right here, Jay. What happened? What caused it?"

Tears continue running down my cheeks as he gently rubs my hair. "The-they don-don't want m-me." I sob.

He lifts me up onto his lap until I'm straddling him, wrapping his arms around me, and pulling me tightly into his chest. Nick's grip tightens around me like a bear hug. A warmth invades me, and my breathing slowly starts to calm down.

"Luna, I want you. I want you for the rest of my life. I never want you to leave me. I never want to give you up. I want to keep you with me at all times. I never knew what living was until I met you. I was alive, but being with you, I can say I'm finally living. I have a purpose in my life now. You're my purpose." He sniffles. "I want to make you happy for the rest of your life and to take care of you. I want you to find solace in me. I want to wipe away all of your tears. I want to be the cause of all of your laughs. I want you to love me more than anyone else."

His voice cracks. "And I-I know that's selfish, but I *don't* want you to love anyone more than you love me. Because I will never love anyone more than I love you. You are the reason I breathe and the reason I continue every day." His voice lowers, barely above a whisper. "So, Luna, if they don't choose you, I do. I want that to be enough for you. *I* want to be enough for you. Please say I'm enough for you." I feel his tears fall on my cheek, and his words silence me and my cries.

I've never felt love like I do from Nick. I don't love anyone more than I love Nick. I love this man and every-thing he is. No matter how annoying he gets, I'll always endure it because he's worth every fucking migraine.

I push against his chest and straighten my spine to look him in the eyes. They're bloodshot red and brim-ming with tears, as if whatever I say will make or break him. I love having this kind of control over him. I see that I affect him just as much as he affects me.

"You're enough for me. You'll always be enough for me."

Then he pulls me back into his embrace, slamming his mouth into mine. His beard tickles my chin. It's filled with intensity and love. His tongue slips into the space between my lips, sliding against mine.

I never want to give this man up or experience what it's like to be unloved by him.

"I love you, Luna James Beitar," he whispers against my lips.

"I love you, Nicholas..." I drawl.

He chuckles lightly. "Cole. My middle name is Cole."

I smile widely. "Nicholas Cole Beckett. I love you so much it hurts."

"Now you know how I feel."

After telling Nick about the conversation I had with my mom, he held me in his arms, embracing me and reminding me he will always choose my side, even if I'm wrong. Which was *so* not the point, but I'll take it anyway.

"Wait, you said you wanted to tell me something. What was it?" His brows clash with each other.

"Oh, yeah. It doesn't matter." He shakes his head.

"Yes, it does. You sounded excited." Until he walked into the room and saw me in a ball, clawing at my throat, trying to breathe. "Please, tell me."

He lets out a deep sigh. "So, I had my meeting with Coach today."

I forgot about that. "How did it go?"

"Good. He wanted me to choose the next captain." He pauses, looking at me like I already knew who he had chosen.

"Dean?" I can't ask him not to choose him just because of our issues; that's not fair.

"Yeah. It wasn't my choice. I told Coach at the beginning of the season that I thought Dean would be a good fit. After these last couple of months, I don't believe that anymore." He rubs his palms up and down my thigh, soothing my nerves. "Coach said unless I could give him a real reason pertaining to the team, he was choosing Dean. I couldn't think of anything besides how he treats you. I'm sorry."

I shake my head and climb back on his lap until I'm straddling him, wrapping my arms around his neck. "Don't be. I love that you would do that for me regardless, but it's personal. Don't let that affect your team.

You can't bring your personal life into your career. It's not fair to the team."

His hands find my waist and slip under my shirt. "Yeah, but you're my team too. You and me. We're a team. It already affected that."

"It didn't. I promise." If anything, it makes us stronger.

"Okay," he says, before kissing me again.

I pull back. "Wait, is that it? He just wanted you to pick a captain."

A smile grows on his face. "I got an offer."

My brows shoot to my hairline. "What! Really? Oh my God! Nick!" I tighten my grip on his neck, and we tumble onto his back. "I'm so proud of you! Congratulations, babe!"

I push my palms into the bed to hold myself over him. "Where?"

His smile slowly fades. "Seattle."

Seattle? That's 3,000 miles away. A forty-five-hour drive. That's so far. "Wow. That's great." I add, less enthused. I didn't know what to say. I know I should be happy for him, but that's so far away. "When would you start?"

The air was thickening in the silence. "They want me to join in the spring," he says finally. He quickly sits back up, holding me firm in his lap. "Look, I told them I wouldn't decide without you. So, let's talk about it, okay? Nothing is set in stone."

"How long do you have till they want your final answer?"

"Monday."

"Monday? Nick, that's one week to make a life-altering decision!"

"I know, but we'll figure it out."

I run my hands through my hair, trying not to stress myself out again. "Hey, babe. Breathe." He reminds me while rubbing my arms up and down.

"Yeah, I know. This is just... a lot. I have finals this week, and then I have the showcase this Saturday. But this is such a big deal, and I don't want you to think I don't care about it because I do. I *really* do, Nick. I promise."

"Hey," he beams. "I know you care. We don't have to talk about it today. We have a couple of days to think about it, okay? We'll figure it out."

"What about school? Are you going to finish, or will you just drop out?"

"Hell no. I'm this close to getting my degree. I'll just finish online. But that's only if we go." I love that he says *we*. That he's even including me in this decision. I know he's waited his whole life for this opportunity, and now it's finally here.

"Your mom would be proud of you," I say, cupping his face.

He closes his eyes and looks at the ceiling. "I hope so."

"She is. Trust me. If I'm proud of you, I know *she's* proud of you."

"What would I do without you?" He grins.

"Be lost."

"Yeah, you're right."

I don't know what the future holds, but I'm happy I get to experience it with Nick. I can't really express how much this man has changed my life. He's helped me in ways I didn't even think I needed help in. I don't know much, but what I do know is that I'm glad I met him. I'm glad my brother brought him to my dance studio.

"I love you, Nicholas Cole Beckett."

"I love you, Luna James Beitar."

Then he kisses me again. I'm the luckiest girl in the world.

Chapter 34

Luna

It's finally D-day. The winter showcase. I'm currently in our dressing room, fixing my hair. The auditorium is packed with people. I saw my parents arrive, but Dean and Gia haven't. Not that I'm surprised, but a part of me hoped they would. A deep, deep part of me.

I shake my head, tossing all of my thoughts out the window. There was no room to think about anything except this performance.

"Hey, Luna. There's someone at the door for you!" Giselle screams out.

I stand at my vanity and run to the door. "Gia?"

"Hey." She greets me softly. "I know how important this showcase is to you. I just wanted to support you."

What was I supposed to say to that? At first, I had hoped she would come, but now that she's standing in front of me, that fury and rage are building up again. I just can't stand to look at her anymore.

Before I can speak, I hear someone calling my name down the hall. "Luna!"

It's Nick. How does he do that? Show up right when I need him to. "Nick."

He walks right past Gia and lands a kiss on my cheek. "I wanted to wish you good luck. I also brought you these." Handing me a bouquet of roses.

"God, you just love your cliches, don't you?" I joke, sniffing the roses.

"You know I do." He looks at Gia and back at me. He's staring at me as if he's asking if I want her here. I gently shake my head. "Gia, I think we need to find our seats."

"I wanted to tell you that I broke up with Dean." She sputters out.

"When?"

"The night of the dinner. You were right. I should have never chosen Dean over you. I couldn't see how badly you were hurting. I just wanted him so badly that it didn't matter to me at the time. But that night, it was like you splashed a glass of cold water in my face and woke me up." She takes a step towards me. "You matter way more than a relationship with Dean does. Luna, I'm so sorry. Please, you have to believe me."

I did believe her, but the problem was that I just didn't care anymore. "I forgive you, but we're not friends anymore. It was so easy for you to lie and betray my trust like that. I don't see how I could ever forgive you again."

She looks at her palms and back at me. "You're right, but I'm not ready to give up on us yet. I'll give you time."

I knew we could never come back from this, but I would love to see her try. So, I give her a small nod, and then she leaves.

Nick quickly grips my face and kisses me, molding his lips with mine and stealing the breath from my lungs. I hold onto his waist for balance. I could stay like this for the rest of my life. Nick breaks the kiss first. "I'm so fucking proud of you for setting your boundaries."

I can't help but smile. "Thank you, but seriously, I have to get ready."

He kisses my forehead. "You're going to kill it."

"I'll see you after." Then I turn back into the dressing room and run to pull my light blue skirt on.

I've waited years for this moment, right here. This performance is everything. I'm not just doing it for myself but for Cassie as well. I know that everyone thinks

I'm holding onto dance because I can't let Cassie go, but that's not true. Cassie is the reason I got into dance. She helped me find my love for ballet.

Maybe I didn't want to let go of Cassie, but I also knew that this was something we would both cherish for the rest of our lives. We both wanted to dance till the day we died, and she did. She just wasn't able to accomplish the goals she wanted. I'm doing this not just for me but for her too. It's not because I can't let her go, but because I loved her. I miss what she represented, and I miss how she made me feel like the most important person in the room.

I glance at the ceiling. "This is for us, Cassie." I whispered, hoping somehow she heard me.

"Alright everyone, places!" Madam Christine belts.

Then everyone runs on stage and into the wings. I listen to the announcer give the introduction for the performance.

This was it. This was my moment.

"Ladies and gentlemen, *Serenade*." There's a loud round of applause, and then the music starts.

We finish taking our bows, and then we all run off the stage. As soon as we get backstage, everyone screams. I can't believe it's over. We spent months on this choreography, and after thirty-five minutes, it's officially over.

"Luna!" My eyes are on Nick as he walks into the room. I run and leap into his open arms, wrapping my legs around his waist. "Fuck! You were amazing. I mean, I knew you could dance, but you were a different person on stage."

I pull back to look at the huge smile on his face. "You really think I was that good?"

"Hell yeah. Babe, that was amazing. Can you do it for me again later?"

I shake my head. "You're stupid." I drop my feet back to the ground. "I just can't believe it's over already."

"Me either. I'm serious. I really want to see it again." I laugh.

I grab his bearded chin with my thumb and index finger and pull his lips to mine. His arms wrap around my waist, bringing me closer to his chest. "I love you." I say against his lips.

"I love you, too." A grin shines brightly on his face.

"Luna Beitar?" I pull out of Nick's arms and see a lady wearing a navy blue flowy dress standing a few feet away from us. "Are you Luna Beitar?"

"Oh, yes. I am." I respond.

"Oh, great. We've been trying to get in touch with you for the past couple of months."

"You have? How? Why?"

"Well, we've seen videos of your dancing, and to say we're impressed is an understatement. I'm sorry I haven't introduced myself. I'm Carol Rodriguez from the Los Angeles Ballet."

My jaw unhinges. "Oh my god." I whisper, more to myself than to anyone else.

She laughs lightly. "I can say you're not the first to give us that reaction. Anyway, you've been on our radar for the last couple of years. You're an exceptional dancer. We sent out a letter with information a couple of months ago with an offer, but we haven't heard anything back. Normally, we take that as a no, but we just couldn't let you slip through our fingers."

"Letter? What letter?" THE ENVELOPE! "Oh my gosh."

"The envelope you keep saying you'll get around to." Nick whispers against my ears.

Carol looks between the two of us in confusion. "I'm so sorry. It came in a yellow envelope, and I didn't know what it was, so I hadn't gotten around to opening it."

She smiles. "Well, then. Why don't you go home and read that letter, and then give me a call? We have much to discuss." She hands me a business card with her email and phone number on it. "I look forward to hearing from you soon. Oh, right. Stunning job out there tonight."

"Thank you!" I scream internally.

Los Angeles Ballet was Cassie and I's dream ballet company. I know most people want to be in New York, but Cassie and I have always loved LA. It's a vibrant lifestyle. The culture. Everything.

I turn around to see Nick with his arms open wide, ready for me to jump into them, so I do. I grip onto his neck as he twirls us around. I couldn't believe this was happening right now. This is everything I've ever wanted.

"Wait, Nick. Stop. Stop. Stop." I pat his shoulder. He stops twirling. "What about your hockey offer?"

"What do you mean?" His brows furrow.

"Nick, your offer is in Seattle. My offer is in LA. What do we do about that?"

"We'll figure it out. Look, I told you. Where I go, you go. Where you go, I go. There's no separating us. Do you hear me?" I nod my head. "I'm so fucking proud of you, Jay."

"Thank you, *Cole*." I retort.

"Cole? Why are you calling me by my middle name?"

"Because you called me mine. Plus, Cole is a sexy name." I lean forward and run my tongue from his cheekbone up to his brow. I have no idea why I did that, but I don't regret it when his face morphs, darkening his features with lust and want.

"Fuck. We need to get home." I laugh as he starts to carry me out of the dressing room.

"Wait!" I shout, laughing. "I need my stuff."

He runs back into the room, and I point at my vanity, where my duffle bag is resting. I had packed up all of my stuff before the show, so I could just grab it and go. Nick quickly grabs it off of the chair and throws it over his shoulder before running back out the door.

He comes to a halt when we make it outside. "What is it?" I turn in his hold to see my parents standing by my car. Nick lets me slide down his body, setting me back down on the ground. "I thought you left already."

"We were waiting for you." My dad says, walking to me with his arms wide open. "Sweetheart, that was beautiful. I loved every second of it."

"Thank you, dad." I hug him back.

I released myself from his hold. "Why haven't you answered my calls?" My mom asks, still standing in front of my car.

"I've been busy. Plus, I didn't want to talk about what you wanted to talk about." I shrug.

"Oh gosh, Luna James. Please just stop it. Dean and Gia broke up. That means you can put all of this nonsense behind you."

"No! No, I can't, and I'm done trying to explain why I can't. It's not worth the drama or the headache."

"What, you can date his captain, but he can't date your best friend? That doesn't make sense, Luna James." She chirps, crossing her arms over her chest.

"You're damn right, mom." Everyone's mouth falls open, including Nick's. "Dean made me feel like shit while he hid his relationship with Gia. He gaslighted me into thinking I was the problem. But it wasn't me, it was him. He was the one keeping this secret from me. We don't keep secrets from each other. He did!" I huff as the rage seethes. "Why can't you see the problem? He lied! He went on and on about how I'm being dramatic and making everything about myself. He knew what he was doing and just didn't give a damn. So, no. I don't forgive him. I'm sick and tired of you acting like he walks on water. He doesn't! So, if you're done berating me, I have to go celebrate with Nick."

I kiss my dad on the cheek. "I'm proud of you, kiddo." He whispers in my ears before returning a kiss to my cheek.

Then I grab Nick's hand and walk to my car. I push the button on my keys to pop my trunk open and throw my bag in. I feel hands wrap around my waist.

Nick gently tugs on my ears with his teeth."I'm going to fuck you so hard tonight."

"Is that a promise?" I tease.

"Why don't we go home and find out?" Then he shuts my trunk.

Chapter 35

Nick

As soon as we get home, I keep my promise and fuck Luna until she can't take it anymore. She finally fell asleep after two hours. I've been up, watching her peacefully sleep. Watching her sleep has become my new favorite hobby. I could do it for a lifetime and never tire of it. When she's having a good dream, she does this thing where the corner of her mouth will rise just an inch. It's like she's smiling, but not fully. It's one of the cutest things she's done.

We really need to talk about our future, but I put it on the back burner for the night. I want her to be proud of the amazing performance she gave tonight. I was so fucking proud of her. Watching her dance is something entirely different. Even if I wanted to look away, I couldn't take my eyes off of her.

I slowly edge my way off the bed, trying not to wake her. She shuffles in her sleep, but she doesn't open her eyes.

I walk to the desk in the corner of her room and grab the yellow envelope. Its killing me to know what offer she received. I know how illegal this is, but it's not like she's going to report me.

Actually, she might.

Regardless, I grab the top of the envelope and place my index finger under the tab that's sealing it closed.

"What are you doing?" I jump with a low screech.

"Geez, Luna. You scared the shit out of me. What the hell?" I roar as I try to catch my breath.

"Well, you shouldn't be going through my mail. You know I can report your ass, right?"

"You won't, though. But you *should* open this. It's killing me to know what's inside of it." I throw the envelope on the bed.

She looks down at it and scoots her back against the headboard until she's fully sitting up. "Can you open it?"

"You literally just got on me about opening your mail. *Now* you want me to open it?" My brow arches in confusion.

"Yeah, because I'm asking you to. Pleaseeeee." She pouts.

I shake my head and then grab the letter off the bed again. "Fine."

I slowly tear the top of the envelope open and pull out a stack of papers with a brochure that says *Los Angeles Ballet*. I quickly glance over the letter, which basically states they would love to have Luna come join their dance company. It also says she would sign on as a soloist. I'm not entirely sure if that's good or not, but I know she wants to be a principal.

Is that better than a soloist or worse?

"What does it say?" Luna blurts, sitting in anticipation.

"They want to sign you on. They say they would love to have you as a soloist in their dance studio." I look up from the paper. "What's a soloist?"

Tears swell in her eyes. "Really, they said that?" She jumps from the bed, still naked, and grabs the paper from my hands. "I mean, it's not principal, but I can work my ass off to become a principal. Oh my gosh! I can't believe this! They want me to join their studio!"

Then she lets out a shrill screech. "Fuck! Luna, my ears," I bellow, covering my ears.

She covers her mouth, hiding the wide grin tattooed across her face. "I can't believe it! Why did I not open this sooner?"

"Your guess is as good as mine." I shrug.

"Nick." Her smile drops from her face and is replaced with a worried gaze. "Your offer from Seattle—I can't just let you decline your offer, but I can't decline this one either."

"Yeah, I know. So, I'll wait," I add.

"What do you mean?"

"Luna, you've waited your whole life for this moment. I haven't seen you this happy about something in a while." I say, grabbing her arms and pulling her into my chest. "I want you to sign with the company in LA."

"No, Nick. Don't do that. Don't put me before yourself. You've waited just as long to get an offer from a team. It's not fair for you to give up your dreams for me."

"I'm not giving up on my dreams. I'm just pushing it back. I can wait a couple of more months. I don't need to be signed right away. I still have school. You have what, another year and a half?" I sigh. "If you want this, take it. I'm not asking; I'm telling you. I refuse to allow you to let this fly right by you. Sign the damn paper, Jay," I demand.

Luna pushes out of my arms and sits up. "I love you. I don't want to lose you, and I feel like I will if you don't sign with Seattle. Later down the line, you'll resent me for keeping you from signing with a team that wanted you," she cries.

My hands find her cheeks. "I will never resent you, and you will never lose me. I don't know how many times I have to tell you. But I will keep saying it until it sticks. I want you for the rest of my life. Your success is my success, and vice versa. When you win, I win. I promise. I'm so fucking happy and proud of you."

I kiss her lips softly. "I can promise we'll never have to worry about separating."

"So, I should sign?" she asks hesitantly.

I muffle my laugh. "Yes, Jay. Sign the fucking paper. Now." I growled.

She smiles again, takes the paper to the desk, and hovers her pen over the bottom line. "Oh wait. Should I get a lawyer to look this over first?"

"Yeah, that's actually a pretty good idea. I have one on retainer you can use." I pull out my phone and pull up my lawyer's number.

"Tell me you're rich without telling me you're rich," she quips.

"Shut up."

Luna has a meeting with my lawyer to go over the contract today. So, I'm trying to find something to do with my time. I offer to come along, but she says she wants to do it by herself.

I'm so fucking proud of my girl. She's starting to see herself the way I see her: strong and confident. I know she's still working through her insecurities, but it's a start, and that's all that matters.

My phone starts to ring in the middle console.

Unknown number.

Who the hell is calling me?

I hit answer. "Hello?"

"Is this Nick Beckett?"

"This is him. Who's this?" I probe.

"Hello, Nick. This is Mike Tranvessli with the San Francisco Falcons. I've been trying to get in contact with you about possibly signing with us," he answers.

I abruptly pull over to the side of the road, hugging my car to the curb while cars honk as they pass by. "Did you say San Francisco?"

San Francisco was in California. It's not Los Angeles, but it's pretty fucking close, right? What, it's like a five-hour drive? I couldn't drive five hours every day, but I could find a happy medium for us.

The man continues to speak. "Yes, San Francisco. We're a new team. We just became official a couple of years ago. We would be honored to have you join our team. We'll be in town this week, and we can have a meeting to go over all the other logistics. Will you be free?"

"I'm sure I can make myself free," I answer.

"Great. I'll email you the details. See you soon." Then he hangs up.

This is perfect. I personally have never heard of the San Francisco Falcons, but I'd be stupid to turn down the most perfect offer. It would be in California with Luna. I just want to be wherever she is. So, if I have to join an unknown team to do it, so be it.

Don't get me wrong. I would much rather be joining an elite team everyone knows and loves, like the Boston Bruins. But it doesn't matter as long as I'm with Luna. She's all that matters to me.

I put the car in drive again and pull off. Arriving at the stadium, I quickly hop out and run to Coach's office. I knock on his door before opening it. "Coach? You in here?"

When I walk in, there's a man wearing a black and white suit sitting in the chair directly in front of Coach. He has his hand resting under his chin and his ankle on his knee. The way he's lounging, I assume he and Coach are old friends.

"Oh, sorry, Coach. I didn't know you had company. I'll come back later."

"Beckett! Get your ass in here." He shouts before I can close the door. "I was just about to call you in. Apparently, you're popular in the NHL right now."

The man in the chair stands up. "So, this is the infamous Nicholas Beckett." He drawls, holding his hand out for me to shake. "I'm Johnathan Reeves."

I grip his hand and give it a firm shake. "It's just Nick. I'm sorry. All due respect, but am I supposed to know you?"

A laugh bubbles in his chest. "You're funny, kid. I don't suppose you should. Not that it matters. Our team knows *you*, though."

My brows scrunch. "Your team?"

"Los Angeles Kings," he states.

My grip loosens in his. There's no way. "You've got to be fucking shitting me."

He laughs again. "Like I said, funny kid. Well, we drove a long way to make this deal with you. Actually, I lied. I flew here, but semantics." He shrugs. "We've seen your film. We were at your last game as well. Not that you knew about it." I look at Coach, wondering what the hell this guy is talking about.

"We wanted to see how you would play without knowing we were there. If you knew, you might have changed tactics to impress us. Which you didn't need to do. We're already impressed. You're a good player, kid. An even better captain. You command your team with such authority and respect. I saw how they all listened to you. They trusted you, and that's hard to come by with captains. I hear you've only been captain for a year. Is that correct?"

"Yes, sir," I affirm.

"Well, I'll be damned. You command your team's respect with only a year's worth of you being captain. Imagine what you could do with a longer amount of time with your team," he adds.

"What do you mean?" I ask, confused.

"Nick, we want you to join our team as captain. Well, co-captain. We already have a captain, but he would be honored to have you on board with him. We both watched your film together, and he was just as impressed with you as I was. So, what do you say?"

I couldn't believe this. None of this seems real. They're standing in front of me, offering the dream of a lifetime. I want to say yes right here, right now. But all I can think about is Luna. I know she would want me to join, but I need to hear her say it.

"This sounds amazing." He gives me a pleasing smile. "But I have to talk to my girlfriend first."

He looks at Coach. "Kid has a girlfriend?" Then he looks back at me. "No offense; it's just that most players who want to join the NHL typically joins single. They don't typically want to give anyone a free ride."

I fight the urge to deck the guy by just insinuating Luna's a gold digger. "Luna isn't like that. Her family isn't broke, and neither is she. Also, she's a dancer who's already been signed. Even if she was a gold digger, I wouldn't mind. Not if it's her."

He looks me up and down and smirks. "I respect it. I meant no disrespect. Look, take the time you need to figure it out. When you do figure it out," he pulls out a card from his pocket and says, "Give me a call."

He looks at the coach one more time. "It was good seeing you again, Coach."

"You too, Reeves," Coach replies as he takes a seat back in his chair.

I look at the card in my hand. This feels unreal. I feel like I'm living someone else's life.

"What are you still doing standing in my office, Beckett? Get your ass home and talk to that girlfriend of yours!" Coach orders.

I flash him an award-winning smile and run back out to my car. I pull out my phone and text Luna.

Luna J <3

Are you home yet?

no, I'm at your house

I got here a couple of minutes ago

Where are you??

on my way home to you

Chapter 36

Luna

After meeting with Nick's lawyer, he told me the contract was a solid deal. He said it probably wouldn't get any better with my age and where I'm at in life right now. So, I called Carol and told her I would sign the contract. We met at a cafe and talked about my move to LA and other things.

I can't believe this is my life. I've waited so long for this moment, and to think it's finally here is driving my brain insane.

Nick texted me forty minutes ago that he is on his way home. I can't wait to tell him I'm officially a soloist at the *Los Angeles Ballet Company*. Everything is falling into place. I'm not a principal, but I could get there in due time. Not to mention, I'll have Nick by my side. There really is nothing that could go wrong. Except maybe Nick not getting any offers besides the one from Seattle.

I really want him to make it as a hockey player. He deserves it. Especially after all the shit he's endured with me, losing his mom, and my stupid ass family drama. I don't think there is a single world in this universe I'm in and don't have Nick by my side. I can't even imagine it. He has become my whole life.

There's a knock at the door, and I quickly jump up from the couch to answer it.

When I pull the door open, Dean is on the other side of it. "Dean?"

"What are you doing here?"

"I'm waiting on Nick," I reply, crossing my arms over my chest.

He shakes his head. "What the hell happened to us, Jay?" he mumbles. "When Cassandra died, we promised to always be there for each other. We swore that nothing would separate us. Then Nick comes into our lives, and all of a sudden that oath is moot?"

"Don't do that. Don't you dare blame Nick for your actions. You did this. Not him. Did you know Gia came and apologized? You haven't. I don't think you understand what the hell the problem is. That has nothing to do with Nick and everything to do with you. So, what's the point in arguing with you anymore?"

"We're not even dating anymore. Gia and I," he explains.

"She told me."

His mouth gapes. "When?"

"When she came to my winter showcase," I answer. I would be lying if I said I wasn't bitter about Dean not coming to the showcase. But what did I expect? We weren't even talking.

"Fuck, the winter showcase!" He groans, running his hands down his face in guilt. "I'm so sorry I wasn't there."

"Don't be. It wasn't important to you, so I didn't expect you to remember it anyway."

"Jay don't be like that. Come on, you're my twin. We're supposed to be able to move past this. What do I have to do?" he begs.

I shrug my shoulders. "I have no idea. But I know I shouldn't have to tell you either. Besides, I'm not sure how I can just forgive and move on. You said some pretty shitty things along the way, and you just expect me to forgive and forget because you're my twin?" I shake my head. "That's not how this works."

I want to forgive Dean. He's my brother, but I couldn't. He's right. We promised to always be there for each other after Cassie's death, so what happened? He started to treat me like shit because he was sleeping with Gia.

"Luna, have you noticed I'm not bitching about you dating Nick? I told you how much being captain means to me. Nick was my way in, and you fucked that up." What is he talking about? "Yeah, I heard he tried to convince Coach not to give me the captain position. I wonder why that is. Probably because he feels the need to stand up for his girlfriend, right? That's why I came over. Now why the fuck would he do that, Luna?" He puffs out a harsh breath.

I remember Nick telling me about asking his coach to give the position to someone else. I don't know why Nick would do that. Regardless of how I feel about Dean right now, he would be a damn good captain. I know it, and so does Nick. I can easily tell him that I told Nick not to do that, but his mouth starts to move again.

"So, yeah. Who really got fucked in this situation? I'm trying to look past this because I want us to move on, but for some unknown reason, I always have to lose shit for you to end up on top. I'm sick of it. So, no. Fuck *you*,

Luna. You don't want a twin? Wish granted." Then he stalks back to his car.

Something deep inside of me wants to chase after Dean and apologize, but I can't get my body to move. A part of me feels guilty. Like I'm the one who's been fucking up this entire time. But I'm also not the person who told him to lie to me. I didn't tell Nick to *not* go to bat for Dean for the captain's position. He did that all by himself. How am I the one to blame for *his* actions?

So instead of chasing after him, I shout back instead, "Fuck you, too, Dean!"

He doesn't turn around. He just gets in his car and drives off.

I walk back into the house and slam the door behind me. I'm sad that I just lost my brother, but what am I supposed to do? I can't keep telling him what he did wrong. I shouldn't have to. Why doesn't he understand? I love Dean, but I refuse to live the rest of my life putting everyone's feelings above my own. I matter just as much as they do.

From this day forward, I will be protecting my peace at all costs. So, if that means not talking to Dean or Gia, then so be it.

When Nick arrives home a couple of minutes later, I instantly wrap my arms around his waist. Nick has been my light for the last couple of months. He's constantly making sure that I know I'm enough. I never have to be someone else when I'm around him. He accepts me for who I am, and I love that about him.

I pull back, stand on my tiptoes, and kiss him. I fuse my lips to his and show him all of the love I feel for him.

He pulls away as he tries to catch his breath. "That's how I want to be welcomed home from this day forward." He grins.

"Deal." I return my lips to his.

"I have some news I want to talk to you about," he whispers against my lips, setting me back down on my feet.

"Me too, but you first." I pull him to the couch and let him sit down first, and I straddle his lap.

"I got two more offers today."

"Oh my gosh, Nick! That's amazing. Where?"

"That's the best part." My brows wrinkle. "They're both in California."

"This isn't some sick joke, is it? Seriously?" I ask, pushing my palms into his chest as I try to keep my cool.

"Yeah, but there's more."

"How can there be more?"

"One of them is from the Los Angeles Kings."

My arms loop around him as I shriek into the crook of his neck. "Nick, that's so great!" I straighten my spine, settling my hands on his cheeks. "Wait, what do you want?"

"Honestly, I would fucking *kill* to play for the LA Kings." Thank God. I'm not sure what the other team is, but I don't know if I could handle him not being in LA with me. "Plus, being with you in LA is a plus."

"Perfect because I officially signed with the Los Angeles Ballet. Your lawyer said the contract looked good and I should take it. So, I met with Carol and signed."

He grips my cheeks with both of his palms. "I'm so fucking proud of you."

My heart flutters when I hear that. I've had multiple people tell me they were proud of me, but when Nick says it, it holds more value. "Thank you, Cole."

He rolls his eyes. "You're never going to let that go, are you?"

I smile, interlacing my fingers behind his neck. "I can't say that I am."

"So, does that mean we're moving to Los Angeles?"

I nod eagerly. "I'm not going to miss Boston."

"Me either." Then he pulls my lips back to his. "Oh shit, wait." He grits, breaking the kiss. "I forgot to give this to you the other day. Dean gave it to me when I went to meet with Coach. With everything going on, I forgot. I'm sorry, babe."

He hands me a wrapped package he pulled from his hockey bag. "Is this my present from my parents?" He gives me a soft nod.

Standing from his lap, I walk over to the counter and slowly rip the paper off. I become emotional as I take the photograph out of the package. It's not just any picture; it's the one of Dean, Cassie, and me. All of us were sitting on the front porch, laughing. Dean is sitting in the center with his arms over both Cassie's and my shoulders. I have a smaller version of it on my nightstand, but this one is bigger with a walnut wood frame.

On the bottom of it, it says, *No matter where we go, we'll always have each other*. It was something Dean and I had always promised each other. We would always be there for each other. No matter the distance,. Something he brought up earlier.

Things have gotten so crazy between us. I really don't want him to be out of my life forever. Maybe one day it'll all work out. I really hope it does.

Nick ran his palm up my back. "Are you okay?"

I nod. "Yeah. I'm fine." I set the picture on the counter and whirled around to wrap my arms around Nick's neck again. Rising on my toes, I return my lips to his.

I don't know what my future holds, but I know that as long as it's with Nick, I don't care.

We're moving to Los Angeles and starting our lives together. I have Nick by my side, and the value he adds to my life is beyond description. What he did was fill a void in my life. He was the medicine I needed to flourish and improve myself. Physically and mentally. I could tell him, but some things were better left unsaid.

I'd rather show him for the rest of our lives.

My phone buzzes, breaking our kiss. "One second," I murmur. I pull my phone up to see a text from Gia. "It's Gia."

Gia Mia

I know you're not talking to me, but I

I need someone to talk to

What?

I don't really want to do it over the phone

Can we please meet?

Gia, I'm not ready to talk to you yet.

I still need space

"What is she saying?" Nick asks.

"She wants to meet up." I look up at Nick. "Should I?"

He shrugs. "I don't know. That's up to you, babe."

My phone chimes again.

Gia Mia

I'm pregnant...

What the actual fuck?

Acknowledgement

Grecia—Kiddo, thank you for the countless nights we spent sitting on my terrible couch, reading each chapter. Giving your opinions and feedback.Also for the encouragement to continue writing and publishing this book. Your patience and help are what gave me the motivation to finish this book. Although it took a lot of time, you helped make my dream a reality. To say I'm grateful for you is an understatement!

My beautiful beta readers— Thank you so much for all of your help with this book. Thank you for giving me your complete and unfiltered honesty. This book would not be what it is without your help. You guys really did help, and there are not enough words in the world to describe how thankful I am to you all. Your words of encouragement are what gave me that last push to finish this book and publish it. So, Thanvi, Parnika, Bailey, Kate, Noelani, Anni, and Madisson, thank you! <3

Readers— Thank you so much for giving my book a chance! It really was a journey. I rewrote this book three times before I felt like it was finally ready to publish. It's been such a dream of mine to publish a book. To finally be able to do so is actually mind-blowing. I struggled with wondering if this book was good enough or if people would even like it. So, you just buying it means the world to me! I really hope you like or even love this book. I love all the comments and critiques. If you have them, share them!

Samantha- You are truly God-sent! This cover is so beautiful, and I just love it. Working with you was truly the easiest part of this journey. You're incredibly talented, and I can't wait to work with you in the future. Seeing these designs from the mock-ups had me so excited to see the final results, and you did NOT disappoint! Thank you so much for being a part of this journey with me!

God—I'm a very religious person, so there's no way I'm not going to shout out the big man upstairs! Helping me through my tears and fears about this book. He truly carried me and made sure that I persevered. I owe it all to him!

Happy Reading!!

About the Author

P rincess Berry is a debut indie author. Better Left Unsaid is her first story. She loves writing in her free time and just recently took a chance on herself by publishing her first book.

Born and raised in Los Angeles, California, Princess is the middle child of six. She recently graduated from Oklahoma State University before moving to South Korea for a year to teach English as a second language. Now, you can find Princess somewhere in Florida, working at Walt Disney World. If she isn't working, Princess will spend her free time listening to music and reading either a dark or a sports romance.

For more information, follow Princess on Instagram @princessboffcial.